THE
BODIES
WE
WEAR

THE
BODIES
WE
WEAR

JEYN ROBERTS

ALFRED A. KNOPF
NEW YORK

THIS IS A BORZOI BOOK PUBLISHED BY ALFRED A. KNOPF

Visit us on the Web! randomhouse.com/teens

Educators and librarians, for a variety of teaching tools,
visit us at RHTeachersLibrarians.com

Library of Congress Cataloging-in-Publication Data
Roberts, Jeyn.
The bodies we wear / Jeyn Roberts. — First edition.
pages cm.
Summary: After a powerful new drug causes havoc
and deadly addiction, seventeen-year-old Faye trains to take revenge
on those who took her future and murdered the boy she loved.
ISBN 978-0-385-75412-5 (trade) — ISBN 978-0-385-75410-1 (lib. bdg.) —
ISBN 978-0-385-75411-8 (ebook)
[1. Revenge—Fiction. 2. Drug abuse—Fiction. 3. Love—Fiction.
4. Science fiction.] I. Title.
PZ7.R54317Bo 2014 [Fic]—dc23 2013042352

The text of this book is set in 12-point Sabon.
Printed in the United States of America
September 2014
10 9 8 7 6 5 4 3 2 1

First Edition

To Kaliya, You know I'd do it all again.
Here's to life.

ONE

People say when you take Heam, your body momentarily dies and you catch a glimpse of heaven.

I was only eleven years old.

I saw something else.

I saw hell.

—+—

I like it when it's dark. There's not much light here. The city is constantly surrounded by clouds and shadows, even in the afternoon. But at night, there are no dusty streams of sunlight to try to warm my face. This is the way I prefer it. The light shows my flaws. My skin becomes translucent; the dark circles under my eyes grow darker.

Not all of my scars are visible.

These are easier to hide.

The soapbox preacher stands apart from the crowd.

He must be well over six feet tall, which gives him an advantage, along with the packing crate beneath his shoes. Shoulders tower over heads, his long black jacket reaching past his knees, disappearing into the crowd. His collar is gray and crooked, but his hair is immaculately cut, short and close to the scalp.

"Heam is not the salvation of heaven, my children. It is not the proper path. Do not follow false gods."

He speaks with passion and saliva, his mouth spewing a steady spray of words and liquid, forcing the few onlookers in the front row to step back several feet. They must be followers of his flock; no one else has the patience to stay out in the rain. The majority of people, always in a hurry and hidden under their umbrellas, step past him, keeping a safe distance, as if his enthusiasm might be catching.

It never stops raining here. Always moist and humid. My hair lies flat against my scalp; raindrop diamonds drip from my bangs. I barely notice it anymore. The long jacket I wear keeps my skin from growing too damp. Sometimes I believe I can see mold growing on the bodies of people who stand too still.

He is right. Heam is not salvation. But neither is he.

I don't know what it is about me that catches his eye, but as I step away from the stragglers, he jumps down off his makeshift podium and moves through the crowd as they part like the Red Sea.

"You," he says. "Yes. Stop. Tell me, child, have you been saved?"

Two people close in the gap, so I have no choice but to pause. Their eyes are gray, empty. One of them smiles, yellow teeth glowing dull under the streetlight. The faint smell of decay passes through his lips. They put their hands up to touch me, but hesitate. I'm wearing sunglasses and my jacket is pulled tight against my neck. They can't see my markings, but still they know something isn't quite right. Animals can sense when a human is sick—damaged. These people are no different, sheep being led to the slaughterhouse. Maybe they can smell me? Taste my aura? To them I might be the demon they've heard so much about.

I turn around just as the tall man reaches me. He stops a few feet away, face feverish and shiny.

"Young girl," the preacher says. He's ecstatic. Girls are drama queens, he's thinking. They cry harder. Maybe he'll get the show he desperately wants. He's found the person he wants to exploit. He's more confident than his flock. They shy away, but he stands his ground. The sheep are smarter than the wolf tonight.

I won't make it easy on him.

"Jesus loves you, my child," he begins. "He died for all your sins, and all he asks in return is your love. Your obedience."

This is not a conversation I planned on having tonight. I shift from one foot to the other, shuffling my weight around, what little there is. Some days it feels like the entire planet's shoved against the small of my back.

"You have the wrong person," I say. It's my one and only warning. If he's smart, he'll listen.

"Even the most troubled child can be turned in the right direction," he says. "All you need is for someone to tell you the truth. Do you know the truth?"

He grabs my arm as I walk away, pulling me hard, determined to have his silly showdown.

Wrong move.

I step forward, grabbing his fingers as they try to wrinkle my jacket. My grip is brutal and I see his eyelashes twitch as he tries not to flinch. I peel his hand away, pushing it back toward his own body. The whole episode takes only a few seconds; not even his followers notice or hear the sounds of his bones creaking as I squeeze harder. I lean in until I'm inches from his face. The decay on his breath is strong. With my free hand, I pull down the top of my shirt until part of my upper chest shows. His eyes come to rest on my scars, thin purple-and-red spiderweb patterns, covering the spot where the heart beats inside my chest.

His eyes widen and he steps backward, pulling hard, desperately trying to free himself from my grip. I let go at once. No one else sees what I revealed; they only watch as their pauper savior backs down from the fight.

I lean toward him, whispering so only he can hear. "I said you have the wrong person. As you can see, there is no saving me. My soul is gone."

Turning, I walk away, leaving the congregation soaking in the rain as the sky opens up and tries to wash away their sins.

I don't have to walk the alleys but I do it every night on the way home. It's out of my way and I could easily take the train. Most people prefer not to walk these streets at night. You can't see it beneath the streets but it's there, the green-and-yellow subway, whisking people safely to their homes, keeping their eyes blind to the reality of this city.

Not everyone seeks revenge in the most obvious places.

I'd like to say that they recognize me in this neck of the woods. I'd like to brag and say my message has become adamantly clear and that they tremble in fear at my footsteps and run the second their eyes meet mine. If the police actually bothered to patrol this neighborhood, they'd bow to me in respect and buy me coffee. But that would be a lie. I am no more important to them than a discarded burger wrapper from the local fast-food restaurant.

Invisible.

Just the way I've planned it.

"Excuse me?"

Okay, maybe not fully invisible.

I turn; a small girl with a red umbrella stares up at me. She's ten, maybe eleven. I narrow my eyes, waiting for her to speak. She's holding on to some papers, flyers, maybe. She could be bait, another religious group sending their tiny congregation members to trick us sinners. But her eyes are wide and blue; she's suddenly unsure why she bothered to stop me. What on earth possesses her to be out this late? Looking past her, I see a woman that's probably her mother a ways down the block. She has flyers too and is talking to a man who doesn't seem to care what she's saying. He pulls out his phone and accepts a call, turning his back on her.

"Excuse me," the girl says again, regaining my attention.

"Yeah?"

Her fingers are trembling. She takes a flyer from the top of her pile and thrusts it toward me. "Have you seen my brother?"

It catches me off guard and I reach out, taking the paper. A large MISSING is stamped across the front. A boy, possibly my age, quiet-looking, with glasses and short blond hair. He looks bookish, the type of kid who shouldn't be missing. Maybe he wandered away from the library one evening, never to return.

But someone loves him—this little girl with her cold shivering hands and tiny voice. She looks at me, eyes sparkling with hope that I might be the one who will feed her a small bit of information.

"No, sorry," I say.

"Okay, thanks," she says. "Can you keep the flyer? Just in case? If you see him, please tell him to come home."

I nod, fold up the paper, and stick it in my back pocket. The little girl turns and heads back down the street to meet her mother.

So many missing people in this city. If you took a picture of every single one and put it on a flyer, there would be enough to paper the galaxy.

There are bad people out here that make blond-haired, glasses-wearing boys go missing in the dead of night. No one bothers to stop them.

Am I after revenge? The short answer would be yes. The real answer takes longer.

I almost walk past without seeing them. A couple of Heam abusers, gutter rats, so to speak. The girl can't be older than twelve, small, pale, and thin; her body looks translucent against the brick building. The boy might be older; it's hard to tell, especially when he's barely able to hold his head high enough for me to see his face.

If I hadn't been looking, I would have missed them. Gutter rats learn to hide in the cracks so the dogs won't find them. These kids have crawled between the metal Dumpster and the wall. The smell of rotten food and mold is overpowering; I have to cover my nose with my hand to get closer. The walls are sticky with slime and dirt. It rained earlier and both kids look wet. Wilted.

The girl is not breathing.

"How long has she been like this?" I ask.

The boy doesn't answer. He's wearing the dazed expression of someone who has just seen heaven.

Is she still under? It's possible. There's not much you can do at that point except wait the few minutes for the cycle to end. To try to resurrect someone while they're under is signing their death sentence. The shock is too much.

"Hey!" I grab the boy and shake him hard enough to get his attention. Blurred eyes switch from the sky to the walls before finally seeing me.

"So pretty."

"When did you swallow? Did you drop at the same time?"

"Huh?"

"The girl!" I shake him again. He needs to hear me.

"You're hurting me." He sounds surprised.

"Focus! Tell me about the girl. Did you swallow at the same time?"

He finally understands. "Yeah, I think so. She might have gone first. So beautiful. Have you been? My grandmother's waiting for me. I saw her. She was dancing. The sky was so bright. Sun. It burned my eyes. So beautiful."

I let go of the boy and he slumps against the wall. He won't be moving for a while. Even if his legs did work, I doubt he has anywhere to go.

But the girl still isn't breathing.

I stretch her out on the ground. Her hair drifts in the rainwater; long tangled swirls fan out from beneath her head. Tilting her head back, I pinch her nose and take a deep breath. Exhaling directly into her lungs, I watch her fragile chest rise slightly beneath her dirty clothing. I breathe into her a second time.

Nothing.

My hands find the front of her jacket and I yank it open, tearing at the buttons on her shirt at the same time. I can see the marks growing on her chest. Spiderweb veins, purple and red, spread out against her pale skin. Tiny cracks in a dam, starting at the center of her heart, creeping steadily across her chest and toward her shoulder.

She's going to die.

No, she is dead.

I place my hands on her chest, palms down, and I begin the rhythmic compressions of CPR. One, two, one, two, one, two. Thirty times.

Breathe twice. Her lungs rise and fall.

Up and down.

The boy slumped against the wall starts humming softly to himself. An old song. Maybe his grandma used to sing it to him?

I go back to the compressions, counting under my breath. I can feel something pop and snap beneath her skin. I watch her face grow whiter with each passing second. I can almost see right through to her skull. Even her eyelashes look pale as raindrops pool in the corners of her eyes.

I change position and press my mouth against hers, ignoring the hint of strawberries on her lips. That taste. The smell. It makes my heart slam against my chest. It makes me crave, yearn, desire. Memories flash behind my eyes. Colors. Silver. Black. Cold fingers creep along my neck. Suddenly I'm seeing stars and the edges of my vision start to darken. I'm going to scream but there's no air in my lungs. Everything I had was transferred into her.

I'll wait for you.

Where?

Her eyelashes flutter.

And then her eyes open.

I'm right down in her face and she panics, cracking her head against the ground as she tries to understand where she is. I pull away from her, putting my arms out to try to keep her from hurting herself.

"It's okay," I say. "I'm not here to hurt you. You overdosed."

I speak softly to her for several minutes before the

words begin to sink in. She eventually allows me to help her up, until she's leaning against the side of the building beside the boy. He still hasn't noticed her. But that's normal. When you take Heam, everything else ceases to exist.

"What's your name?" I ask her.

"Beth."

"That's a pretty name," I say. "I'm Faye. Do you know what happened to you?"

She shakes her head.

"You overdosed," I tell her. I pull back her shirt a bit to show her the scars. Tears instantly fall. "But it's okay, you're going to be fine."

I'm lying.

I don't tell her that it'll never be the same again. People will treat her differently, like a monster they want to shove back in the closet. Those scars will never go away, a constant reminder of her evil deeds. She will lose family and friends. If by some fluke she manages to live beyond her childhood, she'll be fired from any job the second they see her markings. There will be no justice for her either. There are no rules to help Heam users. Only prejudice.

She'll never feel right inside her body. There will always be the nagging feeling that she doesn't belong. It'll be like she's living with someone else's body. She's no longer an owner. She's been reduced to tenant status.

She'll never stop craving.

I find the small bottle lying half under the Dumpster and pick it up. There are a few tiny drops at the bottom; the silver-colored liquid clings to the glass. The boy is right. It is beautiful. Even now I can imagine myself tilting the drug to my lips and letting that power coat the inside of my throat. The veins in my chest pulse and grow itchy. It takes all my strength not to start scratching till I bleed.

So easy.

I throw the bottle at the Dumpster as hard as I can. The thin glass splinters and droplets instantly dissolve into the rainwater.

I don't ask her what possessed her to try Heam. Everyone's answer is different and they all make perfect sense at the time. Who am I to judge?

"Will you come with me to the hospital?" I ask her.

She shakes her head violently, enough to finally catch the boy's attention. He sees me for the first time and his eyes grow big.

"Are you a cop?" he asks.

"No. I'm only seventeen. Bit too young to join the force."

"Are you an angel?" the girl asks.

"Not even close."

The boy's eyes fall upon her brand-new spiderweb veins. The high is going away and reality is kicking in. I can't help wondering what his grandmother would say about this.

"Do you have somewhere to go? A home?" I ask. "Can I take you someplace?"

"No hospital."

"Okay," I say. "No hospital. But you need to get out of the rain."

"I can take her to my place," the boy says. "My mom's working nights. She can sleep on the couch."

"What about your family?" I ask her. "Do you want me to call someone?" I'm happy to hear they have homes. A lot of the kids here don't. At least they'll be safe tonight.

"They won't notice. They never notice."

"Okay." I reach out my hand and help her to her feet. The boy puts his arm around her protectively. I walk slowly with them to the end of the alley to make sure he can handle her on his own. Her legs are shaky but I think she's steady enough to get home.

"Thank you," the girl says.

"Don't mention it." I reach into my pocket and pull out some bills, shoving them into her hand. "Take the train if you need it. Or get a cup of coffee. Hot and black. It'll help with the dizziness."

I don't tell them that drugs are bad and they shouldn't be doing them. I don't believe in blind preaching.

I don't tell her that she'll probably be back here next week and swallowing again. Heam is far more addictive than any other drug on the market. It's cheap—twenty bucks a hit. It's easy to find. The odds of her getting clean are a million to one. I also don't mention that her odds of overdosing are much higher now that she's been through the first round. Scientifically I could explain that her blood will eventually break down and neurons will start sending bad messages to her brain. She will literally go crazy from use.

It's also not my right to point out that the odds of me finding her again when she needs me the most are, at best, astronomically against her.

I don't say any of those things. She doesn't need another lecture.

"Keep her warm," I say. Then I slip off into the night, the steady drizzle erasing my existence.

—+—

My last stop of the night takes me past the dark bar on the corner where my life ended six years ago. I've never been inside the place but I can imagine it well enough. The bar is made of wood, with rows of glasses hanging high above the bartender. The mirror is caked with dirt, the kind that no longer washes off when you take a cloth to it. Drunken men line the stools; I can't imagine there would be many women, except perhaps a waitress or two. Old men, barstool prophets, they spend their time speaking of days when the city was a better place. Back before the Heam addicts, prostitutes, and dealers took over. They probably talk about who's in charge, what they're doing wrong, and how they personally would make things better.

Big talk for small men. But everyone needs dreams to pass the time.

There's also a dead man sitting inside, tucked away in the corner booth, drinking. He doesn't know he's dead yet, but none of that matters. His days are numbered.

I'm going to kill him.

TWO

I don't hear the guy until he's right behind me. That's real talent. It's usually hard to sneak up on me. He doesn't scare me, though. It's almost as if I knew he was there all along.

"You sure you want to go in there?" I can practically hear the smile in his voice. It's his shadow that gives him away. It stretches out before me, shifting as he leans against the building.

He's not concerned; if anything it's as if he finds it amusing that I'd think about it in the first place. There's something familiar in his voice, yet I'm positive I've never heard it before.

But I understand his point. This bar isn't exactly the type of place a girl would go into willingly.

"I can handle myself," I say. Turning, I'm surprised to see he's not much older than me. Maybe eighteen or nineteen. I was right, I don't know him. Never seen him before and I'm good at faces.

He smiles. The light reflects off his green eyes. He distractedly massages his neck with pale fingers.

I turn my back on him. "What makes you think I was planning on going in? Do I look like a party girl?"

"Nope." He moves till he's standing beside me. His black jacket doesn't do a good job keeping him dry. His hair is stuck to his scalp, wet and black; it covers his ears and overlaps the collar. Beads of rain glisten on his neck. "You look a little jumpy," he adds. "I thought maybe you were debating sneaking in."

"I don't sneak," I say. "And I'm not jumpy. If I wanted to go in, I would."

"If you say so."

I turn to say something nasty but he's still smiling and not in a smirky way. He's amused, but he's not laughing at me. And I finally get it. I must look a little odd standing under the streetlamp in the middle of a downpour. I'm like the soaking-wet dog that's too stupid to run into the house when it's called.

"You look soaked," he says. "If I had an umbrella, I'd help keep you dry."

"I'll live."

The rain continues to fall. I glance upward, but all I can see are the gray clouds above us, and the constant pattern of water as it cascades down by the buckets. I like the rain at night. I love the way it reflects off the lampposts, giving the white light a fuzzy halo. I like the way the puddles jump and vibrate, like a million water bugs having a frenzied party.

If it ever stopped raining, I think I'd feel lost.

"Besides," I say. "Look who's talking about sneaking. I didn't even hear you come up. Do you always walk up to people from out of nowhere and start conversations?"

"Sometimes."

"You should wear a bell or something."

He laughs.

The silence swallows us. He's still beside me, waiting for me to say something. But what does he want to talk about? Why? Normally, I'd assume he wants something. Spare change? Directions? Is he planning on mugging me? Something worse? Why else do strangers come up to you out of the blue? If he's looking for a date, he's going to be awfully disappointed. I beat the crap out of the last guy who thought I was into that sort of thing. I may be small, but I'm feisty enough to hurt someone. I don't train every morning for nothing.

He rubs his hand through his hair, slowly, as if checking for something. Strands of hair get stuck between his fingers. Absently he tugs on his dark locks a few times, almost as if he's never felt his hair before. When he pulls his hand away, his hair stands out like devil's horns. But the rain quickly weights the strands down and back into place. I watch him lick his lips. He's waiting for me to speak. To make the next move.

"I was just looking for someone," I finally say. "Not that it's any of your business."

"In there?" He sounds a little appalled and that makes me feel better.

"It's possible."

"You don't look like the type of girl to keep that sort of company."

Now it's my turn to smile. "And what kind of girl do I look like?"

He literally looks me over from the top of my head to my boots, pausing a bit too long at the middle for my taste. He spends a long time looking in my eyes, until I become the first to break the gaze. Direct contact always makes me nervous. He nods his head, tilting it to the side, when he's finally finished sizing me up. "Sad. Forlorn. Not in an emo sort of way. No, I'm getting that wrong. You're not a stereotype; you're cooler than that."

He's not looking directly at me when he says this. He's staring at the bar. One of the neon lights is flickering, and his face changes from blue to normal over and over. Fingers run along his jawline.

"Wow," I say. "You can really read me like a book. Very insightful. Anything else you want to add?"

"I'll bet you never carry an umbrella," he says. "You're probably damp all over. But you think that's okay, don't you? It's what you're trying to achieve. It's a shame you live here. I'll bet the sunlight would look wonderful on your body."

My cheeks burn, although I'm not overly sure he's paid me enough of a compliment to embarrass me. In a way, I can't help thinking I've been insulted.

"That's the oddest thing anyone's ever said to me," I answer truthfully.

He shrugs and then steps closer again, until he's just

inches away from me. I can feel the heat radiating off his body. He's at least a foot taller than me but he leans down until his lips are breathing softly in my ear. "The person you're waiting for. Are you sure he's in there?"

I close my eyes and a face flashes across my mind. A face I won't name because if I do, I might hear his voice in the furthest corner of my mind. I don't want to remember.

I'll admit it. I have a lot of ghosts. But so does everyone else. Right?

The rain continues to fall. He's touching his hair again. I wonder if his hair is a different color when it's dry. A dark chestnut perhaps.

"What's your name?" I ask. All these personal comments flying back and forth. It's time we're properly introduced.

"Chael."

"That's a unique name."

"Is that a bad thing?"

"No, just different. Didn't say I didn't like it."

He touches his shoulder this time. Pulls at his shirt like it doesn't fit properly. Either this guy is nervous or he's one of those people who just can't be still.

"What's yours?"

"Faye."

"That's a pretty name."

"Um, thanks."

His head perks up as if he's heard something. Pulling a mobile phone out of his back pocket, he looks at it, frowns, and then turns his head, staring out into the falling rain.

"Well, Faye," he says. "It's been a blast meeting you but I've got to run. I'm sure we'll cross paths again. Promise me you won't go into strange bars while I'm gone. I'd never forgive myself if you got into trouble."

I widen my eyes in mock surprise. Who, me? Never!

He bows in an over-the-top gallant manner, which might be charming but he trips over his feet as he turns to leave, giving me that crooked grin one more time before disappearing off into the rain.

Weird guy.

———+———

It's ironic that I live in a church. Of course, God hasn't resided here in years. One might argue he was never here to begin with. The big front door rocks on its hinges; the old wooden doors are swollen from years of keeping out the rain. The lock constantly creaks and it takes several twists of my key to make it open. One of these days it's going to fall off in my hands. Inside, the electricity has a mind of its own, only working when it wants, which is practically never. The heating system is messed up, so in the winter the pipes freeze and the floor becomes shiny with a thin film of ice. The summer is a sauna of humidity, leaving my skin perpetually soaked with small beads of sweat.

In the winter I live like some relic from an ancient feudal time. A fire burns in the fireplace all day and night and we stay as close to it as possible, the light flickering across the pages of my homework while I curl deeper inside my blanket. But luckily, it's not winter right now and the rain, although cold, is bearable.

We can't even complain because technically we're not supposed to be living here. No one wants an old, dusty church. When the city condemned it, God moved away. He packed his bags and headed for someone else's church. I hear it's beautiful there.

My key finally turns and I open the door and step inside.

"You're late."

I smile. "I doubt you were worried about me."

"Just because I know you can take care of yourself doesn't mean I don't worry. There are still plenty of unsavory people out there."

I walk past the row of wooden pews, many of which are cracked and not safe for sitting. They are covered in a fine layer of dust and cobwebs because neither of us is very good at being clean. The marble floor beneath my boots is scratched and unpolished. There is no altar at the front of the church, just a makeshift living-room area complete with a couch and chair where Gazer likes to read. The fireplace is dark and piled with dry logs. The power must be out tonight, because there's an oil lamp burning, and I can see his profile peering intently into one of the many books he rereads on a regular basis.

Tonight it appears to be Thoreau. *Walden*.

"Do you have homework?"

"Some. Not much. I'll get it finished before I go to bed."

"Good. Do you want me to look anything over?"

"No. I'm going to head up. It's been a long day."

"I'll see you in the morning, then. Bright and early."

Gazer takes care of me. He's been my guardian from the moment he found me in the alley and breathed air back into my lungs six years ago. It's a good thing he took me in. No one else wanted me.

I don't remember much about my parents. I was young when they took my father away. The courts were so quick to judge him. It didn't matter that he had a family to take care of and no one wanted to hire him because he had a back injury. He'd lost his job after the accident, and the disability checks had long since dried up. He started taking Heam to escape his pain. Then he started dealing. Small-time stuff, but in the end, he owed the wrong people a lot of money. I remember my mother and me standing beside him after the verdict. He leaned down to hold me and I could smell the cheap cologne on his skin. The scent was familiar and it made me feel safe. I have no pictures from my childhood and I can't visualize what his face looked like, but I can still remember that smell on his clothes. Sometimes if I try hard enough, I can picture his eyes, sad and tiny beneath dark lashes. But it depresses me, so I try not to think about it.

He didn't complain when they took him away. He couldn't stand upright because of his injury but he still walked away with his head held high.

My mother held my hand so tightly my fingers were pink jelly beans poking out from under her chewed nails.

He didn't look back.

And I don't want to talk about my mother, so don't ask.

Upstairs, my room is dark and cold. I was right, the

21

electricity is out and I light the candle beside my bed before pulling back the covers. Kicking off my shoes, I crawl into bed, jacket and all, and curl up on my side.

I should get up and at least brush my teeth.

The flame bounces and jerks when I exhale. The bedside table has seen thousands of candles; years of built-up wax scars its pitted finish. The tabletop is bumpy, so the candleholder doesn't rest properly. I once carved the initials of the boy I loved in the soft wax with my fingernail.

But he's dead too.

I'm thinking of that little gutter rat and I can't get her face out of my mind. Beth. Such a pretty girl, it's a shame she doesn't have a chance. I hope they made it home or that she's sitting somewhere warm. It won't be long until the addiction begins to scratch away at her. Is the boy taking care of her?

Will she survive?

I can't help wondering if people thought the same about me.

—◆—

"Don't hurt her. Please. She's just a girl. Hurt me instead."

Laughter. Always laughter.

The man leans over me, touching my chin with rough fingers. Pulls my face up to meet his stare. There's something funny with his eye. He twitches, spasms that make his lashes flutter like some crazed Venus flytrap. I'm amazingly calm. I know I should be afraid but I think I'm past that instinct.

Beyond fear.

I can hear my friend Christian pleading from some-
where behind me. He's begging them to let me go. To take
him instead. His words are silenced by a loud smack. I
can't turn around to look. The man is still holding me.
He's breathing heavily and I can smell alcohol and sour
air when he exhales.

"You want a piece of candy, little girl?" He holds the
bottle out in front of me, giving it a small shake. Silver
liquid spills against the thin vial. For a moment, I forget
all about the dirty man or that Christian's making wet
gasping noises behind me. All I can see is the bottle and
its contents. I think it's very pretty. I wonder how the man
manages to get that liquid to turn that color.

I smile, only because I don't know any better.

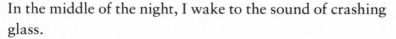

If I could turn off my brain, I'd use that feature before
going to sleep. Dreams are useless anyway.

In the middle of the night, I wake to the sound of crashing
glass.

Outside on the street, a man is screaming.

In the other room, I hear Gazer's drawer slide open as
he grabs his gun from its hiding spot beneath his shirts.
I hear him move toward the window, carefully drawing
back the curtains. Gazer's mostly being cautious; the odds

are good that they will just kill the man straight out and then leave. They don't usually go after witnesses; people in this neighborhood never rat them out. Men like them have nothing to fear. I'd get up to join Gazer but my bed is warm and I'm still half-asleep. Besides, I know he'd just shoo me off with a wave of his hand. Gazer is the protector of everything holy inside this church. I am just his disciple.

Eventually the screams stop and Gazer never fires his gun, so I go back to sleep.

—+—

In the morning we train.

I wake about a minute before my alarm is set to go off. Years of early-morning practice have given my body an internal clock. I never sleep in and I never take days off. Even on Sundays, when Gazer says I should take a break, I still rise before the sun and head down into the bowels of the church to practice.

Death never takes a day off. Why should I?

I get dressed quickly, ignoring the dampness that tugs at my bones, and find my running shoes hidden under a pile of books. Pulling my hair up under a baseball cap, I head downstairs and into the kitchen. It's not really a kitchen, just a makeshift room that has a small Coleman stove and a refrigerator that clanks and rattles and always sounds like it's about to take its last breath.

I grab a quick drink of water and then head out the

door. The rain instantly hits my face, but it's not enough to slow me down.

I hate running. I hate the burn in my calves and the way the sweat stings my eyes. I don't like the way my lungs feel, like they're about to collapse after a few miles. But Gazer says I need to do it because it keeps my body in good shape, and doing something I hate builds character. He also says that running is spiritual and clears my mind, leaving me in full control of my body. Once I learn to master my body, I can truly learn to master the fighting skills I require.

Gazer believes me when I say I want to let sleeping dogs lie.

"Revenge is not a worthwhile dream," he agrees. "The man who spends his life focused on retribution often misses his own true calling."

That would be fine if I wanted to live a long and worthwhile life. But someone like me can't have the wants and dreams of others. Someone like me is cursed, forced to spend her life sitting on the sidelines, only wishing she could play the game. Free will only works as well as the hand you're dealt.

I hear the sirens before I smell the smoke. The fire truck zooms past me and I watch without slowing down. When it turns the corner, I know I should go straight and finish my run. But instead I follow it, heading down toward the water, where the older storefronts are.

The fire is raging out of control, sending thick black smoke straight up and into the gray rain clouds. The building used to be a grocery store, owned by a nice Asian man and his wife. They lived in the back but now they're standing on the street, their arms wrapped around their children, who are all barefoot and in their pajamas.

I wonder who they pissed off.

I approach them carefully, holding my hand up against my face to try to block some of the heat. "Did everyone get out?"

The man's wife starts talking in Cantonese, pointless because I can't understand her. The man tries to calm her down, but she starts pulling away from him and gestures toward the building.

Someone is coming out.

A figure emerges from the smoke and flames, a child in his arms. A hero. A few onlookers cheer and the firemen rush over and grab the child from his arms. The child is whisked away, along with his incoherent parents and other siblings. They load the child and the mother in the back of the ambulance. The father and two other children stay behind for questioning.

Then the firemen turn to the hero of the morning. They try to pull him toward the ambulance but he shakes them away.

He's the guy from last night. The one who acted like he'd never felt his own hair before.

Chael.

When he looks up, he sees me. Lips turn up a bit in a half smile. He winks.

It's short-lived. The firemen aren't taking no for an answer. They grab him by the arms, talking to him about smoke inhalation and possible lung damage. They need to take him to the hospital just to make sure. They pull him past me and he winks again. There's a smudge of soot on the bridge of his nose.

The police finally take over and start pushing the crowd back. I allow them to steer me across the street, where I can get a better view. The mother is gone now, off to the hospital. I hope the child is okay.

With a loud crack, something in the building gives way, wood splinters, and it starts to collapse in on itself. Flames shoot higher. If the firemen don't get it under control soon, the entire block could go up.

It's quite possible the shopkeeper was unable to pay for protection and this is the retaliation. The Heam gangs are strong in this neighborhood and they rule it by forcing people to use their stores as fronts, as places where dealers can sell Heam out of rooms in the back. This particular street has at least five stores that I know of that cater to the gangs. And with the way sales are booming, they are always in need of new businesses.

I scan the streets and sure enough, I see a couple of dealers halfway down the block. They're leaning against a burned-out car, doing nothing to hide the reason they're there. A couple of gutter rats approach them and they make a sale, fully aware that the police are watching them. That's the way things are done down here. No one cares enough to actually try to clean up this part of town. There is too much violence and illegal activity; the police are overwhelmed, unable to do anything about it, even if they have evidence.

It's possible that someone tried setting up business inside this store and that the owner refused. I find that hard to believe, though; he looked too timid to deny anyone. He's got family too. Refusal to sell Heam could carry the heavy fine of the gangs' targeting his kids. The people in this community know this. They rarely say no.

Sometimes children get involved in more ways than one. When they arrested my father, he owed the wrong people a lot of money. He got put in jail, so they came after me. Whether their intentions were to make me an addict or to kill me, either way they succeeded in getting back at my father.

The shopkeeper is still on the street, along with two of his children. I wonder what items he mourns. If it were his wife, I'd imagine she'd be visualizing the photo albums, baby shoes, and other treasured items that are now lost. Maybe even a love letter tucked away in the back of the closet, inked in fine calligraphy. But what does he regret? I look at one of his children, the daughter, and think about Beth. I wonder how she survived her first night. It's possible her family threw her out on the street. It wouldn't be the first time such a thing had happened.

I should have gone with her. I should have made sure she'd be okay.

So tiny.

The shopkeeper's daughter stares at me, sucking her thumb, holding on to her dolly, perhaps the only thing she owns that's left in this world.

What kind of heaven awaits her?

Gazer is waiting for me when I get back.

"Good run?" he asks.

"There was a fire," I say. "I stopped to check. The grocery store down by the water. You know the one that sells the Chinese cabbage you like."

Gazer frowns. "Shame," he says. "Now I'm going to have to go across town to find some. Probably get charged a fortune too."

I shrug and go over to the coffeepot and pour myself a cup.

"Was there anyone there?"

He's referring to the gangs, of course. He knows they like to stick around to watch their own handiwork.

"A few," I say.

"Did they see you?"

I shake my head. "They were too busy selling to a bunch of gutter rats."

He nods. "Good." Turning, he heads toward the stairs. "Drink that and hurry up. We'll have to keep it short today. Don't you have a test to take?"

"Only in biology," I say. "That's the easy stuff." I gulp the last of the coffee, burning my tongue in the process. Grabbing a towel, I wipe my forehead and then head downstairs after him to get in a few punches before I have to shower and get ready for the one part of my life that isn't so bad.

At least some of the time.

THREE

I go to Sebastian Clover High School. It's one of the top schools in the district and very private and expensive. They didn't want me, of course. At least, not in the beginning. It took a lot of persuasion and a few recommendations from both my old school and an appointed government caseworker who follows my life from a distance. They pushed the "pity this poor child who is really a victim and not at all a drug abuser" spiel.

So in the end, they changed their minds. They wanted me. Everyone wants a sinner.

They even gave me a scholarship, and as long as I maintain my grades I can continue to attend school. As long as I don't resort to my old druggie ways.

I am a blank slate.

I don't have problems with school. It's easy. All I have to do is listen. All I have to do is write down what they expect me to write. I sit in the back and silently take notes. I very rarely raise my hand, preferring to keep to myself. But I like school. There's only one right answer and I find comfort in that. I wish life were that easy. My grades are very good, although most of the teachers still seem wary of me.

In school I wear a uniform. A pleated dark blue skirt and white blouse. Knee-high socks or tights and black Mary Jane sneakers. My face is scrubbed clean until it shines and I pull my long dark hair back in a ponytail. Makeup is not allowed. No dangly earrings. I look normal. Like everyone else. Well, almost.

No one ever waits for me at my locker. I don't have friends. That's just the way I like it too. Friends complicate things. They want to do things with you after school and on weekends. They expect you to go with them to movies and hang at the coffee shops, pretending to study. They want to know your feelings and share gossip and whatever else girls do when they're together. I don't belong to that world. It confuses me. I don't understand why such mundane things can be so interesting. How can something as simple as a brand-new outfit or sky-blue eye shadow work girls into such a frenzy?

Some of the girls pretend to be friendly but I try not to encourage them. Besides, they'd probably end up asking questions that I'm not prepared to answer. This is something I've been explicitly told to avoid.

There were rules when I joined this school. Rules that were created specifically for me and I have to follow them.

Rule one: I am never, under any circumstances, to

reveal to the other students that I have overdosed on Heam. I'm not to mention that I ever tried Heam nor can I ever mention the drug's name, even in a lesson.

Rule two: Under no circumstances am I ever to remove my clothing in the presence of other students. They must never see my scars and I must never mention them. Because of this, I have been given special permission to skip gym class. A lie was created stating I have terrible asthma and because of this I am excused. Instead, I am to spend the period in the library studying. Even while off the school grounds I should take precautions with my clothing by wearing shirts that cover my chest completely. Not that I've ever had to worry. The kids at Sebastian would never dare to step inside my world.

Rule three: There are to be no relationships with students of the opposite gender. Although it was never stated, I believe it has a lot to do with rule number two. I'm also advised to keep my friendships formal at best. Keep my socializing down to a science.

Rule four: I am never to talk about my parents. If prompted, I am to say that both parents died in an accident—even though the administration knows my mother is still alive. Although I'd never say it to the school's face, to say Dad died accidently is closer to the truth than anything else.

Rule five: Maintain good grades and never criticize the school. I am to constantly remember that I am a guest here. And even the nicest visitors sometimes overstay their welcome.

There are consequences to my actions and if I break these rules, I'm gone. They won't give me a second chance and I doubt there's a single school in the district that will take me if I mess up. Most schools have a zero-tolerance policy when it comes to Heam usage. There are no second chances. There are some groups that try to fight the stigma associated with Heaven's Dream—Heam's official name—but they're fighting a losing war. Hard-core users will always be ostracized.

But even with all these rules, I like school. It's a chance for me to be normal, well, at least pretend to be normal. I get to wear the school uniform and walk down the halls. It's amazing I ever made it this far.

As I sit in the back of the classroom, the teacher drones on about the importance of algebra but I'm not listening. I'm thinking about Chael. Is it a coincidence that I've met him twice in less than twenty-four hours? Is he following me? It's possible that I screwed up somehow, let down my invisibility guard, and now they're aware I exist. There's even a chance they might recognize me, although I've gone to great lengths to disguise all traces of the child I once was. With the exception of the soapbox preacher, I've never gone out of my way to let anyone see my scars. Could someone have seen me in the crowd last night and tattled on me?

No. That's impossible. Even if someone did recognize me, I'm still nothing but a single girl in the crowd. A hard-core Heam abuser who managed to go straight.

Not a threat.

Not yet.

I'm so involved in my thoughts I don't hear the teacher call my name.

Not the first time.

Not the third time either.

What I do hear finally are the giggles. When I look up from the doodle on my notebook, they are all looking at me. Several pairs of eyes. Lots of smirks.

"Um. Yes?"

"The answer would be appreciated, Faye."

I look at the board. There are scribbles of x's and y's and a bunch of numbers. I have no idea. The silence grows and all I can hear are the sounds as people fidget in their chairs to get a better look.

"Forty-three?" I finally say. Of course it's wrong; there's no way I can possibly be correct. A huge breakout of giggles confirms it.

"Silence," Mr. Haines snaps.

No one listens.

"Can I be excused?" I ask. When Mr. Haines raises his eyebrows, I give him the best pity face I can muster. "I'm not feeling well today. Sorry."

He waves a hand at me and I pick up my binder and pencil case. There's only five more minutes left of class, so it's safe to assume he doesn't expect me to return. I hear the murmurs from behind my back as I walk down the aisle and toward the door.

In the bathroom, I go into the stall and lock it behind me. I sit down on the toilet and rub my temples with my fingers. I wasn't lying when I asked to be excused; I'm really not feeling great. My head is suddenly pounding and I wonder if I inhaled too much smoke earlier.

The bell rings and instantly I hear the muffled noises

34

as the kids gather in the halls to rush to their next class. The door opens and a girl comes in, stopping in front of the mirror. A few seconds later I hear a thud as someone else enters, kicking at the door.

"Get out of here," the girl hisses. "This is the ladies' room, idiot."

A low throaty chuckle. "Give me the money you owe me and then I'll leave."

Inside the stall, I perk up my ears and hear the girl as she steps back against the wall. "I told you, I don't have it. You need to talk to Jesse."

"Maybe I'd rather talk to you."

"Leave me alone."

It only takes me a second to decide that today, I'm going to break some rules. Unlocking the door, I step out into the middle of the action. The girl is Paige LeBlanc, one of the more popular girls, and she's backed up beside the hand dryers and staring at a guy I've never seen before. He's not a student; the leather pants he wears are not part of the school-issued uniform. He's greasy too—hair, face, probably even underneath his jacket. His clothes are expensive but dirty; he screams "dealer" from miles away. He definitely doesn't seem the type that Paige would hang out with, even if she was being daring and trying to shock her rich parents.

I walk over to the sinks and carefully put my binder and pencil case down on the porcelain counter.

"The girl asked you to leave her alone," I say. "I suggest you listen to her."

The guy looks me over and I can see the delight in his

35

eyes. He's finding this hilarious. Two pretty Sebastian Clover girls. He's going to enjoy tormenting us.

I smile back, nice and proper.

"Get out of here, girlie," he says to me. "Go take an exam or something. I've got business here."

I step between them. Technically I'm not breaking the rules. I've been told not to interact with the other students. Since he obviously doesn't go to school here, I've got a solid defense for my actions. "Make me."

The guy laughs like he's just discovered a pile of gold under his mattress.

"She asked you to leave," I say again. "Now, I suggest you listen to her or I'll have to force you."

"You?" The guy can't stop smiling. I'm looking forward to watching that grin disappear from his greasy face. Paige continues to cower behind me, but I can tell she's completely shocked. I doubt we've ever said a single word to each other. She probably doesn't even know my name.

"Try it," I say. "It's okay. You can hit a girl. I know you can. I give you permission."

The guy steps forward to brush me aside, but I move to the left, grabbing his arm, bringing my leg right in front of his. It's a simple maneuver; he's still smiling stupidly as he trips, crashing against the sink, and falling hard on his knees.

"Bitch!"

Now I've got his attention. He gets up on his feet, looking at me with surprise, still pretty sure I'm not something he needs to worry about. The idea that a girl could kick his ass is completely beyond his comprehension. He swings

36

at me with his right. I block it, and give him a sharp jab back, straight in the nose. His head snaps back, hitting the hand dryer, sending Paige scrambling to the other side of the bathroom stalls.

Now he's concerned, but it's too late. I punch again, another jab to the nose. Something breaks. He screeches, grabbing his injury with his hand, shocked to find blood pouring down his face. When he lunges at me, I step back and to the side, grabbing his arm and using the force of his body to propel him forward. He's moving too fast and he can't stop from crashing against the wall.

"Open the door, please," I say politely to Paige. She complies.

I pick the greasy guy up and toss him out the door like he's nothing but a rag doll. Walking back over to the sink, I wash my hands carefully. Who knows when that guy showered last?

I pick my binder and pencil case up off the sink and head out the door, which is still being held open by Paige.

Thirty seconds later she catches up to me. The shock has worn off.

"That was amazing," she says. "How did you do that?"

I shrug and keep walking. Continuing this conversation can get me in real trouble. I glance around, but there isn't a teacher in sight to witness my naughtiness.

"I mean, really incredible," she says. "I'm sorry about all that. Trevor is a real jerk. He shouldn't even be here. And I don't owe him money. I can only imagine what you're thinking. I'm not that kind of person."

"What kind of person is that?" I ask.

She pauses. "Not the kind to hang out with gutter rats like that."

"He's not a gutter rat," I say. "He's a dealer."

"Yeah, whatever, they're one and the same, aren't they?"

"No."

"I didn't realize you were such an expert."

I stop walking and turn toward her. She's looking at me curiously, trying to figure out what my story is.

"Dealers are scum," I say. "They destroy lives. They want to become dealers. They're greedy bastards. They earn money off of death. Gutter rats are victims. They have pain. Problems. Issues. They may choose Heam, but they don't always pick their path. Sometimes it's forced on them. Sometimes they just don't know any better."

She studies me, finally deciding that her disagreement isn't worth the fight. "I suppose," she says. "I never thought about it that way."

I turn and walk off. I've got English next period and I'm going to be late if I don't hurry.

"Hey!" Paige just won't leave me alone.

I keep walking.

"Hey, hold up." She runs up and falls into step with me. "I'm sorry," she says. "I really didn't mean to offend you. You're Faye, right?"

I nod, surprised she knows my name.

"Thanks, really," she continues. "I'm having a party Friday night. Would you like to come? I can introduce you around to a few people. It'll be fun."

"I'm busy," I say. Parties? The school would have a fit. Technically there is no rule about who I hang out with in my free time, but I'm sure that would change if I ever started. Besides, what on earth would I do? I may have the body of a teenager, but my mind is old. How would I talk to any of them? I've already proven, in the past five minutes, that I can't even hold a conversation without becoming hostile. Could I really sit for an evening talking about boys and clothing?

Not a chance.

"Okay, well, think about it," Paige says. She writes something down in her notebook as we walk, impressive considering she can barely keep up with me. Tearing the sheet loose, she shoves it into my hands. An address and phone number.

She's not going to take no for an answer. I can see the problem already forming.

She stops at her classroom. Mine is just a few doors down. The bell rings and I start running.

"See you," she calls back.

I should throw the address out. I have no business keeping it. But I find myself slipping it into the pocket of my skirt for safekeeping.

It might be nice. Being normal.

—+—

The rest of the day goes by quickly. I always eat alone at lunch but it doesn't take long before I notice Paige sitting a few tables down. She's with a group of her friends and they're all looking at me intently. Especially her boyfriend, Jesse, the one who apparently owes the greasy Trevor money. Of course she told them. Suddenly I feel like there's a great big red flag flying over my head.

But the teachers don't notice. No one pulls me into the office to ream me out.

Jesse goes out of his way to walk past me at the table. I look down at my book, making it obvious I have no intentions of talking with him. He slows down, even pauses for a second to take a better look. I continue to ignore him. Finally, he walks off, but not before caressing his hand gently across my shoulder. A quick move, probably missed by everyone except me.

What does he want from me?

After class I head home. If I'm quick enough, I can put in a few hours of training before homework and dinner.

I need to stick to what I'm good at. Focus. Everything else is just another distraction.

——+——

The silver liquid touches my tongue and I'm happy that it tastes like strawberry candy. Such a perfect flavor, I wish there were more of it. Like a glass of soda. I'm very thirsty from all that crying.

The men around me are laughing. One of them bends down until he's inches away from my face. His eyes are beady and dark. I don't like them. When he smiles, I see his teeth, white, behind his stubble. But there's nothing happy about him; his eyes don't sparkle, and they remain dead and cold. It makes me nervous and I begin to sniffle again.

"Your daddy was a bad boy," he says to me. "And

since he doesn't have any money, we take our cut out of blood instead."

"Hey, leave her alone," someone else says. I think it's Christian but I'm not fully sure about anything anymore.

The man grins again. His teeth are very white. I can't stop looking at them. They grow in size. If he opens his mouth, he might swallow me.

But things are changing. I can hear my heart beating in my chest, pounding against my temple, with each beat; I'm worried that it might explode. At eleven years old, I'm not entirely convinced this can't happen.

Pound. Pound. Pound.

I look over and I see that they've got Christian down on the ground. He's struggling with them but he's too weak and they've got his arms pinned behind his back. Another man, the one with a long scar along his forehead, has Christian and he's pried open his mouth with his fingers. Someone else pours some of the strawberry candy onto his tongue and it splashes against his teeth. He's no longer pleading. He's staring straight ahead, and our eyes meet. I can't look away. I want to but I can't. His green eyes are full of hatred. Sorrow. Confusion. Too many emotions. It hurts my head.

The strawberry taste is now rancid on my tongue. I swallow, trying to get it out, but it's like syrup coating my throat, and it won't go away. And everything is growing hazy. My eyelids have grown heavy, weighted down by the buckets of tears I've cried. Suddenly my legs are no longer supporting my weight, I tilt to the side, and in slow motion I see the ground reach up to meet me.

And I'm lying on the concrete, staring up at the stars.
Pound. Pound. Pound.

The man with the scary smile leans over me. "Have a nice trip," he says.

A billion colors light up the sky, like fireworks Mom once took me to. I watch them, trying to decipher the colors I don't recognize, but there are simply too many. I think I've stopped breathing; my chest is no longer rising and I'm slightly aware of the burning sensation inside my lungs. But I see blue and pink and red and silver. Lots of silver.

Pound. Pound. Pound.

I want to reach up and touch the colors as they float down toward me, taunting me to pick them up and put them in my pocket. But I can't move my arms; they're no longer under my control. It's okay. I don't need them anyway. The sky is dipping down to meet me.

Everything is beautiful.

Pound.

And suddenly it stops.

No more heartbeat. No more sky. Nothing but blackness.

And then . . . fire.

—◆—

A pounding at my door.

"Faye?"

Another knock.

I sit up, the dream falling away, tangling myself in my

bedsheets. I look at the clock. Almost seven. It's dark outside.

Shit.

Gazer is at my door, knocking again.

"I'm fine," I say. "Just fell asleep."

A soft silence.

"Dinner is on the table. Come down when you're ready."

"Okay," I say.

I wait till I hear his feet recede down the stairs. Climbing out of bed, I head straight for the bathroom, cursing myself in the mirror. I shouldn't have fallen asleep. That was stupid. Now I've gone and missed practice and I've still got a ton of homework to do before I can go out tonight.

These late-night hours are starting to wear me down. I'm a teenager; I'm supposed to be in my prime. So why are there heavy circles under my eyes? I splash water on my face and wet down my hair.

I head downstairs to try to eat something. I'll need my strength for what I have planned tonight.

FOUR

"You're not ready."

I'm sick of those words. I hear them constantly.

And I totally disagree.

But Gazer always says it. No matter how much I train, no matter how many times I manage to land a killing blow, he ends each session with those three words.

You're. Not. Ready.

"Why not?" My current standard reply.

"Because you're not ready."

I walk over to the wooden mannequin and remove the knives sticking out of its chest. One blade in particular is embedded so deeply I have to use my foot as leverage to try to pull it out. Now, that is what I'd call a decent death blow.

"I can throw a knife better than you," I say. "You even admitted it yourself. And my hand-to-hand combat is off the wall. I can fight. You've trained me well and you know it."

"You're decent enough," Gazer says. "But it takes a lot more than fighting to succeed."

I grab the soft cloth kept specifically for wiping down the blades. I start polishing the knife, admiring the way the silver shines, the way it reflects my eyes. There's something very beautiful about a sharp weapon, especially one as deadly as this one. This tiny thing in my hand is powerful. With the right guide, it can take a life. And some lives are worth taking.

"Yeah, yeah," I say, and I wink at my reflection in the knife. "It takes heart and brains and all sorts of other things. I'm ready physically but I suck in the mental department."

It's a well-known argument. We have it weekly.

"Yes," Gazer says. "The fact that you're so nonchalant about it contributes even more to my argument. You have a lot more to learn, Faye. You're still too much of a child."

Ouch.

"I lost my childhood six years ago," I snap.

"No, you lost your innocence. Your childish ways are still up for debate."

I stamp my foot, which I know really does reinforce his views, but at this point I don't care. "You know what they did to me. You understand why I have to do this. How can you sit there and say I'm not ready?" I wave my knife around but Gazer isn't threatened. He knows I'd never hurt him. Of course, he also knows that even though I'm one tough cookie, he could still probably take me out in a heartbeat. He did teach me everything he knows.

The people I want to kill aren't as well rounded as Gazer.

But my mentor isn't going to go down without a fight tonight. "Faye, no one knows your desires as well as me. I'm not your enemy here. I want to protect you. When I took you in, I agreed to help. You were so small, and there was so much hate in your heart. So much fire. I thought if I could help you learn to protect yourself, I might be able to save you. I might be able to make you understand you're better off forgiving and moving on. That life has more meaning than the scars on your chest. But sometimes I think all I've done is add kerosene to that fire."

"You've helped me become a warrior," I snap.

"I've made you more hateful," he argues back. "All I wanted to do was give you confidence. Help you grow stronger so you'd be prepared if you were attacked again. Until you can learn to let go of that hate, only then will you be ready."

"I'm not going to forgive them for what they did to me."

Gazer shakes his head slowly. "Then I can't do anything more for you right now." Turning, he gathers his books and heads back upstairs.

I'm left fuming by myself, which is usually the way these conversations end.

For the life of me, I can't understand why Gazer seems to believe I need to forgive these people. How on earth is it supposed to be revenge if I don't have the satisfaction of watching them bleed? I push the wooden mannequin back

46

into its resting place in the corner and stare at it. It's a poor excuse for a human: wood, with carpet wrapped around its shoulders to mimic flesh and blood. In my mind, I envision the dead man at the bar, his crooked smile and short hair. I remember him standing over me, and for a second, I'm eleven again, full of fear and helplessness. Pulling my arm back, I punch the dummy as hard as I can, feeling the pain in my knuckles where flesh meets wood.

If it were really his face, I would have broken his nose. I would have felt the cartilage snap beneath my knuckles and seen the surprised look on his face. Only then would I pull the knife from behind my back and finish the task.

"Remember me?" I whisper to the empty room. "You took my soul. Now I'm returning the favor."

But the wooden dummy doesn't respond and suddenly I'm feeling foolish. Gathering up the rest of the weapons, I put them back in their proper spots and head upstairs.

I've got better places to be.

—+—

Gazer ignores me when I tell him I'm heading out. He's curled up by the fireplace again, his nose in a book. How can he sit there night after night and read his life away? All he does is live inside those books. He hardly ever goes outside. He has no friends. There must be fire in his heart too. I know his past. I know what they did to his wife.

How tiring it must be to be him.

If I were him, I'd hunt down each and every one of them and take their lives slowly and methodically.

I wouldn't waste my time reading, that's for sure.

It's raining as usual as I slip out the door and into the night. Drizzle hits my face and I tilt my head up appreciatively. My training session was particularly rough tonight and the rain is refreshing. It cools my burning muscles and actually wakes me up a bit. I first started training with Gazer when I was eleven. I used to get so exhausted I'd sit down and cry. Then I learned about the healing property of rain. When I went outside and stood in the middle of the dilapidated-church parking lot, the coolness of the rainwater would wash away some of that pain. I'd stand in the parking spot marked RESERVED FOR MINISTER and feel the exhaustion and soreness drip off my body and into the ground beneath my feet.

Heam was invented when I was five years old. It was created by two chemistry students in a university in Switzerland who were looking for something that resembled crystal meth, LSD, and Ecstasy. They wanted a new drug that would be easy, trendy, exciting—something that anyone with a little background in mixing chemicals could create cheaply and effectively. What they got was Heaven's Dream, or Heam for short.

Heam works in ways that no drug has ever worked before. It targets both the brain and the spinal cord, attacking the central nervous system, and breaking apart everything that allows us to live. Within five minutes after someone takes the drug, the body begins to shut down. Breathing grows shallow, the heart beats slower, body temperature drops, and the body enters a catatonic state. Shortly after, all communication between brain and body ceases and the person ingesting the drug . . . dies. The victim will be dead anywhere from two to ten minutes before the brain and body kick back into action. If you look at it in computer terms, it's as if the body goes through a reboot. Everything shuts down and then starts up again. Although it's been tested repeatedly on lab rats and chimpanzees around the world, scientists still don't quite understand how this drug does this. There are plenty of theories but no real answers.

The dangerous thing about Heam is that not all users become addicted. There have been cases of people dropping once or twice and then never trying it again. For many users, there are no side effects. No withdrawals. No consequences.

But there is always the risk. The next level.

For people who do get addicted, it is a never-ending world of pain. They completely cease to function in the normal world. They will do anything to get Heam: steal, sell their bodies, even kill. They are unable to keep jobs. Family means nothing to them. Babies have died, forgotten in their cribs. Spouses tear each other apart for one more hit.

Addicts live in a semi-delirious state between the real world and the heaven their mind shows them. They can live this way for years. But their bodies grow weaker. Their hair starts to fall out. Nothing else matters, except scoring their next hit. There is no solid data on long-term Heam abusers. The drug is still only twelve years old.

Scientists do know a few things. Statistics suggest that one out of a hundred users overdoses. Their body never reboots and they remain dead. With proper medical attention, the occasional overdose victim can be brought back, but with grave consequences. Like myself, they end up with battle scars in the form of red spiderweb veins across the chest and shoulder and an addiction to end all addictions. This is why so few Heam overdosers can kick the drug. It's worse than alcohol. It makes heroin look like a baby's bottle. There is nothing in the world that can come close to the cravings a Heam addict suffers. These cravings never subside. You can't ignore them and no amount of time will make them fade.

Sounds crazy, right? Who on earth would willingly take something that technically has to kill them in order to work? Especially with such crappy odds of overdosing. One out of a hundred isn't very good.

The risk was apparently nothing compared to the results.

When early Heam users came back to life, they brought stories with them. They'd seen an amazing place while they were dead—a world of peace and beauty that had no ugliness or suffering. They often reported feeling completely happy and relaxed. Many of them saw relatives who had died. They saw angels and their bodies floated on the air. It was the out-of-body experience to end all experiences.

They saw the white light.

They reached out and touched it. They felt its absolute warmth.

Heaven.

Euphoria.

And they were fine. No problems.

Overnight it became the world's biggest threat and salvation at the same time.

Suddenly people who had never thought of taking drugs were lining up in the streets for the drug that would let them glimpse the afterlife. Little blue-haired grandmothers were overdosing on Heam and children were being rushed to the hospital in shocking numbers. People stopped going to work and children started dying because mothers were neglecting to feed them.

Religious groups were torn. Here was the proof of heaven's existence that the devout had been asserting for thousands of years. The afterlife existed and you could see it for a cheap price. But others began preaching that Heam was not the path to salvation, that just because you saw heaven didn't mean your soul would go there when you died. God had made heaven elusive for a reason and humans were not meant to test God's plan. Taking the drug quickly went from being an answer to being a sin, but even that didn't stop people from using.

In fact, it made things worse.

Debates raged around the world. Atheists and scientists alike argued that Heam was not a pathway to heaven but a chemical reaction in the body. It was the mind's way of coping with the body's shutdown. The images people saw were only brain waves and neurons misfiring in the seconds before death occurred. It was nothing but a nice dream to have while you were dying.

No one listened.

The Church of Heam sprang up. It was a place where

one could worship and get high at the same time. Governments tried to shut it down but new congregations kept growing. It's now considered a cult by most countries, so the church has gone underground, its followers dropping Heam in secret. But it still exists.

And people continued to die.

But no one seemed to care.

Then a select few began to report seeing another place. One of evil and sadness. Of fire and brimstone. Pain. It only confirmed people's beliefs that there really was a heaven. If heaven was God's great world, then it was only natural that its opposite existed too.

And did society really fall into chaos and anarchy? No, of course not. People still work jobs and the government still functions. But the world is different. Heam changed everything.

Heam is illegal and the punishment for creating and distributing it can mean a life sentence. In some countries, it can result in the death penalty. After so many years, it is now considered a taboo, and there is no easy way out. Heam addicts are not forgiven. They don't get the breaks that other drug abusers get.

No second chances.

A drug that the world hates and loves at the same time.

I always wondered: if those two university students could have seen the future, would they have gone ahead with the drug? It's hard to say. They're both dead now, victims of their own invention. They never lived long enough to see the horror they unleashed.

I stand across the street from my favorite bar and watch the doors, wondering how long I'll be waiting tonight before I see my prey.

The dead man inside the bar is Montague Rufus. Most everyone calls him Rufus, never Monty. He's forty-three years old. His hair is blond, he likes to slick it back with gel, and his eyes are dark buttons that sink deep into his head. His eye twitches constantly and his hands sometimes shake from years of drug abuse. He doesn't touch Heam but sticks mostly to the weaker drugs. He drinks constantly. His blotchy red nose is a testament to his disease.

He likes to wear an old leather jacket that has burn holes on the sleeves and a pair of cowboy boots that have broken more than their share of fingers. He never fights fair.

I know everything there is to know about this man. I've spent a long time watching him. He's the man who, six years ago, destroyed my soul.

He's not an important person but he likes to believe he is. A middleman—his job is to regulate the Heam dealers for the neighborhood and report back to his boss. He is trusted enough to pass on the money but not trusted enough to be given more power. Sometimes he's given jobs that require a little more nastiness. Like going after the children of people who owe money. He likes to drug them, ensuring they will become addicts, gutter rats. I also know he's been responsible for making people disappear now and then.

He does his job well and lives in a nice house in a good neighborhood. He has no family but has no problem giving prostitutes regular business.

There were four men there the night I saw hell. I have made it my life's goal to personally destroy each and every one of them.

I will leave Rufus for last. My plan is to go through the list, eliminating every single one until Montague Rufus is the only one left. I want him to know I'm coming. I want him to fear me.

But not just yet. Not until I feel I'm ready. I don't want to screw up. Until then, I will continue to watch and wait, taking notes, following their moves, and learning everything there is to know about my enemies.

"I see you're predictable, at least."

The words make me jump, and I spin around with one arm raised in defense and the other gripping the knife hidden behind my back. Chael stands a few feet from me, an amused expression on his face.

This is the second time I didn't hear him.

"You scared the hell out of me," I snap.

"Sorry," he says, but he's not.

"What are you doing here?"

"Hanging out. You?" He tugs at a stray strand of hair that's fallen into his eyes. He reaches back and pulls up the hood of his jacket until his already-wet hair is covered. He tugs at the sleeves, pulling them down and over his fingers, which look cold and wet.

"I'm beginning to think you're following me." I remember how he winked at me this morning as he pulled the child from the burning building. It's a bit too coincidental that he's here again.

"Or perhaps you're following me," he says. "Or it's just a small world and we can't help but bump elbows every now and then."

"Why would I follow you?" I ask.

"Why not?"

I shake my head and beads of water drip down my cheeks. Being elusive and avoiding the question only means he doesn't want to answer.

"You were a real hero this morning," I say. Maybe if I ask the right questions I can get some answers. "Why did you save that child?"

He shrugs. "I couldn't not save her. Building was burning. Nasty stuff. You would have done the same thing."

"Maybe."

He smiles. He knows I'm lying. "I bet you would have gone in, flames or not, if I hadn't come out when I did. You could never stand by and let a child die."

"Oh, so you talk to me for a whole total of five minutes in two days and now you've got me all figured out?"

"Yep. Pretty much." He winks again.

"I could eat babies for breakfast. Or stab old ladies on the train for all you know." I'm annoyed now. Yes, he's saying nice things about me but I don't like the fact that he's so smug about it. He thinks he knows me. He doesn't. I want to make this perfectly clear.

"Sure you could." Chael picks up the drawstring of

his hoodie and twirls it around in his fingers. He wraps it tightly around his pinkie until the finger turns bright pink; then he releases it and starts up the process again, with his ring finger this time.

"I'm not a good person," I say to him finally. "So stop pretending like you know otherwise."

"Okay, miss, whatever you say."

From down the street I hear a familiar voice.

"Excuse me? Have you seen my brother?"

The little girl is still handing out her flyers. She's got her red umbrella and she struggles with it while trying to hold the papers with her cold fingers. People hurriedly walk past her as if she's contagious or something. No one wants what she's selling. As if sensing my stare, she looks up and spots me. She turns and starts walking toward us.

Chael pulls his hoodie further down over his face. "Hey, you want to go get a cup of coffee? My treat."

My first thought is to say no because part of me thinks he's really missing a few brain cells, considering his behavior, and the other part is still half-convinced that he's following me. But, if I look past the constant fidgeting and drawstring twisting, there's something in his eyes that makes me reconsider. His eyebrows are deeply furrowed and he's chewing on the inside of his lip. He's hiding something. And I want to know what.

The little girl is closing the distance when he turns his back to her. He shoves his hands in the pockets of his jacket and gives me a grin.

It's cold out and a cup of coffee really does sound good. It'll give me a chance to dry out a bit before returning to my street corner. I was planning on following Rufus home tonight. I do that at least once a week to keep my stealth tactics updated. He's never once seen me and you learn the most about a man when he doesn't realize he's being watched.

And I have to admit, I'm very curious about Chael.

"Okay," I say.

Chael reaches over and takes my elbow and heads me down the street away from the little girl, her depressing flyers, and the red umbrella. In a way, I'm glad. I didn't want to tell her I haven't seen her brother tonight. She gets enough bad news from everyone else. I don't want to add to it. I hear her voice but whatever she's saying is lost in the sound of the rain.

We go to the little fifties diner a few blocks away. It's an okay place. I've been here a few times before. It has these little working jukeboxes on every table. If you pop in a quarter, it'll play a song. Mostly stuff from the fifties. Elvis. The Big Bopper. Ricky Nelson. Pat Boone. Personally, I don't like the music of that generation. It's too damn cheerful.

But we squeeze into a booth. My pants stick to the faded vinyl seats and a small farting sound escapes when I unstick myself, forcing me to fake-cough to cover the sound. Chael doesn't notice or he pretends not to. Instead, he focuses on the jukebox and I hope that he doesn't play anything because it'll only make me roll my eyes and probably dislike him.

Thankfully, he spares me. He picks up the sugar dispenser and twirls it around in his fingers and then starts stacking some of the little creamers, keeping himself busy until the waitress comes by to take our order.

I get coffee. Black.

Chael orders coffee and a piece of cherry pie. No ice cream.

I keep the menu and flip through the pages, looking at the pictures, not really seeing them. Most of the items have stupid names that reflect past celebrities. The Big Bopper Double Whopper Tuna Melt. Marilyn Monroe Milk Shakes. James Dean Chicken Tacos. Chael starts ripping apart a napkin with his fingers. When he's got a tiny pile of shredded paper, he starts tearing apart a second one. And then a third.

The waitress brings our coffee. She goes back for the pie.

I wait.

Chael has a large pile of destroyed napkins. He pauses only to start opening creamers and dump them in his coffee. The brown liquid quickly grows lighter. Then he adds a large amount of sugar. Coffee sloshes over the side of the cup and he cleans it up with a fresh napkin.

This is turning out to be the most boring coffee date I've ever been on. Of course, considering I don't socialize, it's also technically the first coffee date I've ever been on. Definitely not memorable. I would have expected there to be a little more talking.

"You must drink a lot of coffee," I say when he first lifts his cup up to his lips. He pauses, watches me with bright green eyes that look a little puzzled. I smile.

"No, why?"

"The caffeine? You fidget enough," I say, nodding in

the direction of the shredded napkins and stacked creamers. "You can't seem to sit still."

"Nervous energy," he says.

"And you play with yourself a lot."

"What?" He looks seriously alarmed and it takes me a few seconds to realize how my comment must have sounded.

"I don't mean that way. I mean you're always touching yourself. Oh crap, I don't mean that either." I'm blushing now, my cheeks burning. I can't seem to get my words out properly. "It's like you're always pulling your hair or wiggling your fingers." I point to his hand, which is beating a rhythm on the table. "You're doing it right now. It's like you're not comfortable with your body."

He leans forward, his eyebrows raised in surprise. "That's an odd thing to say. Why would you say that?"

I shrug. "I don't mean anything nasty. Sometimes I don't think enough before I speak. No filter between brain and mouth."

"Maybe this isn't my body," he says, and then he laughs a bit too hard. "It could be a loaner." The waitress brings over his pie and he immediately digs in, breaking apart the crust with his fork. Cherry filling sticks to his lips.

"You're weird," I say, my cheeks slowly growing less flushed. "But that's not an insult. It's a compliment. I like weird."

He gives me a half smile. His green eyes sparkle underneath all that dark hair.

"Where are you from?" I ask, trying to remain nonchalant. "I haven't seen you around before."

He pushes his pie plate out of the way. He seems to have lost interest in it after a few bites. "I grew up here but I've been away for a long time. Just recently came back."

I take a sip of coffee. "Where did you go?" A few gutter rats walk by outside, their eyes hollow. Everything about them attracts the darkness. Even the shop light won't touch their skin. One of them looks in and stares right at me without seeing. So young. It's not fair.

"Just away," Chael says. "Nowhere special."

"Why did you come back?" I ask, still looking out the diner window. A car with a busted back window slowly drives by, splashing the sidewalk with rainwater. "I mean, if I managed to get away from this city, I'd never come back."

"Where would you go?"

I shrug and take a sip of coffee. "I dunno. Somewhere warm? Somewhere I'm not going to be judged for who I am. Maybe Africa. Or New Zealand. I hear things are better there."

"Not really," he says. "Heam is everywhere. Even the warm places."

"Oh? You're an expert on Heam? You learned this during all your travels but you still don't know why you came back?"

Chael doesn't say anything for a long time and finally I tear my gaze away from outside and look at him. He's watching me carefully. His head tilts to the side and he runs his fingers absently through his drying hair again.

"I'm not sure why I came back," he says at last. "It wasn't my choice but at the same time it was my only chance."

"That makes no sense."

"I'm complicated that way."

Chael reaches into his pocket and pulls out some cash, which he tosses on the table. Standing, he smiles down at me but shakes his head when I make a motion to get up.

"Stick around, why don't you?" he says. "Take a break tonight. Let the bad guys rest. No one will die tonight if you're not around. I promise."

I give a short choking laugh. "What makes you think I'm after bad guys?"

"You're after Rufus and his friends," Chael says. "That's why you're always outside the bar. You're studying him. Waiting for him to make a mistake. Maybe even waiting for the perfect opportunity. But you're not going to get them first. They're mine."

I'm halfway out of my seat but he pushes me back down with his arm. I'm so surprised that I let him do it. "How do you know—"

"I know a lot about you, Faye," he says as he heads over toward the door. "You don't want to go down this path. Trust someone who knows. Leave Rufus to me. You don't need that revenge. It's not your salvation."

"Who are you?" I scream after him. A few other patrons look up from their dinner stupor in shock.

Chael stops, his hand resting on the door handle. "Blue skies. You'll figure it out. It's okay, honey bunny."

And he's gone. Just like that.

FIVE

Sleep doesn't come easy. I can't stop thinking about Chael. How does he know so much about me? Have I been wrong all along? Do they know who I am? Have they been waiting for me to slip up all this time? If so, why are they sending Chael after me and not coming themselves? Surely, I'm not so intimidating that they've had to hire someone to take me out. Rufus may be a coward but I know from experience that he likes to deal the death blow himself. Especially when it comes to young girls. Didn't he already prove that six years ago?

So why Chael?

I'm a wreck when I finally drag myself out of bed for school the next morning. There are dark marks under my eyes and my cheeks look more hollow than usual. I can barely keep my brain focused as I pour my morning coffee. Half of it ends up on the floor and I have to hunt around for some towels. It's mornings like this that I wish either

Gazer or I were a little more practical in the cleaning department.

The church feels damper than usual this morning if that's even possible and I'm shivering in my yoga pants as I start my warm-ups. Gazer is still mad at me and he shows that anger through our workout, forcing me to do the most mundane and physically challenging tasks. Push-ups. Sit-ups. One hundred squats and then a five-mile run before I'm allowed breakfast. I do it all without complaining and I don't say more than a few words to him. Our anger works both ways.

I barely make it back in time to have a quick shower and head off to school.

—+—

Paige is waiting by my locker. I spot her in the distance and immediately look around guiltily to see if any teachers have noticed. No adults in sight. That's a good sign but at the same time I'm wondering why I've bothered being so careful these past few years. No one seems to be paying attention to me in the slightest. It's been a complete waste of time being in this paranoid state.

Even if the teachers have become more relaxed, I will continue to follow the rules. I don't want to get kicked out of school. It's important to me. It's the only link to normalcy that I have. Without it, I'm not sure who I'd be left with.

A monster.

"Hey," she says when I approach.

I nod at her, brushing past to get to my locker. There

could be security cameras. I ignore her as she waits for me, hovering at my back to get a peek at the contents. There's nothing there to impress her. No mirror. No token gifts from boys. No stickers, pictures, or any of that crap that the other girls seem to love. My locker is like a prison cell, bare and lifeless.

"You don't like me much, do you?" Paige asks as I slam the door closed.

"Never said that," I say.

"Then what is it?"

"What's what?"

"Why do you act like you can't stand to be around me? Is it because of Trevor? I told you already. He's a major jerk and I don't have anything to do with him."

"It's not Trevor," I say. "He's a nobody. I just don't want friends."

Paige's mouth draws itself into a surprised O. She's wearing a very nice lip gloss that makes her lips a perfect pale pink. "Everyone wants friends."

"Not me."

"I don't believe you."

I shrug. "Suit yourself." I turn and start walking to class. She struggles to catch up. "Come to my party."

"Why?"

"Because I want you to come."

I spin around, hoping to catch her off guard, and it works. She takes a step back cautiously. "I'm not interested in your games. If you want to go slumming, find someone else. I'm sure Trevor has friends who will be more than happy to entertain you."

"Is that it?" She rolls her eyes, showing off her lovely blue eyeliner. "I'm not slumming. I could care less who you are or what your parents do. I'm not a snotty little rich princess and I have no intentions of becoming a gutter rat either."

I shrug. We've arrived at my English classroom, a class she's thankfully not a part of.

"Come have lunch with us," she calls out. "Make up your own mind about us first. You'll see. We're a lot of fun to hang out with."

She's determined, that's for sure. Ignoring her, I head into class. Maybe I will have lunch with them. It could be nice to have someone to talk to for once, even if I do have to monitor everything that comes out of my mouth. Sitting at my desk, I glance up to see Mr. Erikson, the English teacher, staring at me suspiciously.

Maybe not.

Besides, what would I say to them? It's not like I can tell them anything about myself. The school warned me against these things. I'm not even supposed to mention Gazer. Originally the administration put together a backstory for me, featuring good wholesome parents who had excellent-paying jobs and loved me to death. But they abandoned the idea, deciding that it would be too complicated for me to remember, and that it was better if I just ignored everything and everyone.

Never tell.

My motto.

The bell rings and everyone gets settled. Mr. Erikson begins to talk and I immediately lose all focus. I'm too

65

tired to listen to him drone. I've already read the book, a modern-day love story. She eventually leaves him to go live in the woods like a wild animal. I remember being fascinated with it when I was younger. I've never seen a forest. I couldn't imagine what living in one would feel like.

Peaceful.

I wish I'd gotten more sleep last night but I just couldn't stop thinking about Chael and the comment he made to me before he left.

"Honey bunny."

Not the world's most original term of endearment. My dad used to call me that when I was little. I used to hate it and get angry, puffing out my cheeks and telling Daddy to stop teasing me. Christian overheard my father once and he used that expression every chance he had. Outwardly I used to get angry but inwardly, well, coming from him, I loved it.

Honey bunny. A sign of affection. Teasing. Something you'd see on a greeting card. Something even a sarcastic stranger might use.

Chael really does have nice green eyes. It would be a shame if he turned out to be the enemy.

Trying to stifle a yawn, I rest my chin on my hands, letting my hair fall into my eyes so I won't look so obvious.

It would be easier if I weren't so tired.

I'm in a very small room. No, correction, I'm in an elevator but it's not moving. I can see the buttons on the

wall, ranging from numbers one to twenty-three. The emergency phone is there but it's not working. There isn't any power except for a small light in the ceiling above my head. I pick up the phone but only hear dead air. I press some of the buttons but nothing happens. I seem to be stuck between floors.

I have no idea how I got here. The last thing I remember is my heart trying to beat its way out of my chest and the man who gave me the liquid that tasted like strawberries. He gave me Heam. I know this. I may be young but I'm not stupid. I've heard my mother talking about it and I know my father went to jail because of it. You're supposed to see heaven. I heard about heaven from stories my grandmother told me.

"Don't tell her that," my mother used to say. "You're filling her head with nonsense. There's no such thing. I'm not raising her to believe in that crap."

"She has a free will and mind," my grandmother would respond. "She can think for herself. Look at her life. A bit of goodness won't hurt her."

"There is no God," my mother would say.

"The world is full of opinions. That is yours. I have mine. Let her reach hers on her own."

They would argue this back and forth and eventually my mother would throw up her arms in disgust and go somewhere. The bar. The store. The kitchen to finish the dishes. Anywhere but near her mother, who was too old-fashioned to tolerate. Grandmother would pick me up and I'd curl into a ball in her lap and listen to her stories.

Heaven was supposed to be a place where angels

floated on clouds and played harps. There was no sadness and everyone was peaceful and happy. I always figured it would have lots of ice cream and every bed would be warm and soft.

I look around but I don't see any angels. Maybe this elevator will take me up to the clouds. But it's not moving. Why isn't it moving?

And why am I so cold?

I try calling out, my voice tiny and hollow, the feeble sound bouncing around the confines of my cell. I call out Christian's name. My mother's. I hear something and immediately shut my mouth to listen.

The noise starts small. A scratch. Faint. Then again. Louder this time.

I press my ear up against the smooth doors.

I listen.

Scratch. Scratch. Scratch.

A whisper.

Pound. Pound. Pound.

Something smashes against the door, denting the metal. I scream and back up against the opposite wall, my back pressed against the chrome railing. The walls are made of mirrored glass and I can suddenly see my own horrified expression staring back at me a thousand times.

A sharp spike breaks through the metal with incredible speed. I dodge the rod and it breaks through the mirror, sending bits of silver glass raining down around me. Another pole slices through; the sound of metal scraping against metal fills my ears and I scream again. There is something on the other side of those doors and it screams back at me, denting the metal with its claws. My heart slams against my chest, threatening to rip itself out of my body.

Pound. Pound. Pound.

I'm so cold. Icy water flows down my back, my spine. My fingers are so frosty I can't feel them. My feet have frozen to the floor; they won't move. My entire body won't move. I can't breathe. There's no air inside of me. The room grows hot and the metal turns red and begins to sweat in front of my eyes. But I still can't move and my hands are shaking so badly I'm positive icicles are going to form on my fingertips and break off, smashing to the floor.

Another pole. This one strikes me, piercing my wrist and hand. I drop to my knees, reaching for my wound with my good arm, trying to pull myself free. The pain is enormous. It fills my body; I can't think or even see properly. Everything around me turns bright red. I want to scream but I can't. I am beyond words. Beyond breath.

And then the shadows come.

They crawl up along the walls, their eyes reflecting in the bits of broken mirror that surround me. Long and black, they have no form, but I can see the claws on their fingertips and the tails that trail behind them. They laugh and whisper obscenities. When I open my mouth to scream again, one of them slips into my mouth, coating my throat. I begin to choke, unable to fight against the darkness that tears its way into my chest.

Another pole pierces my stomach. I can feel the blood pouring out of my body, dripping along my legs and pooling in my shoes. My hands are covered with the stuff and I start pressing the elevator buttons in panic, but my fingers only manage to leave behind sticky prints and accomplish nothing else.

The walls break away, opening up to complete darkness. I'm not falling but I'm not moving either. I curl up the best I can with the metal rods piercing me, trying to make myself as small as possible. Blood drips away from my body into nothingness.

Then in the distance I see my father. He looks the way he did the day they led him away to prison. He's tied to a cross and bleeding everywhere. His eyes roll around in his skull until he's looking right at me. His mouth opens but no sound comes out.

I try to scream but just like him, my own voice has been stolen.

The shadows dance around me, whipping my body with their darkened arms and scaly tails. They cover me completely until there is nothing.

"You're a pretty little piece of sunshine," something whispers in my right ear. "I'm going to swallow your soul and devour you for all eternity."

I open my mouth and try to scream again. Scream forever because no one is going to hear me.

—+—

"What the hell?"

I open my eyes and discover I'm back at my desk and everyone is turned around and watching me. My mouth is

70

open and although I'm quiet at the moment, I'm pretty sure I was screaming a few seconds ago. The look on everyone's faces confirms it.

"Faye?" Mr. Erikson is looking at me. The book is still in his hands but he's forgotten it's there.

"I'm sorry," I say. "I was up all night. Not sleeping well."

There are several snickers and whispers.

"Please see me after class, Faye," Mr. Erikson says. He turns his attention back to the rest of the class. It takes a few minutes but eventually the students turn around in their seats and I'm temporarily forgotten.

The bell rings and of course there are stragglers, kids taking their dear sweet time at their desks because they're dying to overhear my talk with Mr. Erikson. But he shoos them away, telling them to get the hell out of his class. For a teacher, sometimes he's kinda cool.

I stay at my desk with my books piled neatly in front of me. I don't want to be here but he's standing between me and the door and I can't get past him without confrontation. So I wait, hoping he might forget about me, but of course he doesn't.

"Is everything okay, Faye?" Mr. Erikson closes the door and comes over to sit down at the desk beside me.

"Yes," I say. "Just having some bad dreams."

"Anything you want to talk about?"

I shake my head.

"It's only natural considering the hell you've been through."

No pun intended. There's no way he could possibly know that I didn't visit heaven when I died.

"You know, I don't care much for the way things have gone for you," he continues. "I'm not really in a position to criticize, but I know your records and I know what you've been through. The way they treat people like you is abysmal. They never really give you a chance to recover. I wish I could say we've grown into a more cultured society but we haven't. We'll forgive a mother who drowns her children but we won't forgive a young girl who had no choice in becoming an addict."

I look at him in surprise. What he's saying is very unpopular. He could get fired for even suggesting that the school is treating me poorly. He knows it too. He's giving me power over him. I could turn around and report him. Of course, he's probably counting on the fact that they probably wouldn't believe me.

"I had a younger brother who died of a Heam overdose," he says. "He was an addict and he died. It's amazing how simple I can make that sound. Not a day goes by when I don't miss him. But I never looked down on him or treated him like a second-class citizen."

I stand up and brush some lint off my skirt. "Thank you, Mr. Erikson, but I'm okay, really." I gather up my books. "It was a long time ago and I'm better now. I'm sorry about your brother."

Mr. Erikson nods and stands up himself. Walking over to the front of his room, he sits at his desk as the door opens and new students come in, laughing with each other over some joke. They stare at me for a second before heading to the back of the room.

"If you need help with anything," Mr. Erikson says, "you know where my office is."

"Thank you," I say.

"Be sure to get more rest," he adds as I head off toward the door. "No more sleeping in class."

"Okay."

There is always going to be the odd person who wants to stand up for me, but I don't want their help.

I'm a pretty little piece of sunshine. I know those words. I hate them.

—+—

I was eleven when I saw hell. Torn apart. Blood dripping from my body. Monsters in the shape of shadows terrorizing my mind. Not something anyone ever wants to experience.

I have no idea how long I was dead. But when I came to, Gazer was kneeling over me, his hands resting on my chest, trying to jump-start my heart. I was lying in a puddle of water, my skin frozen beyond feeling, and Gazer's hair dripping on me. The streetlights reflected off his face, and all the water droplets in his hair shone like a million diamonds. He looked like what I thought an angel might look like.

"You're going to be okay," he said in a very calm voice.

And I believed him.

He helped me up carefully, his arms around my shoulders, and he took off his jacket and wrapped it around me. It was heavy and it smelled faintly like cigarettes. It didn't really do much to warm me but the largeness made me feel covered and safe. I curled up inside that jacket and looked around.

The bad men were gone.

Christian's body lay sprawled out a few feet away.

He wasn't moving. No chest rising up and down. His eyes were half-closed and he stared up at the sky, the rain falling onto his face. There were tiny pools of water in the corners of his eyes. Hands clenched, arms spread out, he looked like a small downfallen Jesus without his cross.

"Is he dead?"

Gazer nodded. "I'm sorry," he said. "I couldn't save you both. But understand me, there's nothing in the world I wanted more to do."

"Is he in hell?"

"No," Gazer said. "Why would you think that?" He paused when he saw the tears instantly spring into my eyes. He leaned forward, his fingers touching my cheek, studying my expression, which fell apart at his touch. He waited, pulling my body close as I shook and sobbed. We sat together in the smelly alley and the rain continued to fall.

"You didn't see heaven, did you." Not a question.

I shook my head.

"What did you see?"

"Monsters." My body trembled and I couldn't control it. I wanted to tell him about the shadows and the way the metal pierced my body but the words wouldn't come out.

My teeth were chattering too hard. I swallowed several times, wondering if the shadow demon was still inside me.

"You know none of that stuff is real. What you saw. It's not heaven or hell. It means nothing. It's more like a realistic dream that your brain invents to try and fight off the drugs."

I know he was trying to make me feel better but it didn't work. My grandmother used to tell me that the most evil people went to hell because God punished sinners. That meant I was evil. I had no idea what I'd done to become bad but I did it. Maybe it was because I let Christian die. Maybe it was because of something I did before and couldn't remember. But I was doomed. Evil. I had seen hell, and nothing Gazer said could make me think otherwise.

"What happened to the bad men?" I finally asked. I thought of the man with his leather jacket and his big smile and how much I hated him.

"They left," he said. "I scared them away. They won't come back."

"I'm going to kill them," I said.

Gazer didn't say anything. He pulled me tighter and we sat for a while longer until the ambulance arrived, the bright red lights flashing against my face. The EMTs came and Gazer convinced me to let go of him so they could take care of me.

"Don't leave me," I said.

"I won't," he promised. "I'll be right over there. You're not alone."

They pulled me away from Christian's body and split

us up. One of them stayed with my newly dead friend; the other brought me to the ambulance, where he sat me down on a stretcher in the back of the vehicle. Gazer came over and joined us, trying to fill the paramedic in on the details. He told him how he found us alone and managed to use CPR to bring me back. He didn't mention the bad men.

The paramedic checked my vital signs and did a few other things that I didn't quite understand. I was perfectly fine until he tried to pull my shirt up over my head. Only then did I resist. I was still scared.

"Come on, miss," the paramedic said. "I need to check you. If you're uncomfortable, I can make the man go away. This will only take a second."

"I want him to stay," I said. I had never met Gazer before; hell, I still didn't know his full name, but I felt safe with him around. There was something in his eyes, a certain kind of sadness that made me feel secure. Without him by my side, I probably would have completely fallen apart, especially with what came next.

When the paramedic peeled off my wet shirt, I saw the veins. A spiderweb-like pattern that started at my chest and stretched outward, stopping just below my neckline. Many of the veins crisscrossed up over my shoulder. They were dark red, almost purple.

"Jesus." The paramedic whistled. "What the hell are these kids thinking these days? They keep getting younger and younger." He wasn't even speaking to me anymore. "I mean, come on, she can't be older than twelve. How old are you, kid?"

"Eleven," I whispered.

"What on earth made you try Heam? Just how stupid are you?"

"I didn't," I said. My lower lip quivered. The tears were threatening to push their way forward again. Why was I being blamed for this?

"I believe she and the boy had the drug forced on them," Gazer said, coming to my rescue.

"What the hell were they doing out this late at night?" the paramedic asked. "Where are their parents? If these were my kids . . ."

"But they're not your kids," Gazer answered. "And I don't think you should continue this conversation. You're clearly upsetting the girl."

"Whatever," the paramedic said. "Not my problem. We'll take her to Sacred Heart. You going to come along? You know her parents?"

In the end, I didn't go to the hospital. When they brought Christian's body into the ambulance in the large black bag, I began screaming. I thought the shadows had gotten to him. No amount of coaxing by either Gazer or the paramedics could keep me under control. Besides, there wasn't much more they could do for me. I'd survived the overdose; the only thing left to do was contact my mother. No hospital in the world would waste the bed space to keep a new Heam addict under observation. Gazer finally convinced them that he'd take me home.

I stood there, holding Gazer's hand, watching the ambulance take my best friend away.

Christian was thirteen, two years older than me. We lived next door to each other and he often took care of me because our parents were never around. He was the most beautiful boy in the world in my eyes. I had such a school-girl crush on him. We had gone out that evening because both our mothers were working late shifts and we wanted to meet his father when he got off work. We had done it dozens of times; sometimes his dad would take us out for hot chocolate and donuts. I loved Christian's dad like my own father. I was always welcome at their dinner table, especially since my mother was often working two or more jobs to try to put food on ours.

We'd taken a shortcut through the alley that night and found more than we bargained for. Four men looking to get revenge against a man who died before paying off his debts. Funny how quickly life could change with a simple wrong turn down a darkened street.

"Will they bury him?" I asked when the ambulance turned the corner. They no longer had the flashing lights on.

"Maybe," Gazer said.

"Can I go to the funeral?"

"You'll have to ask your mother."

I nodded. My chest was itchy and burning at the same time. I kept touching the spot over my heart, tracing my fingers over the veins, thinking how odd it was that the skin didn't feel different. There was a hollow feeling in my stomach and I was thirsty. I wanted something. It was as if my brain were screaming at me. I remembered the strawberry liquid, remembered how good it tasted on my tongue. I wished I had some more. If I had more, maybe the excruciating hunger in my mind would go away.

I thought it was funny that I didn't feel any emotions. I should be sad. I loved Christian. Why wasn't I crying? I had bawled my eyes out a few months ago when the neighbor's dog had been killed by a car. Christian had hugged me and told me everything was going to be fine.

Now Christian was dead. Why didn't I feel?

I didn't know it at the time but Heam numbs the body and brain, especially after a recent ingestion. I couldn't cry. The drug wouldn't let me. The tears would come later, and they did come. An army of them over the next several years. Sometimes I thought my brain would melt out of my skull from all the grief.

"Come on," Gazer said. "Let's get you home."

Home.

Yeah, that didn't work out well.

My mother took one look at the veins on my chest and no longer wanted me.

That's how I ended up with Gazer. There was nowhere else to go.

SIX

"So what's with the anti-socialness? Are you always this stuck up or are you simply challenged in the life-skills department?"

I look up from my book, not overly surprised to see Jesse standing at my table. Paige is behind him, leaning around his shoulder. It's obvious she's set him up to try to change my mind.

"Maybe I just don't like you," I say.

It was easier when they left me alone. I didn't have to constantly be on my guard. I didn't have to be mean.

This whole bitch process is wearing me down. No matter how much I try to convince myself I'd rather be alone, there's a small voice in my brain that calls me a liar. Maybe it would be nice to hang out just once and try to be normal. But then the itchiness in my chest reminds me that I'm here on this earth for a short time. I have a purpose. Just one. And I will go to my grave once I fulfill it.

Having friends would just complicate things. It might end the loneliness but it would only prolong the sorrow. Which is worse?

"Yeah, I don't believe that," Jesse says, and he pulls out the chair across from me and sits down. Paige continues to stand but she smiles at me. There's something odd in that grin. They've come here for a purpose other than friendship. But what?

I glance around the room but once again the teachers are all off in other directions. I can't help wondering if I've been so good at following their rules that they no longer feel they have to watch me. Or maybe they never cared to watch me in the first place. Have I been paranoid all this time over nothing?

"Paige has been telling me a pretty incredible story," Jesse says. He takes one of the fries off my plate and eats it. "She told me that you had a run-in with Trevor. Left him in nasty bloody shape too. I saw him at the club last night. He looked like he'd been run over by a truck."

I shrug.

"So it is true?" Jesse looks impressed. "She said you were like some sort of ninja."

"Hardly," I say.

"How'd you learn to fight like that?"

"Just did." I'm not about to out Gazer to the two of them. Even though Gazer hasn't been a cop in more than a decade, it still might not look good for him if people knew he'd been training me. People tend to question it when a grown man teaches a girl how to throw a knife properly.

"You can do that all the time?" Jesse takes another fry and chews it thoughtfully.

"Yeah."

"I may have a business proposition. Could be a nice little change for you." Jesse doesn't hide the fact that he's checking me out. His eyes go up and down my body. I know what he's looking for. We may have to wear uniforms at the school but it's still obvious who is rich and who isn't. Jesse sees that I don't have any jewelry. I don't have a pair of expensive shoes. There are no designer sunglasses on top of my head. My backpack is old and worn, most definitely secondhand.

He knows I'm broke. It's not like I've ever tried to hide it.

"What kind of money are we talking about?" I ask.

"A lot."

I wonder what Jesse would consider a lot. He's one of the only students who drive a car and it's impressive enough that even I've turned to watch him as he drives down the street.

Don't get me wrong. I don't care about money. The old saying is "You can't take it with you" and I've always thought about it that way. I'm not saving for retirement since I'm fairly certain I'm not going to live past twenty. So what's the point of worrying about it? Gazer gets enough money off his disability pension to keep us afloat and that's all that matters. So what if we live in a rundown church that doesn't have hot water half the time. So what if I wake up in the mornings unable to feel my toes sometimes. I don't need nice things. I'd probably just ruin them anyway.

But as I sit there, I realize that a bit of extra money could go a long way. I could leave it to Gazer, a thank-you for helping me all these years. I could even give it away; put it toward one of the rare privately funded Heam support centers. God knows they could use the help. I could even use it to buy myself something nice, a sort of farewell gift for me when I leave this world. I've always wanted to eat in an expensive restaurant. I've never had fancy food. Just like the prisoner gets his last meal, maybe I could do something similar?

I glance around again. I can see Mr. Erikson across the room watching me. Not out of concern, though; he seems happy to see me socializing.

"I'm listening," I say to Jesse.

Paige's grin grows wide and she finally sits down next to us at the table. "It's not a big thing," she says. "We just need a little protection."

Jesse waves his hand in her direction, obviously meant to shut her up. It works. She closes her mouth and waits.

"As my girlfriend blabbed," Jesse says, "we do need a bit of help. We did something really dumb and now we're afraid that certain people aren't going to leave us alone."

"You mean Trevor?"

He nods. "Yeah, stupid dealer just doesn't get it. We're not interested. See, that's what happens when you're too polite to the hired help."

"Isn't that what you want me to be?" I can't help smirking. Hired help? Me? The thought is almost funny enough to make me laugh out loud. But I'm professional enough to keep a neutral face.

"God, Jesse." Paige punches him on the arm. "What's wrong with you? It's this sort of crap that got you in trouble in the first place." She gives him a shove and turns to me. "Don't listen to him. He's a jerk. Will you do it?"

"What exactly do you want me to do?"

"Show up at the party on Friday night. We'll have a list of who gets to come in and who doesn't. Trevor isn't on the list. Neither are a few others. All you have to do is make sure they don't come inside."

I pick at the last remaining fries on my plate. Mostly for show. I was done eating five minutes ago. "Doesn't sound that interesting."

"It's worth five hundred."

I get up, collect my tray of cold food, and start to walk away. "Make it a thousand and I might consider it," I say over my shoulder.

Always leave them wanting more. That's probably the only worthwhile thing my father ever taught me before they hauled him away. I wonder if it worked for him. Will it work for me? Time will tell.

I have to admit I'm a little disappointed. Even though I had to reject Paige, it was nice thinking that someone wanted to befriend me. Christian was the last friend I had besides Gazer, and Gazer doesn't count because he's in his late thirties. It's been so long, I've forgotten what it's like to have someone my own age around. I sometimes wonder if Christian and I would have remained friends if he'd lived. But I don't think about it often. It hurts too much.

They haul my ass into the office right after lunch. The vice principal comes and gets me personally. She leads me straight to the principal's office and shoves me through the door.

"I understand there was a bit of a disturbance this morning?" Mrs. Orman, the principal, asks me once we are locked away in her office.

"No, not really," I say. I'm trying to remain calm but I'm worried. This is the first time in three years that they've had to come and talk with me. I've done so well. It would suck to get expelled now, especially when I'm so close to graduating. Only a few months to go. I quickly glance down at my outfit to make sure everything is in order. No buttons missing. My skirt is pressed and wrinkle-free. No scars poking through the cotton. I look like the prim and proper schoolgirl I'm supposed to be. If I smile sweetly, I might even look innocent enough to fool her.

She looks at the file on top of her desk. "Screaming? Disrupting the entire classroom? I'd hardly consider that a small thing."

"I had a bad daydream," I tell her. "I haven't been sleeping well lately."

"You're not using again, I hope."

I shake my head vehemently. "No, of course not."

"Good, because I'd hate to have to remove you, considering you've done so well here. But you understand how important it is to keep a low profile."

"I have been keeping a low profile."

Mrs. Orman nods in agreement. "So far, yes. Let's keep it that way, shall we? Consider this a warning. Make sure you get enough sleep from now on. We need you nice and rested, don't you think?"

"Yes, ma'am."

"Good." She closes the folder and nods at me to leave.

My last class of the day is physics and I coast through it by sitting at the back of the class and pinching my leg every few minutes to keep myself awake. I don't need a repeat of this morning. Most of the hype has died down but there are still a few students giving me unusual looks.

Paige is waiting for me at my locker. I knew she was going to be there. She's alone. I guess they figured Jesse was getting on my nerves. I've got to learn to keep a better poker face.

"A thousand is acceptable," she says. "Will you do it?"

"Okay," I say. "But I've got some conditions."

"Which are?"

She waits. I open my locker and shove my books in. I grab my jacket. "I'm not going to hurt anyone unless they try to hurt me first. So I won't fight someone just because you tell me to. Consider me more of a peacekeeper."

She agrees. She actually looks relieved. I have a feeling this wasn't her idea. Hiring me. Hell, she probably didn't even want the party.

"And I want to be paid up front. And I'm not staying the whole night. I think two a.m. should be enough."

"Okay," she says. "Tomorrow is Thursday. I'll give it to you then."

I grab my backpack. "Deal."

"It's funny," Paige says as I get ready to walk away. "I

thought the reason you don't take gym is because you have asthma."

"Yeah? So?"

"You sure didn't seem winded when you beat up Trevor. In fact, you look to be in pretty darn good shape for someone who can't breathe."

"What can I say?" I slam my locker. "I hate competitive sports."

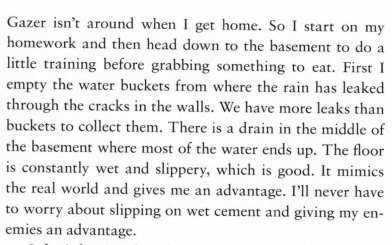

Gazer isn't around when I get home. So I start on my homework and then head down to the basement to do a little training before grabbing something to eat. First I empty the water buckets from where the rain has leaked through the cracks in the walls. We have more leaks than buckets to collect them. There is a drain in the middle of the basement where most of the water ends up. The floor is constantly wet and slippery, which is good. It mimics the real world and gives me an advantage. I'll never have to worry about slipping on wet cement and giving my enemies an advantage.

I don't know what the basement was originally used for. Maybe to keep records. Maybe a place where the nuns used to sleep. It's hard to tell. Now it's just a large room filled with all sorts of exercise equipment that Gazer has managed to salvage and fix over the years. A treadmill is in the corner but it doesn't work anymore. No amount of tinkering can save it now. Gazer keeps saying he's going to throw it out but he doesn't get around to it.

There are mismatched weight sets. A stationary bicycle that's slightly lopsided. In one corner is a small room where we keep the weapons. No guns. Neither Gazer nor I believe in them. Guns are too loud. They bring too much attention.

But we do have the knives. Those are the weapons I work with every day. My goal is to master them. And I'm already very good. Even Gazer admits I'm better than him.

To be a fighter, I need the ability to clear my mind of all thoughts and burdens. Gazer makes me do yoga and meditation. Personally, I hate yoga but I do it because I need to be the very best. But today I'm not able to achieve a clear head, no matter how long I try to maintain downward-facing dog. I can't stop thinking about everything; too many thoughts do circles inside my brain. So after half an hour or so, I grab my towel and head upstairs.

Defeated by my brain.

I decide to start dinner but the stove isn't working. A new leak has sprung above the stove and the water has soaked all the burners and the flames have gone out. I get a new bucket from under the sink and place it on the back burner to try to catch the dripping. Water begins to collect in the bottom, making a hollow thudding noise that sounds like a heart beating. It takes me a while to find matches but that turns out to be a useless chore because I can't relight the burners to save my life.

I kick the stove in frustration, leaving a nice dent and a black scuff mark the size of my foot.

"What did the stove ever do to you?"

I spin around and Gazer is standing in the door.

"Burner light is out," I say. "Everything's soaking wet. You'll have to patch the leak or I'm not going to be cooking for a long time."

"Sandwiches it is."

The fridge is rattling but at least it's still working. I pull out some meat and cheese and Gazer and I get to work with dinner. It's not the first time we've had to fix sandwiches for dinner.

"How was your day?" Gazer finds the chopping board in the sink and rinses it off.

"Fine," I say. I'm not about to tell him about the deal I've made with Paige and Jesse. I don't think he'd be very happy to hear about it. Although I'm not one for keeping secrets from Gazer, this is something he's better off not knowing about for now. When I slip out the door tomorrow night, I'll let him think I'm just making my usual rounds.

"Did you practice?"

"A bit."

"Good."

This small talk might sound mundane, but to me it states that Gazer is no longer angry with me. My little outburst from earlier has been forgotten for now. He doesn't hold grudges and neither do I, aside from grudges toward a few certain men who deserve it. This is why we get along so well.

Gazer used to have a good life. He had a wife and a daughter. He had a job that he loved. He was a cop and from what I've heard, he was excellent. In his room, in the bottom drawer of his desk, he's got pictures from his former life. Hidden away, there are snapshots of him wearing

89

the uniform, smiling at the camera, his arms around his family. He was young, only in his midtwenties, but he had his entire life planned out. He'd married his high school sweetheart and they'd had a beautiful daughter together. They were the perfect couple.

There is one picture I like in particular. A black-and-white photo. Gazer has his arms around his wife, and he's looking down at her in admiration. She's smiling with her eyes half-closed and you can tell there aren't two people in the world who enjoy each other's company as much as these two.

He was in love.

And then he angered the wrong people and she was gone. They came in the night when he was at work and killed her. They killed his daughter too.

Although Gazer knew who murdered them, there wasn't enough proof to prosecute. The killers walked. Gazer lasted with the force for about six more months before finally quitting. The job was no longer inside of him. The will to right evil was gone. He hasn't held a job since. He lives off a small pension and that's why we live here. We can't afford anything else.

This is why I find it frustrating when Gazer tells me I shouldn't spend my life focused on revenge. If anyone should know exactly how I feel, it should be him. I wonder if he lies awake at night, picturing the faces of the people who did this to him. Doesn't he dream of seeing their bodies lying at his feet the way I do?

Gazer doesn't want me to know he still goes into his drawer and looks at his pictures. But the walls between our bedrooms are thin and I can hear the squeak of the wood at least once a week when he thinks I'm sleeping. He will spend an hour or two on the floor, looking at the ghosts of his past, reliving the pain that will never leave him.

Does it make him stronger? I don't know. I don't have any pictures of Christian or my parents to look at. Even if I did, I'd probably burn them. The thought of having to look at those smiling faces places a hollow space in my stomach that expands and can never be filled.

Gazer is stronger than me. But he's stupid too. Those men still walk the streets. When I am done, my tormenters will be in their graves, unable to ever hurt anyone again.

—+—

After dinner, I wash the leftover dishes in the sink with cold water while Gazer retreats to his living-room corner to read his books. We deal with our pain in separate ways. He immerses himself in the written word and I wander the streets. At least he gets to stay dry.

I grab my jacket and head downstairs.

"Don't be out late," Gazer says without looking up from his book. It's the *Iliad* tonight, a favorite of his. The pages are worn and the cover is dog-eared from years of touching. He's pretty much got the entire story memorized by now, not an easy feat.

"I won't."

"And get up an extra hour early tomorrow," he says, and I can see the hint of a smile forming at his lips. "We have to make up for all that lost time this morning."

I will not groan. I will not give him the satisfaction. "Sounds brilliant," I say through clenched teeth.

I may be forgiven but he still wins. Tomorrow he's going to make sure my body aches. Revenge, Gazer-style.

When I step outside, I notice that the rain has finally stopped. It's still cloudy and cold and the air has a fine mist about it that could be mistaken for rain, but it's not. I smile. Such a nice change. I wonder how long it will last.

So there's a spring to my step as I walk down the street. It feels good not to have my hair plastered against my cheeks. I even undo my jacket a bit and let the cool air press against my turtleneck shirt.

I tell myself I'm not heading anywhere in particular but I find myself pointed toward the bar. But I'm not going for Rufus; he's not there. I know this because I overheard him a few nights ago on his phone. There's a shipment of illegal immigrants on its way in tonight he's got to deal with. I will go down to the docks and check it out later before I head home.

There's no real need for me to be there but I still find myself stopping at my usual spot underneath the streetlight. I wait.

But Chael doesn't show.

This is stupid. I'm not waiting for him. I don't even want to see him. He's weird. He never gives me a straight answer and he threatened me the other night. So why is it when I try to think about him, all I can do is picture the way his hair is the perfect length or that his green eyes are always looking at me so intently?

No, stop it. He's trouble.

92

I don't need trouble.

And I'm not going to let him take my revenge.

Rufus and the others are mine.

"Excuse me?"

It's the little girl with the MISSING posters in her arm. She doesn't have her red umbrella tonight and she almost looks naked without it. I smile down at her but she's not smiling back. Instead, she's biting her lower lip and clutching her flyers so tightly the paper is wrinkling in her grasp.

"What's up?" I ask her.

"Why are you doing this?" she asks. "You took a poster. You said you'd tell me if you saw him." She waves the flyers at me; the boy with the glasses stares up at me from xeroxed paper.

Her sudden anger at me is surprising; I'm at a loss for words. "I'm sorry," I choke out. "I don't understand."

"Yes, you do!" She grabs a flyer and shoves it in my face. The boy's forlorn expression stares right into my eyes. "You were with him last night. I saw you!"

I reach out and grab the paper, yanking it from her fingers. I look around wildly but her mother is nowhere in sight. "Okay, you need to calm down and tell me what you thought you saw. I guarantee you I wasn't with your brother. I hold the flyer up and read beyond the MISSING part. Arnold Bozek. Eighteen years old. Been missing for a week. There's a phone number to contact. I look at the boy with the short blond hair and glasses. No, there's no mistake on my part. I've never seen this boy before in my life.

"I'm sorry," I tell her. "I haven't seen him."

"But you talked to him last night," she says. I can tell

by the look on her face she believes what she's saying. "You talked to him right here. Under this light. I saw you two together. I called out but you turned and ran. Why? Why are you keeping him from us?"

She's talking about Chael, but how she could mistake him for Arnold is beyond me. Chael's hair is almost black. He doesn't wear glasses. Only a blind person would be unable to tell them apart.

But it was dark outside and he did have his jacket hood up if I recall. It is possible that this girl might have thought it was her brother. She's been spending so much time looking; maybe what she saw was a type of mirage. She wants to see Arnold so badly that other people begin to look like him.

"You've made a mistake."

"No I haven't," she says, and throws the flyers on the ground. "Don't lie to me!"

"I'm not lying and I haven't seen your stupid brother," I snap back. I've lost patience with her. I've tried being nice and that's getting me nowhere. Time to bring out the bitch. "And stop following me or I'll have a talk with your mother."

I turn and stomp off into the night. I half expect the girl to follow me but she doesn't. When I reach the end of the block, I turn and look. She's still by the streetlight, on her knees, picking the flyers up off the street. They'll be wet by now. Useless. Frowning, I head off toward anywhere but here. It's not my fault.

SEVEN

Friday night and I am stupid enough to tell Gazer part of my plan. I should have known better. He always takes the practical side.

"You can't go to a party," he says. "Not with the kids from school. You know the rules. All it takes is one person to make a comment Monday morning and you'll be kicked out the doors."

"Nothing's going to happen," I say. I haven't told him about the bodyguard part. Paige stopped at my locker this morning and gave me a discreet envelope. It's now hidden between my mattresses. Paid in full. If I don't show up tonight, I'll have to give the money back.

"That's irrelevant," Gazer says. "If you get caught, you won't graduate."

"Who cares," I say. "It's not like I'll be able to get a job or anything."

Gazer reaches out and touches my arm. "Don't talk

like that, Faye. You never know what the future holds. Graduating has always been important to you. Don't give up on that hope now. Not when you're so close."

He's right, of course. Graduating is the one lousy thing I want to do before I leave this earth. At least then I can say that I did something. So when I arrive at the gates of hell, I can look the demons in the eye and when they ask me what I did besides kill four men, I can say at least I survived high school. That's gotta count for something.

But it seems stupid, now that I think about it.

"Maybe I don't think it's important anymore," I say.

"That's not true, Faye," Gazer says. He sits down in his chair and lights the closest candle. "I know you think you're going to die because of what happened to you as a child. I know you think you're doomed and that the gates of heaven are unavailable to you."

Because it's true, I want to argue. But I keep my mouth shut.

Gazer lights a second candle. "The reality of the situation is that none of us know what's going to happen when we die. That's why we live. The illusions you had under the influence of Heam were just that. Hallucinations. Fake."

"No one knows that for sure," I say. "Even the experts can't tell if it's an illusion or an out-of-body experience."

"A lot of this is propaganda, put together by the churches to make people afraid," Gazer says. "It could simply be the brain's way of dealing with the body shutting down."

"It felt real enough to me. You don't understand."

Gazer closes his eyes tightly and it hurts me more than I'll admit to see him like this. I don't like knowing that I'm causing him pain. I want to protect him, lie and tell him the words he wants to hear. He is my family. He's the one person on this earth that cares about me. Loves me. But he'll never understand me.

"I'll finish school," I say. "But I need to go to this party. I've never been invited to anything before. It's important."

I speak the words as a lie, but there is a half-truth there. If it weren't for the money, I might actually believe that they want me. I try to picture myself at the shops with Paige, looking around for the perfect prom dress. Maybe Chael could be my date. He'd show up with a rose corsage. Gazer could break out the camera and take pictures to frame on the mantel. I'd be given a curfew and we'd head off into the night in a beautiful white limousine. At the party, we'd sit at the table with Paige and Jesse and giggle and chat like old friends. Powdering our noses in the bathroom. Dancing to some crappy band. Soft kisses under the moonlight.

The thought is so absurd I have to chomp down on my tongue to keep from laughing out loud.

Gazer sighs as if reading my mind. "I'm sorry, Faye, but I can't allow it. I think it's best if you stay in tonight."

"You're grounding me?"

"Yes, I guess I am."

In the six years we've lived together, Gazer has never once pulled rank. Not once. He's never refused me anything. I open my mouth to protest, but Gazer picks up his copy of the *Iliad* and opens it to the bookmarked page. It's his way of saying the argument is over. Finished. Kaput.

I go upstairs to my bedroom and flop down on the bed. Looking at the clock, I notice that it's just a bit past eight. No problem. I'll let Gazer think he's won. Technically I don't have to be at Paige's until eleven. I'll just wait till Gazer goes to bed and do what every other normal teenager would do. I'll sneak out.

—+—

Gazer taps on my door around ten-thirty. I'm lying on the bed, staring up at the ceiling. A textbook rests on my chest but it's mostly for show. I haven't been studying. Not with all the plotting going around in my brain.

"It's open," I say.

He opens the door and steps inside. "I wanted to apologize for what I said earlier," he says. "I shouldn't have trivialized your feelings the way I did."

"Thanks." I shift on the bed and the textbook slides off my chest and onto the floor. It hits the ground with a good hard thunk.

"And I'm sorry that you feel the way you do and I wish I could fix it," Gazer says. "I love you like my own daughter. I'd do anything to try and make your pain go away."

"I know."

And I do know. I remember the nights following my overdose. Waking up from dreams, screaming, tears falling, and Gazer always being right by my side. He'd pull the covers up tighter and tell me stories from all the books he's read. And he never left my side until I'd slipped back into sleep.

Gazer's been there to fight for me since the moment he took me in. I don't think I'll ever be able to express to him how truly important he's been to me.

Gazer takes a deep breath. "What's happened to us, Faye?" he asks. He leans against the wall and stares down at his hands. "I feel like we're pulling apart. Fighting all the time. It worries me to watch you drifting away. I'm afraid you're going to wander too far and I won't be able to bring you back."

I get up off the bed and go over to him, putting my arms around him and hugging him tightly. The tears threaten my eyes, burning me, and I blink several times to try to keep them back. "I'm sorry," I say. "It's my fault."

Gazer shakes his head. "No, it's mine." He pushes me back and looks into my eyes. "I haven't done my job. I've tried to bring you peace but you won't accept it. You're going to do what you're going to do. I won't stand in your way anymore."

"What do you mean?"

"I mean you're ready. Well, ready as you're going to be. But promise me you'll at least wait until you graduate. Give yourself that at least."

I want to be happy. Gazer has finally said the words I want to hear. But I'm not happy. Mostly because I can tell he doesn't believe them. He's telling me to get my revenge only because he failed at teaching me otherwise.

It's not a victorious moment.

Especially when I know in ten minutes or so I'll be sneaking out my bedroom window.

There are so many things I want to say but I can't stand to say them to Gazer's face when he looks this weak.

"I'm really tired," I finally say.

"You should get some sleep, then." He kisses me on the forehead. "Maybe we'll both feel better tomorrow morning."

I smile and he closes the door behind him on the way out. I listen to his footsteps going down the hall and back downstairs to his books. Within seconds, I yank my jacket from off the floor and grab my gloves from the top of my dresser. I head over to the window.

I wasn't feeling guilty earlier and now I try to push the shame away by concentrating on the task ahead of me. I've never snuck out the window before. I cringe when the wood squeaks as I push up the frame. Cold air hits my face. Squeezing through the small space, I step down onto the ledge, trying not to look down. It's a good twenty feet below. I probably wouldn't hurt myself badly if I fell but I don't want to take the chance and find out. I lower myself by my arms, feeling the muscles straining against my shirt, and drop down to the next ledge. From there I lower myself again and drop down the last ten feet. I hit the ground with a thud and freeze, hoping that Gazer doesn't hear it and come to investigate.

It's not until I'm on the ground that I realize that I'm not getting back inside the way I came down. Why didn't I think of that before? My fingers close around my keys;

if I'm quiet enough, I might be able to sneak in as long as Gazer actually goes to bed tonight. There are many nights when he falls asleep in his chair, his book resting in his lap.

Leave it to me to make things more difficult.

Not much I can do about it now.

Earlier I typed Paige's address into my phone to get directions. I head off toward the train. She's a good forty minutes away. I'll get there a bit late but it's better than nothing.

—┼—

"You're late."

Jesse stands in the living room, a glass of beer in his hand. His eyes are watery and he's not standing very straight. I wonder how much he's already had to drink tonight.

When I arrived, there were so many teenagers hanging around that it seemed pointless to knock. I followed the noise and it led me around to the backyard, where dozens of kids were hanging out, talking loudly amongst themselves. Most of the school must have been there; I recognized a lot of faces, but there were some I didn't. Paige must have invited most of the city's entire population of underage kids.

She lives in a very fancy area of town. I've never been here, never had any reason to visit. You won't find gutter rats hanging in the alleys here. You won't find dealers on the street corners and young girls wearing fishnet stockings and short skirts. Instead, you find large houses and gated communities with landscaping that is maintained by hired help. Paige's home is gigantic, a massive brownstone mansion with a huge yard and a pool surrounded by fake Greek statues. There's even a waterfall, man-made of course, that spills directly into a pond surrounded by rose bushes and expensive-looking patio furniture. It's impressive. I've never before known anyone who owns their own pool.

After gawking for a few minutes, I turned and walked in through the back door, which led to a kitchen, bigger than anything I've ever seen. Another door went into the living room and that's where I found Jesse.

"Sorry," I say to Jesse. "I had some problems."

"We should deduct some of that off your paycheck," he says. His words come out a little slurred but I'm not sure if it's an act or not. His eyes look very alert and not drunk at all. I can't help thinking I'm being led on for some reason. But why?

"You made it," Paige says. She rushes over to stand beside me, a group of girls following behind her. I recognize most of them from school but many of their names elude me. I've spent so much time trying to be invisible; now I'm wishing I'd spent a bit more time so I wouldn't feel so stupid.

Now that the girls are here, Jesse slips away. I watch him go across the room and pull out his phone. He quickly makes a call. I can't see what he's saying but he looks over at me a few times, not even trying to be discreet.

That should be my first warning sign but I choose to ignore it.

"Here." Paige thrusts a beer into my hand. I accept it, but decide not to drink. It wouldn't do me much good to get hammered tonight. It's best to keep my inhibitions at a steady level. Who knows what kind of secrets I might reveal if I get sloshed. I look down at the amber liquid in my glass and wonder. I'd be lying if I said I wasn't curious. I've never been drunk before. Alcohol never factored into my plans.

I take a sip. The liquid burns my throat in a good way. But I stop at that. I'm being paid here for a service. Heaven forbid Trevor sneaks in if I'm puking my guts out in the toilet.

Paige leaves me to go talk to some other girls and suddenly I'm feeling very self-conscious. Even though I've gone to school with most of these kids for years, I don't think I've ever said more than two words to any of them. Now that I'm standing here, in a living room the size of a cruise ship, wearing clothing that's not school-issued, I can't help feeling odd.

And wow, are they dressed. Now that they've been given the chance to ditch their ties and skirts, they've really managed to master the ability to dress in as little clothing as humanly possible. There is a lot of bare skin in this room. Low-cut tops showing cleavage, short skirts that barely cover their asses, and bare midriffs revealing belly buttons. I wish I'd given a bit more thought to my own wardrobe tonight. I'm wearing jeans and a black shirt with a high neck. My scars are well hidden.

They're lucky, these girls with their ability to wear such clothing. I'd give anything to spend a single day in their place. I'd love to be able to stand proud and not be ashamed of my body. Bare skin. I'd love to feel the rain falling on my shoulders.

I am not a monster, but the world treats me like one.

I stand there with my drink in my hand, watching the room, my eyes scanning but never staring at anyone for very long. Paige chats with her friends and some of them turn and look at me curiously but no one comes over.

"Having fun?"

I know that voice. I don't even have to turn around before I open my mouth. "You *are* following me."

"Maybe. Or perhaps I was invited."

I turn my head until I'm facing Chael. "You don't go to my school. If you did, I would have seen you."

"Is everyone here from your school?"

"Mostly."

"I guess I am following you."

"And I suppose you're going to be all mysterious again. You know, I'm getting kinda tired of your tricks. Maybe you should go focus your attention elsewhere." I point toward another girl, who has obviously had too much to drink by the way she's dancing. "There. She's available. Go stalk her."

Chael chuckles and his eyes light up. He's amused. Not quite what I was going for.

"I'll stick to you," Chael says. "You're much easier to find. I don't know where she lives and I can't be bothered to find out."

"But you bothered to follow me."

"You're interesting."

"Apparently. You seem to know a lot about me already. You know I'm going to kill Rufus. What else?" I realize I touched my chest as I was talking.

Chael watches my fingers trail along my shirt. "Yes," he says, and his voice sounds heavy. "I know about that."

"Are you going to tell them?"

"No. What kind of person do you think I am? Don't worry. Your secret is safe with me. I'm here to protect you, not out you."

"I don't need protection."

"We all need protection."

"Not me."

"Why? Because you know how to fight?" Chael gives me a dazzling smile. "Revenge takes more than tossing a few knives around. It takes deliberation and determination. And it takes your heart. That's not something you can easily get back."

"You sound like Gazer."

"He must be a very brilliant man."

A popular song comes on and someone cranks the volume. A very drunk girl gets up on the coffee table and starts dancing. Another boy joins her, his arms wrapped around her waist, and she giggles like crazy and lets him spin her around. Both of them end up flying off the table and onto the floor while everyone cheers.

It just goes to show that having a lot of money doesn't exactly make a person smart.

"God, this is stupid," I say.

"Why? Because they're enjoying themselves?"

"Yeah, being drunk is fun," I say sarcastically.

"It can be. Haven't you ever wanted to just let go like that?"

"Like that?" I point to a guy in the corner who is throwing up in a potted plant. A girl stands beside him, giggling, and petting his back with her hand. "That's disgusting. Who in their right mind would consider that fun?"

"It's more like a rite of passage, I suppose."

I look over at Chael and he's leaning against the wall, his eyes focused on the party. "I guess that's why I can't understand, then. I've never had the luxury of being a normal teenager."

"That's your own fault."

If looks could kill, he'd fall over dead that very instant. "Big talk," I snap at him. "You seem to know everything tonight. Well, you know about me, then. You know I can't do stuff like that."

"Why?"

"Why?" I slam my hand against my chest. "Because of that. I'm not like them. I'm not normal. Rufus and his friends made sure of that."

"You could be normal."

"You could quit being a jerk."

"Point taken."

I'm being a major bitch but I can't help it. If he's not going to play fair, then I won't either. It creeps me out that he knows so much about me but I don't know a single thing about him. Why the need to be so vague about everything?

"Who are you?" I ask. I guess it never hurts to try a straightforward approach.

"I can't tell you."

I pause. "Why not?"

"Because you wouldn't believe me. But trust me, you will figure it out on your own. It's better that way and I'm patient. I don't mind waiting."

"That makes no sense."

"Neither does me being here."

I look into those green eyes, those familiar eyes, but I can't remember where I've seen them before.

"Is it important that I remember you?" I ask.

He nods. "It is. But a little more time won't hurt."

"Does it have something to do with Rufus?"

Chael points over toward the door. "It does. But I think you need to focus on them right now."

I look over and notice that Trevor has arrived. But it's the person he's with that scares me the most.

I said that Rufus was the man I most want to take revenge on. I also said that there were others.

John "Trank" Sheffield. He's short and stumpy and somewhere in his midthirties. He likes them young from what I've heard, and he's low enough to supply the schoolgirls with all sorts of drugs to get into their pants. The night I died, he tried to cop a feel from me before Rufus pushed him away. When he held my arms back so Rufus could put the Heam in my mouth, I could feel his breath on the back of my hair as he exhaled excitedly. His breath smelled heavily like cigarettes and hot wings.

Normally, Trank hangs out over at the strip clubs or down on the street corners where the younger gutter rats peddle their wares for doses of Heam. He's quite a favorite among the desperate young girls. He's been known to give them bad Heam, meaning strawberry-flavored liquid candy mixed with silver nail polish to give it that special gleam. I still find it amazing that he hasn't been killed yet.

He's a disgusting pedophile who deserves to be put to death for his crimes. That puts him at number two on my list.

And here he is, standing right in front of me.

He's walked in behind Trevor and a few others I don't recognize. They're younger, Trevor's age. A motley crew of dropouts and dealers, exactly the kind of trash Paige hired me to keep away from her party. But seeing Trank has caught me off guard. The years haven't been kind to him. There are lots of deep lines across his forehead and at the corners of his eyes. It's been a while since I've seen him, a few months perhaps, and years since I've actually seen him this close. I may follow the men on my list but I rarely get close enough to get this good of a look.

It's not surprising that he's hanging with the kids these days. As far as I can tell, through my research, he doesn't get along well with people his own age. He seems to have trouble talking to them.

But why is he here?

When I see the grin light up Jesse's face, I get a pretty good idea. The two approach each other and slap each other on the back. Jesse reaches into his pocket and pulls out a wad of cash, not even caring if everyone in the room sees him. Trank produces a brown paper bag of something and they make an exchange.

"Your friends are up to no good," Chael says.

"They're not my friends."

"Really?" Chael gives me a grin and starts tugging on his shirt in that weird obsessive way of his. "I would have thought Trank would be on your list, considering what he's done to you."

"He is on my list," I say, wondering how the hell he knows I have a list in the first place. Also, should I be threatened because he knows Trank's name? I decide to try to get him to say more. "Seeing that you know so much about me, I shouldn't have to tell you."

Chael smiles and doesn't take the bait.

Jesse heads off to the other side of the living room, the small package tucked discreetly inside his jacket. He approaches a group of guys who seem awfully eager to see him. But instead of giving them some of whatever's in the bag, he pulls out a notebook and starts writing something down.

People start giving him money. A lot of money.

And he writes more in his notebook. It's almost as if he's taking orders.

"Weird." I look over at Chael and he's watching Jesse too. A frown shadows his face.

"What do you think he's doing?" I ask.

"My guess is taking bets."

"For what?"

Chael frowns again. "I'm not sure," he says, but I think he does know.

Before I can question him further, things start to get a little more interesting. Paige rushes over to Jesse and starts talking to him, but not loud enough for me to hear. She's obviously agitated, waving her arms around. Several times they both look over at me.

Suddenly it's very clear. How on earth didn't I notice this before?

"It's a setup," I say. "I'm here to fight Trevor."

"Looks that way."

"No problem," I say. "I kicked the crap out of him before. I can do it again."

"I don't think he's going to fight fair this time," Chael says, and he points to Trevor's waist. Sure enough, I can see the flash of silver, a knife hopefully, and not a gun, sticking halfway out of his pants.

I didn't bring a weapon tonight. I decided against it, figuring that I wouldn't be doing anything other than babysitting a bunch of drunks. I didn't think Trevor would bother showing his face, not from the way Paige made it sound. She'd said he wasn't invited and didn't even know about it. I'd say that was nothing but a big fat lie.

"That's it," I say. "I'm leaving."

I turn and head toward the door. I don't even bother looking to see if Chael is trailing me; in all honesty, I could care less if he is. He probably already knows where I'm going even though I haven't got the slightest clue myself. All I know is it's time to leave before things turn ugly.

The front door is blocked by boys. Kids that I go to school with that I'm pretty positive have never even noticed me before tonight. They're smiling and laughing and the joke's on me.

Paige comes running up behind me.

"I had nothing to do with it," she says in a panicked voice.

"With what?"

"This. Trevor being here. I had nothing to do with it." She grabs me by the arm and I pull away.

"Faye!" Jesse comes up and throws his arm around me, giving Paige an ugly look. I shove him away and he falls against some of his friends. A look of resentment crosses his face but only for a second. Then he smiles.

"Leaving so soon?" he asks. "That's a real shame because I forgot to mention your contract had a clause in it. See, Trevor here is a little offended that you managed to beat the crap out of him. He wants a second chance to mess up your pretty face."

"Not gonna happen," I say.

"Oh, I agree," Jesse says. "That's why I'm betting against him. But there's a bunch of people here who think otherwise. The odds aren't in your favor tonight."

"They'll be even lower because I'm not fighting," I say. "I'll give you your money back on Monday. I'm not interested."

Jesse laughs. "You say that like you have a choice."

I look around and spot Chael over by the corner. He hasn't moved. He's watching the scene with a look of amusement on his face. He's not going to come to my defense. Of course, he probably knows what I'm capable of doing. The others don't. This is why I can't fight.

I could kill Trevor in a heartbeat.

But I don't want him dead. Aside from being an idiot, he hasn't done anything that would put him on my list.

"I have plenty of choices," I snap at Jesse. "Trust me. I'm going through that door. And there isn't anything that you or your friends can do to stop me."

"If you do that, I'll lose a lot of money," Jesse says. "And so will a lot of my boys. I might let them take it out on Paige."

"So?"

Jesse smiles. "You saved her once. I can't imagine you went through all that hard work just to let her go a few days later."

He's got a point. I glare at Paige and there's a part of me that really does still want to leave. Screw her. She made her own bed. No one forced her to go out with a creep like Jesse. But at the same time, I won't. If there's anyone who knows what it feels like to be trapped, it's me.

"Fine, then," I snap at Jesse. "But when this is over, you and I are going to have a little talk about my commission. The cost just went up. I'd say about fifty percent of the profits."

"And why would I do that?"

"Because everything I do to these guys tonight, I will do to you if you don't pay up." Ignoring the small look of panic in Jesse's eyes, I turn and head back toward the living room. Chael absently plays with a lock of hair, pushing it behind his ear.

"Okay, everyone," Jesse calls out to the crowd. He's recovered quickly for someone who just had his life threatened. "We're going to take the party outside. Bets are still on for the next few minutes."

I look at the group of boys guarding the front door and wonder how many punches I'll need to throw before I manage to clear a path, when arms clamp down around me. I smell cigarettes and whiskey.

"Come on, little lady," a voice whispers at my neck.

Trank has snuck up behind me. My body involuntarily shudders and I spin around, but he's holding me. Our eyes lock and for a second I'm horrified he might recognize me. Does he remember the last time we were this close? Or was I just another gutter rat to torture because he got paid?

I remember that Trank was the one who sucker-punched Christian first. When Christian collapsed, Trank kicked him in the face and split his lip. I remember kneeling down beside my friend, trying to use the sleeve of my jacket to wipe away the blood, before Trank grabbed hold of me. He pulled me back by my arms, just like he's doing now.

Now he stares into my eyes, but there's no recognition there.

I've changed too much.

I imagine breaking away from his grip. A head butt to the forehead first, and when he falls back in surprise, I'll break his nose with my fist. Maybe I'll split his lip like he did to Christian. And when I'm finished and Trank is lying on the ground in a pool of his own blood, I'll kneel down beside him and whisper something in his ear:

"Not so helpless now."

But I don't do any of those things. Instead, I actually allow Trank to pull me toward the backyard, and I'll be damned if he doesn't try to grab my breast on the way. I give him a sharp jab in the ribs as a warning and thankfully he takes the hint.

I pass Chael and he follows us, not saying a word. He's got a weird expression on his face. His eyes are in a faraway place. He's not even fidgeting.

Out in the yard, Trevor and his group are waiting for me. They've got weapons. I see the flash of a knife blade. A metal pipe. Someone else is carrying a screwdriver. Trevor himself is showing off a fancy new tire iron.

The odds are starting to look more in their favor.

EIGHT

"You want some help?"

Chael appears beside me. He's no longer grinning. He's staring at Trank with a look that's probably similar to the one I'm sporting. Disgust. Hatred.

"I think that's against the rules," I say.

"Screw the rules."

I look over at the group of thugs standing beside the pool and realize that as much as Chael's help might be useful right now, I can't allow him to join in. I have no idea if he can take care of himself and I'm not about to risk finding out. I don't want to be responsible for anyone else getting hurt.

Besides, Chael's face is too pretty to get rearranged.

"No, I can handle it," I say. It strikes me that this conversation is completely surreal. How am I going to protect Chael when I'm not even sure I can take care of myself? Why am I being too stubborn to accept help from someone who might be a useful ally when the odds are so unfair to begin with?

Chael nods, and although he doesn't look very happy about it, he does take a few steps back. "I thought you'd say that," he says. "Holler if you need me."

"Some knight in shining armor," I say with a voice that I hope sounds lighthearted.

"I've seen you fight," Chael says. "I'm more concerned about them, to be honest."

"I'm going to kill you, bitch," Trevor shouts from about fifteen feet away. He doesn't seem to want to get any closer.

"Jesse, stop this." Paige has materialized from her hiding spot inside the house. No one is with her. Even her group of friends has left her alone, choosing to come and stand by the pool to watch the show. Paige approaches Jesse, who is still taking some last-minute bets. She's holding her phone in her hands. "I'm going to call the cops if you don't stop this."

Jesse grabs her arm and wrestles the phone away from her. "Shut up, Paige," he says. He turns and tosses her phone into the pool. Paige races over to the side but she's too late. It sinks into the deep end before she can retrieve it.

Paige comes back toward me. There are tears in her eyes. "I didn't know he was going to do this," she says.

"Come on," Trevor says. "Quit stalling."

"Okay," Jesse says, and he holds his hands up to his face as he shouts, "All bets are in. Welcome to Fight Hell. In that corner, light as a feather, our girl, Faye. Pretty as a peach but she needs to learn to dress a bit better. Come on,

Faye; show us something once in a while! Would it kill you to wear a decent shirt? You've got the package. No one is that much of a prude."

The noise is unbelievable. People scream and cheer. A few stoners in the corner hold up their lighters. Someone tosses a beer at the diving board. Glass explodes everywhere.

"And in that corner, weighing in at a hell of a lot more, a bunch of guys who want Faye dead. Let the fight begin."

Jesse cracks open a beer and takes a long drink. Foam splatters against his shirt. This must be the signal for round one because suddenly all four guys are heading toward me.

I put up my fists.

This is the situation I've been warned about over and over. Never let them notice you. I've screwed up bad. This isn't even about high school anymore. I could actually care less if these kids see me beat the snot out of Trevor. That alone will earn me enough respect and they'll probably leave me alone after this. No one is going to tell the teachers about what's happening tonight. Being a witness to this is more than enough to get expelled. Even Paige, who threatened to call the police, is probably bluffing. She doesn't want to get in trouble any more than the rest of us.

I'm more concerned about Trank. He's most certainly not going to forget me after this. All those years of careful watching on my part are about to be ruined. It's going to be harder to stick to the shadows, now that I'm visible.

People continue to scream but I stay where I am. I'm not going to start this fight. Better to let them come to me. But Trevor hesitates; he's waiting for my move. They've stopped about ten feet away, their weapons raised, but they're obviously a little uncertain about how to proceed. It's not every day a group of guys try to beat up on a girl on a bet. I can't imagine they've done this sort of thing before.

The crowd grows restless. People start to boo and toss half-empty cups of beer in our direction. One of them hits Trevor in the face and beer splashes into his eyes. Someone throws a shoe. Another faceless person tosses his shirt.

This is starting to get a bit ridiculous. The guys wait, holding their weapons. Either my fame precedes me, or they're really just a bunch of cowards.

Finally, one of the guys takes a step forward, the one carrying the metal pipe in his hands. Spurred on by the crowd's cheering, he raises his weapon and heads toward me. I raise my hands to protect my face. The audience goes wild. I keep my eyes on him the way Gazer taught me. Never turn your back on an enemy for even a second.

He swings the pipe toward my face. I lean back at the last second, feeling the breeze of the metal as it misses my nose by an inch. When he comes around for a second blow, I raise my arm and deliver a short quick jab straight into his nose. He flinches and blood spurts from his nostrils but he doesn't drop the weapon.

So I go at him again. He blocks the uppercut but I'm too quick, swinging around with my left, a blow that lands squarely on his ear. A good kick to the stomach sends him reeling, dropping the pipe. Unable to keep his balance with the momentum, he steps backward and right into the pool.

The audience goes insane. When the guy breaks the surface, he's met with dozens of beer cups tossed in his face. He makes his way over to the shallow end, where people splash water at him and continue to bombard him with whatever objects they can find.

"That's one," I say to Trevor. I pick up the metal pipe and pass it back toward Chael, who takes it. No need to have weapons lying around on the ground where anyone can pick them up and try to use them on my back. I definitely don't need a weapon myself. I might hurt someone badly with my hands alone. Having a weapon would only heighten that. The last thing I want to do is end up with a murder charge. Not with all these witnesses around.

I don't get a chance for a break. The guys with the switchblade and the screwdriver decide to double-tag me. They split up, trying to come around on each side, hoping that I might get confused or something. As Screwdriver comes in for the kill, wielding his weapon like a knife, I drop to the ground and swing my leg out, sending him flying. He lands on his back hard, his head cracking against the pool cement. A few others rush to his aid, and when they help him up into a sitting position, there's blood all over the back of his blond hair. Someone actually holds up a few fingers and asks him how many.

Now Switchblade stops, unsure if he should proceed. He's got his knife out in front of him but he's seeing the blood dripping from the back of Screwdriver's head. Obviously, he was all into it earlier tonight when Trevor asked him if he wanted to go beat the snot out of someone, but now that he's watching his friends getting taken out one by one, he's not so sure. It never dawned on him that he might be the one to end up bleeding. Now he's looking at me and he's no longer seeing a helpless girl that needs to be taught a lesson. He sees me for what I really am. He's the only one here who seems to have an ounce of brains left.

Never mess with the lion when you're only a giraffe.

From behind I hear footsteps rushing toward me but I'm not quick enough to turn. Something hard slams down against my shoulder and pain explodes across my body. Trevor has snuck up behind me. My arm instantly goes dead from the blow; the lucky idiot somehow managed to hit a nerve. I turn around to face him, trying hard to pretend that my arm isn't useless and that fighting him is still going to be a breeze. Rubbing my shoulder with my good hand, I try to bring some life back into it.

"Hurt, didn't it, bitch," Trevor says. I almost can't hear him over the screaming of the crowd. His eye is still blackened and bruises cover his face from where I shoved him into the restroom sink.

"Nothing I can't handle," I say. "You don't look so good, though. It must really suck knowing that a girl whipped you so badly."

"You won't be singing that tune when I crack your skull," he says, swinging the tire iron down again. This time I manage to duck out of the way. I avoid the next three blows too, mostly out of pure luck. The pain throbs in my shoulder and it's making it harder to concentrate. When the last blow misses me by mere inches, I finally manage to get a sharp jab in at his nose.

The fight has slowed down somewhat due to the fact that he managed to hurt my good swinging arm. I'm not as strong with my left and this is teaching me a very valuable lesson. Although I would never admit to being afraid, I am a little worried that Trevor might actually win. With me being hurt, he's got a very good advantage over me. I can feel sweat dripping down my forehead and my leather jacket is starting to get toasty. It also doesn't help that I can see Switchblade bouncing up and down from the corner of my eye. He's regaining his cool and getting antsy about jumping back into the fight. If he joins, I may have to call on Chael to help.

I'd almost rather get beaten than do that.

I don't know what's worse. My pride or my stubbornness.

Gazer has told me in the past that a warrior has to be equally matched in all body parts in order to be a formidable warrior. I get it now. It never dawned on me that I might lose an arm or a leg, or even an eye in the heat of battle. I decide that if I get out of this, I'm going to spend the next several weeks only fighting with my left arm, until I feel I'm more even.

Trevor circles around me a few times and then tries coming in from the left. I bring up my good arm and block the blow, my leather jacket absorbing most of the tire iron's jolt this time. Raising my leg, I kick him hard, and he screams as his kneecap makes a popping noise. I grab his arm as he falls, yanking the tire iron out of his hand, and I throw it into the pool. I wonder if Paige is going to manage to clean this all up or whether her mother might find the weapons on the bottom when she goes for a morning swim.

Either way, it seems to be over. Trevor sits on the

ground, both hands wrapped around his knee, rocking back and forth, as he clenches his jaw tightly under all that pain. Switchblade has disappeared, deciding it's better to take the coward's way out instead of getting beaten, and Screwdriver is still surrounded by a few girls, all of whom hold toilet paper to his head to try to stop the bleeding. I'm not sure where Metal Pipe went; I haven't even thought of him since he went flailing into the pool. He must have slunk off into the night to lick his wounds.

I turn toward Chael and he doesn't look happy or surprised. I think he knew the outcome before I even started fighting. It makes me that much more frustrated to know that he's been following me, that he seems to know so much about me. I can't be that transparent. My life is not that simple. He seems to know what's going on inside my mind.

In the distance, the sound of police sirens hits my ears. Paige must have found a way to finally call the cops. It's almost comical; the audience starts moving in all directions. Suddenly no one wants to be seen here.

I see Jesse and move toward him, determined to remind him that he'd better have my money waiting for me Monday morning. But he sees me too and manages to disappear into the crowd before I can get close enough to grab him. I twist around, looking for Paige this time. I'm still mad at her, furious, but at the same time it seems clear that she was just a pawn in Jesse's game. Her next set of actions will determine if I forgive her. If she dumps Jesse by Monday morning, I may consider it. But if she stays with him, well, that answer is pretty obvious.

But the crowd is too frenzied, and by the time I manage to push past everyone, Jesse and Paige have both vanished. I slip around the pool, pushing past drunken idiots who can't seem to differentiate between running away and searching for their misplaced bottles. One guy stumbles over to the edge of the pool and the beer inside his stomach suddenly joins the chlorinated water. Another girl sits down in the middle of the walkway, her phone in her hand, crying hysterically while trying to dial a number.

Forget this. Time to leave. I turn back toward Chael but he's gone, invisible in the sea of teenagers. I can't imagine he's left yet; I'm positive he wouldn't leave without me.

I spot Paige over by the back door. She's leaning against the frame, her perfect face splotched and sweaty. She obviously can't figure out what she should do first. She's given up on trying to get people to stay out of her house; now she's doing her best to block the door. Inside I hear the sound of glass shattering.

She gives me a smile of relief when I approach her. I guess she still has hope that I won't hate her after everything that's happened.

"Have you seen my friend?" I ask her. "The guy I was with earlier?"

"You mean the guy with the glasses?"

"Nope, the dark-haired guy. I was standing with him by the pool."

She shakes her head. "I didn't see him. Faye?"

"What?"

Paige actually flinches, as if she's afraid I might hit her. "I'm sorry."

"Save it," I say. "You want to be sorry, find a way to show me later."

I turn and head back toward the yard. The police have taken over the front and I can hear someone shouting through a bullhorn. Time to make an exit.

I see Trank. He's made his way over to the back gate and is scaling the fence. If anyone can worm his way out of a crime scene, it's him. I race around the pool and toward the back. I'm never going to get as good of a chance as this. Might as well follow him and see where he goes.

I jump the fence easily and no one even notices. A few kids are scaling the wood alongside me. The majority are probably stampeding through the living room, trying to get out as fast as possible. I can see the red lights from the police cruisers flashing in the night sky. At least their job is going to be easier now. A lot of the crowd has already managed to escape.

In the street, I can't see for certain which way Trank went; he's camouflaged by panicked teenagers who are trying to disappear before the cops get smart and send a car around to the back. I pick a direction and head through the darkness, hoping it will lead me to Trank. It's very busy; I pass others cowering behind garbage cans, and someone has even broken a lock and entered someone's garage.

I don't like this area. Even compared to the streets downtown, it's too dark without the streetlamps to light my way. I can smell strategically planted flower beds and freshly mowed lawns. These scents are foreign to me. I miss my week-old greasy burger wrappers and drunken-puke-smelling streets. At least there I know where I'm going. Here, I'm blind. Everything is too clean. There are too many trees and bushes and not enough concrete.

A few blocks away I miraculously spot Trank. He's heading toward the train station, walking quickly, his head down to avoid being noticed. It's a bit of a walk still and I wonder if there's a way to stop him before he reaches the train. It'll be harder to follow him once he gets back into the city. Everything is dark here. There are very few streetlamps and plenty of trees to add to the shadows. As we get further away from Paige's house, everything grows quieter too.

The perfect place for revenge.

I start walking faster. The train is still at least five blocks away. A lot can happen between here and there. Reaching into my pocket, I pull out my gloves and put them on. First rule of thumb: leave no prints.

As I walk, I consider everything. Part of me thinks that this is a really stupid idea, for plenty of good reasons. The police are close by. They're probably going to be distracted at Paige's for a while but there is always the chance they'll decide to circle the area looking for stragglers.

I'm out of my element too. I'm not familiar with this suburb and it doesn't help that it's a very wealthy one. People find dead bodies in the city and don't even give them a second glance. But here they will. Of course, I could always try to carry his body somewhere no one will find it.

The big question is—can I do it? I've spent the last six years of my life planning for this. I've rehearsed it over and over in my mind and downstairs when I'm training with Gazer. But can I actually kill someone?

125

To murder someone is to damn your soul. But I'm hell-bound. I have no idea what I did when I was a child but it must have been nasty. Or perhaps I'm being punished for the sins of my parents or their grandparents or some obscure relative who killed the future president of America? Who knows how far these things go back. It's possible that my own father is looking up at me from his own fiery elevator, the metal poles prodding his liver as the shadow creatures tear out his vocal cords. That's beside the point because I know I'm damned. God made that very clear when he sent me to hell all those years ago. There is nothing I can do to cleanse myself and change what is meant to be.

And it's not like I have a future. The world has made that clear by the stupid Heam laws. The real world holds too much pressure once you've seen the great beyond. No wonder people go back. If life on earth has become hell, why not spend what's left of your time visiting your future residence?

Men like Trank don't deserve to live. I can guarantee he's got his own invite to the great below. His ticket is about to come up. A cursed person like me will be the one to take him out. That way everyone wins.

I've started walking faster; I'm only half a block behind him now. There's a shopping center on the right, empty and dark. If I can get him behind there, I might be able to take him out by the Dumpsters. If I toss him in the trash, where he'll be covered in fast-food wrappers and half-eaten pizza, maybe no one will ever find him except the rats and seagulls. I rub my sore shoulder. The nerve is getting better. It'll probably hurt more tomorrow but right now I'm confident that I can use my arm.

"I know what you're doing."

That voice.

Of course he followed me. I should have known better.

"What am I doing?" Actually, what I really want to do is scream at him but that might give Trank a heads-up.

"You're thinking about taking out our little friend over there."

"If you say so, then it must be true." I start walking a little faster, hoping that maybe Chael will see I'm serious and leave me alone.

"I told you before; you're wasting your time."

"Yes, yes, I recall you saying that. But considering you didn't give me a logical explanation, I've decided to ignore your request."

He grabs my arm, spinning me around. "Why are you doing this to yourself?"

"Doing what? Killing someone who deserves to die? You must know who he is. Why do you want to kill him so badly yourself?"

"To protect you."

The answer floors me. I actually stop moving. Protect me? Who the hell does he think he is? I look right at him, trying to figure out if his serious expression is real or this is one big joke. He's not smiling.

"I—I don't need protection," I stammer. "I'm already going to hell. Might as well take out as many monsters as I can on the way out."

"How would you know if you're going to hell or not?"

"I just know."

"No one knows."

"Yeah, well, I do. Now stop talking or he might hear you."

I turn and start walking again. Trank has managed to get further away, so I move faster to try to regain the distance I lost while arguing with Chael.

But Chael isn't going down without a fight. He catches up to me and matches my pace. I wish it were possible to turn my back to him but it's impossible when I need to watch where I'm going. I at least manage to turn my head to the side so he's forced to talk to my hair.

"Why do you think you're going to hell?"

"Because I've seen it," I snap. "Okay, satisfied?"

"No one can foresee their future."

Without stopping, I turn toward him and yank down hard on my shirt so that my scars show. I should have done this all along. It's the most surefire way to turn off a guy. Nothing uglier than an addict. I wait for him to turn around and walk off into the darkness.

But Chael doesn't react the way I expect him to. His mouth doesn't curl up in disgust. He's not surprised either. He's sad. His forehead wrinkles and his mouth turns down in sorrow.

"I already knew about that," he says. "You're not showing me a secret or anything."

"It's one thing to talk about it, another to see. This is what I am. Satisfied?" I let go of the material and the scars disappear beneath my shirt again. Hidden away like a dark dirty secret.

"Very, yes." He shrugs. "Heam doesn't show you your future."

"You know that for a fact?"

Chael gives me a sad smile. "It's not fair what they put you through."

"How do you know I didn't do this to myself?"

"Why else would you be so hell-bent on revenge? No pun intended."

"Yeah, well, then leave me alone while I get revenge on the asshole who did this to me."

"This is hardly the best location. There are cops everywhere."

"They'll be at the party for at least another hour," I say. "There's all that paperwork to fill out."

"And what will you do with the body?"

"I'll figure it out. Maybe I can have a bonfire. If not, I'll dump it in the bushes. I'll drag him all the way down to the river if I have to."

"You're not thinking clearly."

"Don't you try and suggest I'm crazy. Killing Trank will be my first step toward—"

I don't get a chance to finish the sentence. Something blocks my path and I trip, my legs spreading out in different directions as I fall on something hard.

Irony is so sweet.

Somehow, during all our arguing, we were oblivious to Trank pausing to tie his shoelace. And now I've walked right into him.

By the time I manage to scramble back to my feet, Trank pulls himself up too. There's a fresh cut on his cheek from where his face hit the concrete. He stares at both Chael and me, and although it's dark, there's no mistaking the fear and puzzlement on his face.

"Who the hell are you?" Trank asks. I see him slowly moving his hand toward his jacket. He's going for a weapon.

I don't give him the chance. I'm on him in seconds, kicking at his hand. He screams and drops down to his knees, pressing his wounded fingers against his chest. I shove him backward, reaching into his jacket, finding the gun hidden in the inner pocket.

"Yeah, you don't get to use this," I say to him. I turn and throw the gun as far as I can. It disappears about thirty feet away in a pile of bushes. It's not until the metal leaves my fingertips that I realize I've made my first major error. I've tossed a violent weapon into a not-so-violent suburb. Hopefully, it won't be found by some grade-school kids who think it might be fun to try to fire at some bottles. I shouldn't have done that. It's almost like I'm trying to make life worse.

It's not like I'm an expert at doing this sort of thing. Sure, I've rehearsed it in my mind over and over for six years. Every time I've thrown a knife or punched the dummy, I've pictured the faces of my enemies. I won't even lie and pretend I haven't spent many a night thinking of catchy phrases to say as I kill them.

But things never turn out the way you expect them to.

"You're that girlie from the party," Trank says. He looks between Chael and me, trying to figure out what to say next. "The one those idiots wanted to pound on. I ain't

130

got nothing against you. I wasn't involved. Trevor's a sore loser, man. I don't do that sort of thing."

"No, you just like to do other things," I say. "Like torture children."

"What?" Trank brushes his hair out of his eyes. His face is turning slightly pink; the grease on his forehead shines under the moonlight. "I don't do nothing. I'm clean."

"Liar," I say. I'm starting to feel my groove. I look down the street and there's no one within a close distance. No more panicked teenagers. No little old people walking sweater-covered dogs. A traffic light flashes in the distance, blinking green. A car turns down the street, heading in the other direction.

"You're stalling," Chael says.

I pause. "I'm what?"

"Stalling," Chael repeats. He moves closer toward Trank and kneels down beside him. "You know the term. Taking one's time. Refusing to take action."

"I know what that means," I snap. "And I'm not doing it."

"Then why haven't you killed him already? I wouldn't take my bloody time about it. The longer you wait, the better the odds of getting caught. Remember, there are cops all over the place. Just do it."

"Huh?" Trank is obviously confused by the conversation but he's starting to figure out the gist of it.

"Don't rush me," I say.

"But it's so simple."

"Stop it."

Trank starts to climb to his feet but Chael clamps an

arm around his shoulder, forcing him back down. I raise my fists in defense, so Trank doesn't try a second time. He's still trying to fully get a grasp on the conversation.

"I know what you're doing and it won't work," I say to Chael.

"What am I doing?"

"Trying to guilt me."

"Never. I'm simply pointing out that killing someone isn't as easy as you seem to think."

"Hey," Trank says. "Why do you want to kill me? What did I ever do to you?"

"You stole my life," I say. "Six years ago."

"You can't kill him. Look at him." Chael continues to try. "Look how pathetic he is. Can you really take his life? It's not as easy as you first thought."

"You got the wrong dude," Trank says. "It wasn't me."

"Shut up," I say to both of them.

"Maybe he is the wrong guy," Chael says.

"He's not the wrong guy," I snap. My hands are shaking. I can't decide who I want to punch more at this moment. If Chael would just stop talking, I'd be able to concentrate more. Trank is looking at me, and I'll be damned if he isn't putting on the big puppy-dog eyes. Who would have thought a drug dealer and pedophile could look so innocent?

"I didn't do nothing," Trank repeats.

"You took two lives!" I scream. Mistake number two. I shouldn't be so loud. Someone might come to investigate. "You killed me and you killed my friend," I say in a lower voice. "I'm the ghost that's come back to haunt you."

I pull back my arm and punch Trank as hard as I can. He screeches as my fist meets his mouth and he flies back and out of Chael's grasp. He lands hard on his backside, both palms scraping the ground as he looks up at me. The confusion is replaced with fear. He saw me fight earlier. He knows what I'm capable of.

Chael refuses to give up. He stands up beside me and grabs my arm. "You can't do this. Think about it for a second. This isn't as easy as you want it to be. Revenge is great when you're plotting it, but can you really do this? There's no turning back. You can't undo it once you start."

"I want him dead," I say. "I'm not confused about this. Stop trying to mess with my head."

"If I can mess with your head, you're not ready."

"Stop it!"

"Let me kill him for you."

"No!"

Trank has gotten up off the ground and is stepping backward toward the street. He keeps looking between Chael and me and it isn't until he moves between two parked cars that I realize he's about to bolt.

"You people are crazy," he says with a shaky voice.

"Hey!" I say, reaching out to grab him by the jacket and pull him back in.

Trank turns and runs out into the street. The sound of tires squealing invades my ears.

The van hits him.

NINE

Trank's body flies through the air and slams into a parked car several feet away. He might be screaming; it's hard to tell over the sound of the van's engine and my yelp of surprise. His body rolls several times before coming to a stop in the middle of the intersection.

The van doesn't pull over. It fishtails briefly and then the taillights disappear around the corner and out of sight. I didn't even get a chance to see the driver. Whoever it is must be doing something bad themselves, considering they never even hit the brakes.

Trank's body is twenty feet away, facedown on the concrete. I close the distance, pausing above him. He's not moving but I can't tell if he's alive; it's hard since he's wearing a heavy leather jacket.

Chael catches up beside me. He's breathing heavily, although I'm not sure why. So am I. I think the shock of what just happened has made me lose my breath. I inhale deeply, trying to calm my heart, which slams against my chest. I look around but there isn't a soul in sight. The mall across the street is deathly quiet. The few residential houses remain dark. No porch lights turn on. No one comes outside with phones or weapons in their hands. No cars turn down the street. No sirens flash. No shouts.

Nothing.

Quiet.

"Is he dead?" I finally ask. My voice barely breaks a whisper.

"Not sure," Chael says. He kneels down and his fingers wrap around Trank's filthy jacket. Nothing. Chael gives him a slight shove. Finally, he turns him over, and when I see Trank's sightless eyes staring back at the sky, I know the answer.

"Holy crap," I say.

There is a strange-looking indent on Trank's forehead from where his skull met the pavement. Dark red liquid pools on the ground. His eyelashes are bloody.

"I think it's a good idea to get out of here," Chael says. He stands up and brushes the gravel off his jeans.

"What about the body?" I ask. "Shouldn't we hide it?"

"Why? We didn't kill him."

Good point.

"Shouldn't we at least move him over to the curb? This seems wrong." I look around again to see if anyone's watching but the area is still clear. It's almost spooky. Don't rich people ever go out at night?

"Why? Because things didn't go according to your plan?"

"Stop that," I snap. "Quit making it sound like I'm doing something wrong."

"Last time I checked, murder isn't exactly legal."

"You should talk."

"I am talking."

"Fine." I turn and start walking away. "I've had enough of you and your weird obsessive behavior. I've got a train to catch."

It's strange to think that I can walk away from all that but I do. It turns out to be crazy simple. There's no one to stop me. Eventually I hear footsteps as Chael catches up to me. He gets into step beside me but doesn't say anything. Fine by me. I don't really want to talk to him either.

I should be happy. I just got the first step of my revenge. Trank is dead. He's lying on the ground in his own blood and he died knowing that I was going to kill him. I even got to see the fear in his eyes when he looked at me. Okay, so I didn't exactly get to twist the knife, but the deed is still done. He knew I wanted him dead.

Is it possible that he was telling the truth? He looked right at me and there was no recognition in his eyes, even when I told him he'd killed Christian and me many years ago. It bothers me that he claimed he knew nothing about it. If there had been more time, I might have been able to go into more detail. I would have made him remember.

Right?

Or maybe his brain was so muddled up from years of drug and alcohol abuse that he really didn't remember. Or what if giving children Heam was something he did on a regular basis? If so, how many others had he killed?

I won't lie and say I haven't fantasized about this moment for six years. However, I must admit that in my daydreams, Trank always had that moment of clarity, the look of surprise and horror as he recognized me for who I was. That poor little gutter rat with the skinny arms and barely enough meat to keep her warm under her second-hand jacket. I wanted him to look at my dark hair and remember how he once grabbed hold of it and sniffed at my eleven-year-old neck, licking and tasting the terror on my skin.

I wanted him to feel that terror. I'm entitled to it.

How very selfish of me to complain about not getting that.

We reach the train station without incident. There are a few people around; I even see a couple of kids from the party. When they notice me, they head over to the other end of the platform. That makes me smile.

We catch the first train and start the long ride back to gutter-rat territory. The compartment is empty; everyone else goes out of their way to take a seat several cars over. The forty-minute ride seems to take forever. Sitting next to Chael, I decide it's in my best interest to think about nothing. I stare at the window, seeing only my reflection as the train moves underground.

We spend the entire ride in silence. Chael looks straight ahead, deep in thought, his leg and shoulder pressing against mine. For a while, I watch his silent figure through the reflection in the glass. When the train pulls into each new station and stops, his body moves slightly forward and then back into the seat. He might blink a few times; it's hard to tell. Other than that, he's a statue.

When the long ride is finally over, he gets up to let me out. For a minute, I think he might sit back down, but no such luck. He follows me off the train and up the stairs into the night.

"Where are you going?" I ask him. Maybe he'll give me a clue. It would be nice to know who he lives with. Parents? A guardian? And where does he live? I really know nothing about this guy. I know I should ask more questions but I have a feeling he'll just be as closemouthed as usual.

"Can I walk you home?"

Now, that I wasn't expecting. "Um. Sure. I guess."

"It's a bad neighborhood. I'd hate to see something happen to you."

The laughter bursts from my throat before I can stop it. "Yeah, I'm a real weakling."

"I never said that," Chael says with a straight face. "You're confident and a great fighter. I'd be more than a little nervous if I ran into you in a dark alley. But not everything can be solved by fists and ability. There's a lot more to life than just being tough."

"You're doing it again," I say. "You sound just like Gazer. He's always telling me there's more to everything than what I already know."

"How did you meet Gazer?"

I kick at a pebble with my foot. "He saved my life.

And then he took me in when no one else wanted me. My mother threw me out."

Chael slows down for half a step and I swear his entire body clenches. "Why would she do that?"

"Heam," I say. "She couldn't handle my overdose. It didn't matter that it wasn't my fault." I listen to the bitterness in my voice and hate that I can't control it. "My father had gone to jail for dealing Heam. He owed a lot of money to the wrong people. That's why they targeted me. Mom ended up on probation because of her involvement. I guess she was afraid for herself. She thought they'd come after her next."

"That's not fair. You shouldn't make excuses for her bad behavior."

"A lot of things aren't fair," I say. "It's okay, though. I'm better off with Gazer."

We walk. I find a tin can and kick it for about half a block. The noise is loud, and when I look at my watch, I'm surprised to see it's only a little past one. It feels so much later. Gazer might still be awake. If that's the case, I'll have to wait outside. It wasn't raining earlier but now a soft drizzle is trickling down on my face. At least I won't get soaked. I can always try to find an all-night coffee shop or something if it gets worse.

But when we finally stop outside the church, I think I've gotten my first lucky break that night. I go around to the side, where normally I can see the light from Gazer's study area. Through the window, I can see nothing but darkness. It looks like he's gone to sleep. Sneaking in is still an option.

I return to the front, where Chael is waiting underneath the streetlight. His hoodie is down and his hair is just starting to get wet from the drizzle. Diamond droplets stick to his dark locks, giving him a halo effect from the light over his head.

His eyes are dark and his expression is unreadable.

"Thanks," I say to him.

He nods.

Chael smiles, and for a second I could care less that he's so mysterious. The almost-perfect teeth peek from behind soft lips. So familiar. It bothers me. The more I look at him, the more I believe I know him. I've looked into those eyes before. But where?

And even though he's admitted that he stalks me, why do I feel so safe when he's around? That makes no logical sense. I should be charging the guy with a criminal offense, but instead I have to stop myself from jumping into his arms for a hug.

Mixed signals here. Maybe I hit my head during that fight?

"So when are you going to tell me?" I finally ask. "Why you seem to know so much about me and yet I know nothing about you."

"I can't."

"Why not?" I push out my lower lip and widen my eyes. A look I used to use all the time when I was a little girl. A look that used to work on everyone except Christian. He'd laugh and tell me that only dogs could get away with such pleading eyes. But he'd still hand over the last stick of gum or piece of candy he knew I wanted.

140

"I really can't," he says with a bit of a frown. "I'd love to tell you but I can't."

"Why? Will you turn into a pumpkin or melt into a pile of goo if you tell?"

"Maybe," he says with a sad grin. "I have to wait until you figure it out on your own."

"Figure what out? That makes no sense," I say.

Chael steps forward and leans down toward me. For a second I believe he's going to kiss me and my entire body goes into meltdown. It is a kiss but not in the way I think. His lips brush against my forehead and then pull away.

"You'll figure it out," he says. "And when you do, I'll be back."

I watch him walk away, disappearing into the mist and shadows. Turning, I head back around to the side and pull out my key.

And the memory hits me.

——+——

The rain falls on my face. I'm scared, yes, terrified, but at the same time I'm curious. The silver color of the Heam is beautiful and it looks like something my dolls would drink if they were actually living. I can still hear Christian behind me and I wonder if they're giving him the same treat. Rufus is holding on to my arm and I try pulling away. But his grip tightens until tears start falling down my cheeks. He leans in close and his eye twitches several times.

"Why are you doing this?" Christian says. "She's just a kid. She didn't do anything to you."

"They're all bitches," Trank says, and his fingers reach toward me, but thankfully Rufus slaps them away.

"None of that, Trank," Rufus says. "Don't wear the poor girl out before her trip's even begun." He flashes a smile at me. As he opens his hand, I see the vial of silvery liquid.

Rufus lets go of me long enough to open the Heam vial. He holds up the bottle in front of me and I can't stop looking at the beautiful liquid. I've been taught about it at school and my mother tells me every day not to do it. How can something this gorgeous be evil?

I look over at Christian and he's sandwiched between the man with the scar on his forehead and another man with long sandy hair. The scarred man is ugly. Almost grotesque. His scar is a nasty blotchy-looking thing that has eaten away most of his eyebrow. He's pinned Christian's arm so far behind his back it looks like it might break. Poor Christian. I can tell he's trying not to cry. I try again to pull away from Rufus and move toward my friend but they won't let me. They push me away and laugh. I fall to the ground, the cement scraping my knees, cutting me; my blood mixes with the rainwater and disappears into the gutter.

Rufus holds out the bottle.

"Will it hurt?" I ask.

"Only if you want it to."

"I don't understand."

Rufus smiles. Trank grabs my arms and Rufus brings

the bottle up toward my lips. The smell of strawberries hits my nose.

"You're a pretty little piece of sunshine. You'll figure it out."

I look over at Christian. It's the last glimpse I ever get of him alive. Even though he's struggling with his own pain, he's looking straight at me. Smiling.

"It'll be okay, honey bunny," he says. "It's okay."

Honey bunny. One last tease. A plea to try to take away my fear.

The men laugh and Scarface puts his dirty hand over Christian's mouth.

—+—

My head snaps up in surprise. *Honey bunny?*

How is it possible that Chael could know that? He said those very words to me.

There were only six people there that night. Rufus. Trank. Ming. Phil. Four men. Two victims. Christian and me.

My father called me that, but he's dead.

Christian's dead.

Where does Chael fit in?

I turn and run back to the front of the church, hoping that Chael is still there. But the street is deserted. The light shines down on emptiness.

I jog down to the end of the block but he's not there either.

"Chael!" I scream, but not too loud. I don't need to wake up the entire neighborhood.

I hear nothing but the sound of the rain as it falls harder.

"Chael!" I repeat. I look around and slowly start walking back toward the church. No familiar figure appears, and by the time I reach the door, I have my key back in my hand. I twist the lock, grimacing when the door squeaks as I push inward.

I turn again, looking out once more onto the empty wet street.

"Christian," I whisper.

——+——

I made it to bed without incident. I didn't sleep.

There is no way Chael could have been there. He's not one of them, my enemies. I know them better than I knew my own mother. I've spent a lifetime following them. Besides, Chael is too young. He would have been Christian's age six years ago.

But he's not Christian. Christian's dead.

So who is he?

In the middle of the night, I slip out of bed and go into the back of my closet, where I keep my photo album. There are only a few pictures there. One of them is of Christian and me. It was taken shortly before his death. The two of us were at his house and his dad was trying out his new camera. I'm smiling, big and goofy, and Christian has his arm around me. I look like the happiest kid in the world even though my dress is secondhand and my hair is held back with a ponytail holder I found in the Dumpster. I was so thrilled that Christian had his arm around me and I planned on taking that picture to school and telling everyone he was my boyfriend. I carry the photo back to bed with me and light a candle. By the small flicker of light, I stare at it for the longest time.

Christian's hair. Dark chestnut brown. His eyes. Green. His smile. White and pretty. Beautiful and dead.

It's not possible.

I went to his funeral. Gazer held my hand. Christian's parents were kind to me. They hugged me tightly and even offered to take me home with them. They'd heard by then about what my mother did and thankfully she wasn't invited. But I declined. The hatred and desire to seek revenge were already embedded in my brain. Gazer had promised to teach me how to fight. As much as I loved Christian's parents, I knew my future didn't involve being their adopted daughter.

But I would get revenge for their son.

As the candle burns down, I trace my fingers along the initials scratched into the bedside table. Christian's name.

Not Chael's.

Reaching into my jacket pocket, I pull out the flyer that the girl with the red umbrella gave me. Opening it, I stare at Arnold Bozek's face. His short blond hair and glasses. His smile is big and toothy. The nerdy image of someone who would never take Heam but has gone missing just the same. The little girl accused me of keeping him from her.

"You talked to him right here. Under this light. I saw you two together!"

As God is my witness, I've never talked to Arnold

Bozek. I remember when she called out to us and Chael suggested we go grab a cup of coffee. He'd been nervous and pulled the hoodie up over his face but that didn't mean a thing. He's always doing restless stuff like that. That has to be the night she's talking about. There wasn't any other. I don't understand how the red-umbrella girl could possibly mistake Chael for Arnold. They don't look a thing alike.

There are too many questions going through my mind. Funny enough, I don't think about Trank. His death isn't what's keeping me awake. If anything, his death is a relief. It's one less person I have to follow. One less monster out on the streets. I'm glad he's dead.

When morning comes, I must look like a zombie. Gazer sits down while I'm at the breakfast table, my cheek leaning against my coffee mug in a pathetic attempt to try to keep my face elevated.

"Rough night?"

I look at Gazer in alarm but he's not even paying attention to me. He picks up the paper and opens it. I really pulled it off. He thinks I stayed home.

"Didn't sleep well," I say.

"Maybe you're doing too much," he says, and he goes over to the counter to pour himself a cup of coffee. "You should take a break. All this work you're doing. You're too young to look that awful."

"Gee, thanks," I say.

"I'm serious," Gazer says. He comes over with the coffeepot and refills my cup. "Take today off. I don't want to see you go down to the basement. Go do something fun.

Go to the mall or something. Whatever it is normal girls do. Get a manicure. Go to a movie. Do you need money?" He reaches into his pocket, pulls out some bills, and drops them on the table in front of me.

"Thanks," I say.

"You need to do this more often," Gazer says. "Take breaks. They're good for the soul."

"I thought you didn't believe in souls?" I say as I pocket the money.

"Figure of speech. Now, what do you feel like for breakfast? I'm in a cooking mood. Maybe some pancakes? Or how about an omelet?"

"Do we have hash browns?"

Gazer goes over to the fridge and checks the freezer area. "Not sure. When's the last time we cleaned this thing out? I think there's a frozen dinner here from ten years ago."

"If the stupid machine stopped breaking all the time, we might be able to put fresh food in there," I suggest. As soon as the words are out, the fridge shudders and dies. Neither of us looks surprised. It's a daily event around here.

Gazer gives the machine a swift kick and it jolts back to life. One of these days it will probably throw in the towel for good and Gazer and I will be forced to live on crackers and chocolate bars for a month or two before we're able to find a cheap enough replacement.

"Maybe we'd better stick to pancakes," Gazer suggests. "Doesn't that come in a box? Besides, I'm not sure we have eggs."

I get up and poke around in the cupboards until I find

147

the instant pancake mix. Gazer finds some milk that isn't expired. Together we manage to come up with a breakfast that doesn't look like it will give us massive heartburn or food poisoning.

It's a miracle that we've both managed to stay alive this long, considering that our cooking skills together match those of a child mixing dirt in the sandbox. But the pancakes come out almost fluffy and not too badly burned and I find a bottle of syrup sticking to the bottom shelf in the fridge.

"Not bad," I say through my first mouthful of pancake.

"I should have sent you to cooking classes," Gazer said. "I'm not sure what this private school is teaching you if you think this dreck is tasty."

"I never said it was tasty," I said. "But it is edible. That's better than we manage most days."

Gazer laughs and I pour more coffee.

I like mornings like this. It's almost enough to take my mind off of last night's events.

Almost.

A strange noise fills the kitchen area. Someone has just rung the buzzer. Gazer looks at me with surprise. "Wonder who that could be. Are you expecting anyone?"

"Nope," I say, trying to keep a straight face.

I don't follow Gazer to the door. I stay in my chair although my legs start to twitch and I fight an uncontrollable urge to get up and run. This can only be bad news. No one ever comes to visit us since neither of us actually has friends. Gazer parted ways with his old life before I ever met him. There used to be a few guys from the force that would drop by from time to time but eventually they stopped coming around. As time moved on, so did they.

Gazer opens the door and I can hear low voices talking back and forth. A few minutes later, Gazer returns, and he's being followed by two cops in black uniforms.

Uh-oh.

"Faye," Gazer says, and I can see the anger boiling over in his eyes. "These officers would like to have a word with you. Something about a party last night?"

I'm so boned.

———+———

We go into the living-room area to sit down since the kitchen table is full of leftover pancakes. Suddenly the smell of maple syrup is a tad overwhelming. The two officers have identified themselves as detectives Daily and Aggett.

I sit down on the chair and the officers take the couch. Gazer stands over by the bookshelf and he won't even look at me. He asks if the cops want any coffee and they politely decline.

Daily is older and fat. He's of average height but he looks taller because of his girth. His belly sticks way over his belt and his forehead is beaded with sweat even though the church is cool. His mustache is trimmed and neat. He wears a ring on his finger and I wonder if his wife is concerned about his health. Does she lie awake at night worrying about him getting killed on the job or is she trying to come up with healthy choices to keep his heart beating a few more months?

Daily pulls out a handkerchief and wipes his forehead quickly before opening up a notebook with his pudgy fingers. "We just want to ask you a few questions," he says, and his voice is friendly enough.

"Am I in trouble?" I ask. I keep my voice high and breathy, trying to sound worried and slightly confused. I've decided to go for the innocent-girl look. It's worked for me before. I look over at Gazer and he's glaring at me. He knows exactly what I'm doing. But he's not the person I'm trying to convince.

"That depends on where you were last night."

Now I'm really boned. I could lie and say I was here, but Gazer will immediately know I'm full of it. But will it be enough to convince the police?

I look over at Detective Aggett and discover he's not paying attention to us. He's staring at the rows of wooden pews and the dirty stained-glass windows that make up our living area. He's uncomfortable. Maybe he was an altar boy at one point. Maybe he wore the long robe and stood uncomfortably on the platform, wishing he were anywhere except there. I find that people with strong religious backgrounds have trouble being in our house. They look around at the marble and unpolished wood and find it sacrilegious that anyone would ever want to live here. Then when they see that we've put a couch and chair where the altar used to be, they have to clamp down to try to keep the lectures out. Aggett has that look on his face right now. He wants to ask us why we'd ever defile a house

150

of God with our philosophy books and small color TV that no longer works.

I'd be grinning at him in amusement if it weren't for the fact that this is supposed to be serious.

"Faye?"

I look away from Aggett and see that both Gazer and Daily are staring at me.

"Um . . . yeah?"

"Where were you last night?" Daily asks again.

"I was home," I say. "Here. All night."

I've decided to lie. Might as well go all out.

Daily opens up his notebook and flips through a few pages until he finds what he's looking for. "We've got a report of a party last night. A girl matching your description did some damage there. Do you know anything about that?"

"What kind of damage?" I ask.

"Seems like there was a fight," Daily says, and I can hear the amusement in his voice. "This girl took on a few drug dealers. Kicked their asses halfway across the room, if you'll pardon my language." He laughs. "Never thought I'd live to hear a story like that. Gotta wonder what these kids are smoking these days."

"Really?" I say, looking straight at him. I don't dare glance over at Gazer. I won't be able to keep a straight face if I do. "Wow."

"One of the dealers ended up dead," he says, and I immediately lose the smile.

"I'm sorry, officers," Gazer interrupts. "What does this have to do with Faye?"

"A few kids mentioned her name," Daily says. "Personally, I think it sounds impossible, but we have to follow all leads, as you remember."

Gazer nods and I realize he must know these cops. At least Daily. He can't possibly know Aggett; he's too young. But Gazer probably worked with Daily back in the day before he turned in his badge. This could be good on my behalf. If Daily respects Gazer enough, he might not follow this lead through the way he would with someone else. I can only cross my fingers and hope.

"Anyway," Daily says, "we're just checking things out." He turns to Gazer and turns his pen around a few times in his fingers. "Can you confirm she was here last night?"

"Yes, Faye was with me," Gazer says, and it takes all my strength to keep from jumping off the chair and hugging him.

Daily writes a few words in his notebook. "Figured as much. Crazy party, if you ask me. These kids today are nuts. Way different from back in our days. Wouldn't have dared to do any of the crap they pull. Most of 'em were whacked out on booze. From what I heard, a bunch were stoned too. Not the hard stuff, thank God. Found some weed in the bushes, though. Drop and dash."

"What about the guy who died?" I ask. I look over at Aggett and he's still staring at the pews. He's managed to take out his notebook to look like he's paying attention, but it remains untouched.

"Hit by a car," Daily says. "Happened after the party broke up."

"Oh," I say, and inside I'm jumping with joy. Yes, it

152

was an accident, and no, even if they could place me at the scene, I still wouldn't be charged with anything. But at least I've still managed to remain hidden. Even if this gets back to Rufus, there will be no mention of my name.

"Anyone I know?" Gazer asks.

"John Sheffield," Daily says. "You remember him, right? Goes by the name of Trank? Back in the day. Think you ran him in a few times."

"Yeah, I remember him," Gazer says. "Bad blood."

"Yep," Daily says. "No great loss. We should be thanking the poor fool that creamed him. I can guarantee there isn't going to be a big search for the hit-and-run. Should give the idiot that killed him a medal."

Gazer nods.

"Anyway . . ." Daily stands up and all his weight goes along with him. There's a dent from where he sat on the couch. "We should get going. It was good seeing you again, Gazer. Sorry to put you to any trouble. You should come down and have some beers with us sometime. Miss having you around."

"Thank you," Gazer says. "Maybe I will."

I lead the officers toward the front door. It's agonizingly slow because Daily wants to chat a bit more with Gazer. They talk about people they both know. Officers who have retired or died in the line of duty. It's not a happy conversation but Gazer says all the right things to push them along.

I open the door and the cops step outside.

"How can you live here?" Aggett asks.

I'm actually surprised it took him so long to ask.

153

"It's home," I say.

"You couldn't pay me anything to stay here," Aggett says with a smile. "This place just creeps me right out."

I laugh and give him my sweetest smile. "I'm used to it. I've never known anything else."

They leave and Gazer closes the door. It's only then that I notice his hands are shaking.

"Go to your room," he says. "I don't even want to see you right now. I'll come talk to you once I've calmed down."

I'd apologize but we both know that would just piss him off more. I look at Gazer's face and I can't remember ever seeing him look this angry before. I don't question it. Turning, I flee to the stairs and head up to the darkness of my bedroom.

TEN

"What were you thinking? Do you have any idea what kind of trouble you could have gotten into last night?"

Gazer is still fuming. To give him credit, he did wait a few hours before coming up to punish me. I say punish, because it's obvious he doesn't care to hear my side of the story. He's been yelling at me for the past ten minutes and there's no sign of slowing down. I sit on the bed and watch him fume. I deserve this. He's right to be angry.

He's right about many things.

Gazer stops his ranting and finally sits down on the bed across from me. The light from the bedside table reflects off the side of his face and he looks old at this angle. But he's not old. Gazer's in his late thirties, hardly ancient. But some things age a person, forcing him to wither on the inside. With the light glowing dimly in the dark bedroom, he looks ninety. Tired. Gazer is tired. Why haven't

I noticed this before? Am I really that selfish that I haven't spent enough time worrying about him?

"I understand," he says. "I know you probably think I don't and there's some truth behind that too. I have no idea what it feels like to be you. God knows I've tried. We've both shared our own personal hells. I wish I could be more understanding of yours."

"It's not that," I say.

"And it's not fair that you have to grow up in a world that won't let you be normal," he continues. "I can't help but wonder if you would have turned out happier. Less angry. Maybe if you'd been allowed a normal teenage life, you might have given up on these revenge ideas. Time only heals all wounds if you're allowed to move on. I was wrong. I never should have sent you to that school. I should have kept you home. Maybe then you wouldn't have to follow all those stupid rules. Maybe we should pull you out. I might be able to find a tutor to help finish off the year. It'll cost more but maybe we can find a way around it."

"No," I say. "School is good. I have to graduate."

"You're not happy there," he says.

"Yes I am," I say, and I'm a little surprised when I realize it's true.

"Maybe we can find a way to add a little normalcy to your life," Gazer says. "We can try to work around some of the rules so you can do some crazy kid stuff. Go to the mall with friends. These girls who invited you to the party, perhaps?"

"Yeah, that's not going to happen," I say. I give him a small smile and grab my pillow, placing it between my legs and resting my body against it. "Those girls aren't my friends. I was only invited because they knew I could fight."

"What do you mean?"

I tell Gazer everything, starting with the original fight with Trevor and how it led up to the bet. I don't tell him about the money, though. I still don't think he'd approve of me accepting the thousand dollars. So I just leave that part out along with the threat I made to Jesse about giving me a chunk of his winnings.

"I'm sorry, Faye," he says when I'm done. "That was a terrible trick they played on you. But on the bright side, they'll probably leave you alone now that they know you can kick their ass at any given moment."

I smother a laugh in my pillow. "It sucks, though," I say. "I almost felt like I had a friend. It's been so long. I have you, but no offense, you're not really the person to talk to about girl things. I didn't realize I was that type either. But I guess you can take the girl and give her weapons and stuff but somewhere deep inside she still wants to wear makeup and paint her toes pink."

Gazer nods. "Hold on a second, I'll be right back."

He leaves the bedroom and I'm left alone to wait. I toss the pillow against the wall as hard as I can and then pick it up again. This is one of those times when I wish I had a teddy bear or something similar to abuse. Isn't that what girls my age are supposed to do? Cuddle stuffed animals when they're sad and then write in their diaries or something?

I'm not going to sit here and whine about how the

157

world owes me and that I've been cheated out of a normal life. I've never had that defeatist attitude and I'm not going to start now. I get up and go over to the window and pull back the dusty curtains. It's a cold day. The clouds are hanging low, threatening rain, but I can see a single beam of sunlight trying to force its way down to warm the earth. I look at the street below and search around, wondering if Chael is out there watching me. The thought warms me a little.

I'm excited to see him again even if I don't want to admit it. I finally think I know the right questions to ask him.

Gazer comes back with a small box in his hands. He crosses the room and places it in my palm. "For you," he says. "It belonged to my mother. I planned on giving it to my daughter and that means you now."

"What is it?"

"Open it and find out."

I lift the box lid and look inside. A small pendant, slightly tarnished, lies on soft pink silk. It's in the shape of a circle with a cross in the middle, and there are silver bands intertwined tightly to form a tiny design in each corner.

"It's a Celtic knot," Gazer says. "It symbolizes protection." He points to the top right corner of the pendant. "It contains all four elements. Earth, wind, fire, and water. If you wear it, you'll always be safe."

"It's beautiful," I say. I take it out of the box and the long chain tumbles down through my fingers.

I bring it up and over my head. The chain is long enough

that I don't have to undo the clasp. The pendant rests just above my breasts and I pick it up again once it's on.

"If anyone needs protection, it's you," Gazer says with a smile. "I meant to give it to you when you graduate, but I think you need it now."

"Thank you," I say.

"On that note," Gazer says, "I'm going to go do some reading. If you go out tonight, promise not to get the police involved."

"It's a given," I say.

Gazer gets up to go back downstairs. He rubs his hands along his pants before heading out the door. "Wear your warmer jacket. I hear it's going to rain."

And that's it. He's gone and I'm sitting on the bed realizing that he really does understand me sometimes. It just sucks that our situation is so different from everyone else's. Even though Gazer tries to protect me, he knows there's nothing he can do to make me change my mind. By giving me the necklace, he's setting me free.

I think this is probably the closest we've ever gotten to a real father/daughter talk. Thank goodness he didn't try to talk to me about sex or something equally embarrassing.

Either way, I think we can both agree that once in a while it's nice to be normal.

—+—

I'm sitting at the beach. Okay, not the beach. But I'm on a big fluffy towel with a bright sun in the middle and I'm surrounded by vivid colors of pink, blue, and purple. I lie down on my back and look up at the ceiling, imagining that it's a bright blue sky with one or two puffy clouds floating above me. If I try really hard, I can almost hear the sound of the surf as it crashes against the sand. The taste of saltwater in the air. The peaceful breeze against my face.

Almost.

We're in my house and it's raining outside for the fifth day in a row. Our parents are both at work. I told Christian that I wished we could go to the beach because the water is warm and the sun is much better than the rain. At the beach you can run around barefoot and only have to worry about stepping on sharp seashells. Christian agreed and said it's a perfect day to go swimming, although neither of us has ever been near a lake or the ocean. We've never learned to swim either.

Since we can't go to the beach, Christian brought the ocean to us. We've moved the stained couch into the corner and placed the coffee table on top of it. We picked up all the newspapers and magazines from the floor and tossed them in the recycling bin. Christian ran back to his house while I finished clearing a big spot for us to have our picnic. By the time he returns, I've managed to find some leftover lunch meat and cheese from the fridge and I've turned an empty cereal box into a picnic basket. I fill it with some crackers and grab some empty Pepsi bottles from the recycling bin. Filling them with water, we will pretend they are beer and Christian and I will get make-believe drunk.

Christian has found a bonanza of junk back at his

place to create our afternoon getaway. He's spread out the beach towel and he even found an old washtub that is big enough for me to sit in. We take turns going from the kitchen with pitchers of water until the tub is filled. Our beach is complete.

We put on our summer shorts and shirts and sit down to our feast. We eat the crackers, tossing the crumbs at imaginary seagulls. I sit in the tub, squealing because the water is cold, and Christian rushes over and pulls me out, pretending to be a lifeguard. Water trails across the carpet, turning the dirty pink roses a deeper shade of sogginess.

I'm thankful my mother won't be home until much later because she'd never approve of the mess.

Afterward, we lie down on our backs and stare up at the ceiling and I think I'm the happiest girl in the world. Christian reaches over and gives me a kiss on the cheek. Just a friendly kiss, nothing more, but it's enough to make me wish that when I grow older we can live in a place like our imagination and every day will be warm and peaceful.

I miss being innocent.

———+———

I wake from the dream and the rain is pounding on my window. It's a little after eight and I'm surprised that Gazer didn't call me down to dinner. He probably figured I needed the sleep after last night.

I reach over to the bedside table and pick up the photograph. I stare at Christian's face, trying to imagine what he'd look like today. It's been six years. He'd be nineteen now and probably working alongside his father at the factory. Or maybe he would have gone to school like he wanted and become somebody important. He wanted to get an education and his parents supported him. But in all honesty, things like that don't work out the way we plan. It's most likely he would have ended up with the industrial job.

But at least he would have been alive.

Would I still have loved him?

I look at his smile and his dark hair and think about how soft his lips were when he kissed my cheek. I hate the days when I dream of the past. These are memories I no longer want to revisit but my subconscious seems to like torturing me.

I put the picture back down on the dresser and go seek out some warmer clothes. As I get dressed, I can't help thinking that Christian would look a lot like Chael.

Hell, he'd look exactly like Chael.

—+—

Speaking of Chael, I don't see him. I wander the streets but they're empty of his presence. I wander down by the burned-out grocery store. I go by the coffee shop and take a peek inside. I even spend more than an hour outside the bar, though I know Rufus isn't inside. But no Chael.

He doesn't want me to find him tonight.

It's a slow Saturday night. The rain is heavy and most people have retreated to the comfort of their homes. Even the soapbox preacher and his entourage are missing in action tonight. The bars look pathetically empty too. Isn't there a sad song about not wanting to drink alone in the rain? I don't see the girl with her umbrella and soggy flyers. Finally, after a few hours of empty wandering, I'm on my way back, heading slowly toward home, when the boy comes up to me. It takes me a second to recognize him; he's the gutter rat from several nights ago. The one who saw his grandmother dancing in a sky of Heam-colored rainbows. He'd been with that girl I saved. What was her name? Beth. I can't believe I almost forgot. I should have been thinking more about her but I've been so busy. I wonder how she's dealing with her newfound hell.

"Can you come with me?" he asks. He's breathing heavily and his face is flushed, like he's been running for a while. He leans over and starts coughing for several minutes and I can't help wondering when he used his lungs last.

"What's wrong?" I ask, once his hacking spell passes.

"It's Beth," he says. He turns and spits out a lungful of phlegm. "You need to talk to her. She's going to kill herself."

"Okay," I say. He turns and races off down the street and I follow. It must be killing him to have to go so quickly after that coughing fit. We run for several blocks before he stops in front of an alley. It's similar to the one I found her in, just as dirty and smelly. Just as dark.

"She's in there," he says. "She won't listen to me and I can't call her parents. She managed to score some stuff off a guy. She was talking all funny earlier. Said she doesn't ever want to wake up."

"Okay," I say. "Anything else?"

"Nope," he says. "I made her promise to wait until I found you. I didn't know where else to go. You helped her the last time. I just thought . . ." He pauses. He doesn't know what else to say. He's not even sure why he thought to look for me. In a city of a million souls, finding a single one is almost impossible when you don't exactly know where to look. "You knew what to do before. Can you do it again?" he finally says. With the sleeve of his jacket, he angrily wipes away the tears.

"You did the right thing." I reach into my pocket, pulling out a few bills. "Go get us some coffee," I say. It's a good distraction for him and it'll warm us all up.

He takes the money and heads off toward the closest all-night store.

I turn and step into the alley, slowly, letting my eyes adjust to the darkness. There isn't much there. A few large garbage bins, a pile of used carpet, soggy and slowly melting into the concrete. Several darkened doorways. Halfway down, I spot Beth's form. She's cowering in a corner between several black garbage bags and some waterlogged cardboard boxes.

She's got her knees pulled up into her chest, her thin arms wrapped around them. As I get closer, I realize there's no coat around her shoulders. Just a thin shirt that's soaked through. She's shaking terribly. In her fingers is a bottle and I can see the silver liquid shimmering even from a distance.

"Beth?" I keep my voice low and calm. The boy said

she wanted to kill herself. I need to approach this carefully. She may not remember me.

She looks up and I can see she's crying. Through her white shirt, I can see the faint traces of spiderweb-like scars. I wonder how her parents reacted to her overdose. Did they take her in with open arms, forgiving her for her mistakes and offering to get her help? Or did they toss her out on her skinny ass and announce to the world that she no longer exists?

"How are you doing?" I say. "Do you remember me?"

She nods. "You're the girl who saved me. You brought me back."

"Yes."

"You should have let me die."

A slap to the face. And a harsh déjà vu. For months after Gazer saved me, I used to feverishly wish the same thing.

"Do you want to die now?"

"Yes," she says quickly. Then she pauses and thinks it over. I wait patiently. "No," she finally says. "I don't know."

"I understand." I open my jacket and pull down my shirt so she can see my scars. "You're not alone. I've been there myself."

She looks at me in amazement. "When?"

"I was eleven."

She's blown away. She continues to stare at my chest even though I've closed up my jacket again. Part of me wants to give it to her, to keep her warm, but it's the only good rainwear I have. If I hand it over, I might not get it back. I'm generous to a degree but I really, really need my jacket. So I live with the guilt of seeing her shiver.

"Why did you do it?" she asks. "I mean, what made you want to do it?"

I shrug. This isn't the time to tell the truth. I might lose her if she finds out it wasn't my own doing. If I tell her I was jumped by monsters looking for payback, it will only make her guilt that much worse. She needs to find a way to relate to me. "I was curious, I guess," I say. "There were a lot of bad things going on in my life. I was tired of being alone. It seemed so easy. Why did you do it?"

She nods several times, water dripping off her chin. "Same here," she says. "I'm always alone. No one ever pays attention to me. Except Joshua. I don't know where he is. He left when I told him what I was going to do." She holds the bottle of Heam up in front of her and her eyes fill with tears. It's not her face that keeps my attention. The silver liquid calls my name. There is enough inside for five doses. If she takes it, she'll be gone in minutes. "He left me to die."

"No," I say, and I gently take the bottle from her. She allows it, her fingers tightening around the vial for only a second before giving it up. "He left you to find me. I sent him to get you some coffee. I'll bet you could use a cup."

"They kicked me out of school," Beth says. "I undressed for gym class and they had a huge fit. Hauled me into the office and screamed at me. Threatened to call the police. Told me I was destroying everyone's education and that people like me didn't deserve chances. And at home Mom was furious. She says I'm useless now. She won't even let me look after my little sisters anymore. She said she can't trust me and I might end up killing them. She wanted to throw me out but Dad wouldn't allow it. He says I have to get a job, though, to earn my keep. But that's impossible 'cause I'm not old enough."

"You're lucky," I say. "My mom made me leave. I haven't seen her since."

"And my brother slapped me in the head," she says. "He's older and married and really mad at me. He said it's a shame I didn't die because I'm dead to him now. His wife used to be really nice. Now she won't talk to me."

I nod because there's nothing else I can say.

"I stole the money tonight from my mom's purse. To buy the drugs. I figured she can't call me a thief if I'm dead. She'll probably be happy."

"I don't think she'd be mad at you."

We look down at the bottle between us.

"Does it get easier?"

The hardest question on earth to answer. "No," I tell her. "But"—I try to get the words in before the pain and disappointment destroy her—"I've managed to go this long without ever doing Heam again. If I can do it, you can too, right?"

"It's hard."

Her lips are shaking. She's looking at the bottle as if it's got the answer to immortality. Beth's eyes hold such longing it borders on lust. I wonder if I get the same look on my face. Best not to find out.

"I know it's hard," I tell her. "And it's going to be hard for the rest of your life. But it does get a bit easier. You'll see. You just have to be strong."

167

"Why bother?"

Now, that's the million-dollar question. Yes, why bother? I search my brain but it's impossible to come up with an answer that doesn't sound contrived. I fight my temptation demons because I have purpose. I'm going to get my revenge. But what can I offer her for motivation? I know her future. Her parents are right. She is pretty much useless.

"You need to look inside and find that out for yourself," I finally say, wincing at the corniness of the answer. Given more time, I might have been able to come up with something better than that. But I'm on the spot here, and trying to keep a girl from finding more reasons to kill herself isn't as easy as it sounds.

"I guess," she says, but I can tell she's not even close to being convinced.

"There are places that can help you," I say, trying to move in a more positive direction. "I can take you to one of them. It's not much but they're willing to help you deal with the problems."

"Is that what you did?"

I think of the closest local Heam shelter and of the pale-faced worker there who I've referred people to in the past. I can never remember her name. She'll lie for me if I ask her to. "Yes," I say. "That's what I did."

The boy, Joshua, returns with two coffee cups. He kneels down beside me in the alley and thrusts a cup into Beth's chilled fingers. She holds it with both hands and takes a sip. He tries to give me the other cup but I shake my head, insisting that he drink it instead.

"Here," he says, offering me the change.

"Keep it," I say. "And you should head home. Your parents are probably worried sick. It's late and you shouldn't be out."

"They never notice," he says. "And I won't leave Beth."

I reach out my hand and Beth takes it. She looks at Joshua and smiles. "You listen to Faye," she says. "She's gonna take me to a shelter for help. I can call you tomorrow."

"Are you sure?" Joshua asks. Even if this idiot dropped Heam alongside Beth, I can't help admiring his desire to help her. He must really care about her. Good. She's gonna need him. Hopefully, what happened to her will be enough to make sure Joshua never touches a bottle of Heam again.

"I'm sure," she says. She squeezes my hand with her cold small fingers.

—+—

It's late when I leave the shelter. The pale-faced worker, Ramona, has promised me she'll take good care of Beth. She'll even allow Joshua to stay the night as long as he calls his parents first. He came along with us to the shelter despite Beth's protests, but I can tell she's happy he's there.

It isn't until I'm almost home that I remember I still have the bottle of Heam in my jacket pocket. I pull it out and stare at the silvery liquid.

So pretty.

I want to drink it. More than anything else in the world, I want to touch the bottle to my lips and taste the strawberry-candy flavor as it coats my throat. I want to let the sensation overtake me, the feeling of absolute happiness that the drug produces. It would be so easy. All I have to do is twist the top. How my body aches to feel my heartbeat slow as my body carefully shuts down and dies.

The desire never goes away.

The liquid sloshes against the glass and my fingers begin to tremble. My heart pounds against my chest, against my scars, and the uncontrollable urge to scratch at my skin overwhelms me. My hair stands on end, producing goose bumps all over my arms.

Just one more time.

My entire body is begging me.

I hold the bottle up and twist open the top. The scent of strawberries hits me and my senses go into overload. It's better than anything else in the world. An old friend, come to visit me again. It's brought me dreams of sunflowers and daisies and all the beautiful things that every eleven-year-old in the world wishes for.

I tilt the bottle.

The silvery liquid spills into the gutter.

Even after it's gone and the bottle is empty, the desire to drop down to my knees and run my tongue along the pavement is strong. I wash the bottle out in a puddle of rainwater to make sure every drop is gone and then toss it in the garbage.

Another day down.

It's time to sleep.

ELEVEN

I expect to be expelled Monday morning.

So does Gazer.

Neither of us says anything but the thought is heavy in our minds. We sit together at the kitchen table, not talking, not paying attention, but we both know we're thinking about it.

There is a very good possibility that someone at the party is going to blab around the school about my antics. If it gets to the teachers, it'll get to the principal, and that will be the end of my education at Sebastian Clover.

It's a nice morning. Sunny. Of course it has to be sunny. It never rains here when you expect bad news. That would be too much of a cliché. I leave for school early, but by the time I get there, I'm almost late. I guess no one willingly skips along to their doom. Most of us drag our feet.

As I walk toward my locker, I keep my ears open but there don't seem to be any signs of danger. The teachers that I do pass aren't paying attention to me in the slightest. I do witness a few students whispering as I walk past, and someone actually goes out of their way to avoid me, but that's about it. The murmurs and rumors don't bother me as long as they don't get any louder. As for the idiot running off in the other direction to avoid me, that's just funny. Unless he's a drug dealer or Jesse, he has nothing to fear from me.

I seem to be in the clear.

But the day's not over yet.

I make it through my first few classes without anything major happening. I sit at the back as usual, waiting for the intercom to turn on, or a student to show up with a message, or at worst, maybe the police to escort me out.

But nothing happens.

My last class before lunch is biology and it's a class I share with Paige. Part of me wants to skip it. I'm still angry at her.

When Paige comes in, I look at her, immediately wishing I hadn't. She doesn't look good. In fact, it looks like she's been crying all weekend. That's a good possibility, especially if her parents have seen the damage. That is one party she's not going to get away with having.

I focus on my work but that doesn't stop her. Luckily for me, she arrived just as the bell rang and had to sit right down. But then she manages to make a silent trade with the guy who usually sits next to me. He gets up and moves toward the front and Paige slides into the seat beside me.

"I'm sorry," she says with a low whisper. I look up at

the front of the class but the teacher has his back to us. She's talking low enough that he doesn't hear.

I ignore her. Unless she's got a handful of money from Jesse, I'm not interested in her apologies.

"I knew nothing about it," she continues. "I even broke up with Jesse."

That's the best news I've heard in days. I guess that look of surprise on her face Friday night was real. Although it does make me feel better, it's still not enough. She's only trying to make things better because she's feeling guilty.

"Please let me buy you lunch," she whispers. "We'll go out. Leave the grounds. I know this great place close by."

"Why?" I finally snap, louder than I should have. The teacher pauses, his chalk on the blackboard. Up front, a few students turn around and snicker.

I reach down and pick up my pen, pretending to take notes. Paige does the same thing. For the next few minutes, we focus on copying down all the information necessary to pass this class.

"I want to make things right," she finally says in an überlow voice.

Maybe it's the pleading but more likely than not it's the fact that I'm starving. I didn't have much of a breakfast this morning. The thought of leaving the school and having lunch in a restaurant is a million times better than the crappy cafeteria food I've been eating for four years. Maybe she really is sincere, although I still worry there are ulterior motives behind her friendliness.

But maybe a meal won't be so bad.

"Okay," I say.

Paige gives me a brilliant smile and part of me starts that whole fantasy all over again where she's my friend.

Sometimes I think my imagination is my worst enemy.

—+—

Am I really this lonely? I think the answer is yes.

We sit in a very impressive restaurant that's about a ten-minute drive from the school. I've never been here before; it's not the sort of place I would ever be able to afford. The waiter pulls out my seat and even places a fancy cloth napkin in my lap when we sit down. It takes all my self-control not to slap his hands away in embarrassment.

There's an actual waterfall inside this place. I look over at it in amazement. Rocks have been built into the wall and water pours out from a cavern near the top and into a pool below. Even from our table, I can see bright orange fish lazily swishing their tails as they swim around. I want to go over and put my hand into it to feel the coldness. But that would probably be considered weird in such a ritzy place.

I discreetly run my fingertips across the tablecloth instead. I have no idea what material it is, but it's softer than anything I've ever felt before. A waiter comes over and pours us water in real crystal glasses.

Impressive.

Paige doesn't look out of place here the way I must. She calls the waiter by name and doesn't even bother to open the menu to order. I look over mine, confused by the dishes. I've never seen such things before nor eaten them.

Hummus with roasted garden vegetables. Oysters on the half shell served with sourdough bread. Lobster ravioli in white wine. I scan the words but they barely register. Finally, I order the hummus because it's one of the cheaper dishes and I don't want Paige to think I'm taking advantage of her. If I were a bitch, I'd order the lobster, which is more money than anyone should ever spend on an afternoon meal. But no, I wasn't raised that way. I'm polite.

Paige orders the baked brie in balsamic and oil.

"I'm really sorry," she says after the waiter heads off to the kitchen with our orders. "I think that's a horrific thing that Jesse did and I want you to know I had nothing to do with it."

"Okay," I say.

"And I need to thank you again for helping me with Trevor," she says. "It's not fair. The only reason I got involved with him was because of Jesse. I'm so done with all of this. Never again. Why can't men be decent for once?"

Chael's name flashes through my mind. It makes me angry that I automatically think of him, so I reach for my water glass and suck back an ice cube. I crunch it hard between my teeth.

"He was cool when I first met him," she continues. "But then he changed. He started hanging out with a bunch of jerks. Doing all sorts of crap. I caught him talking to some guys last week about Heam."

My eyes widen in surprise and I swear the scars hidden under my sweater twinge.

"You take Heam?" I ask.

Paige shakes her head. "No," she says. "No way.

175

There's no coming back from that stuff, right? It's one thing to smoke a joint, you know. Heam's different."

"Yeah, it is," I say. There's a second napkin on the table, wrapped around some cutlery. I pick it up and pick at the paper band that keeps it together.

"Have you ever done Heam?"

My scars twitch again. This isn't a conversation I should be having. The teachers at Sebastian spent so much time training me in what to say and not say, I get on a huge guilt trip even when there's no one around to witness my sins. This is a conversation that could not only get me expelled, it's likely the school would press charges against me. They'd go off on a tirade about how I'm exposing the students to drugs. Believe it or not, it can happen. I've heard of such cases in the news. Heam persuasion. People have gone to jail.

"No," I finally say, but the look on Paige's face says she doesn't believe me. I shouldn't have hesitated.

"It's cool if you've done it," she says. "I hear not everyone gets addicted."

"I really haven't," I say, but even my own ears cringe at my lame protest.

Paige shrugs.

The waiter brings our food and I'm glad I ordered the hummus. It's the most amazing thing I've ever eaten. The vegetables are crisp and cooked to perfection. I break off pieces of bread and dip it in the chickpeas. Heaven.

"It might be cool to try," she says after taking a bite of her brie. "I mean, a lot of people do Heam and turn out fine. It's tempting. Who wouldn't want to see heaven?"

"What about the people who overdose?" I ask.

"If heaven is really that beautiful, then death shouldn't be feared."

"It's not real."

"I don't believe that," she says. "It's real. That's why the church is so against Heam. They've spent too much time making us all believe we're gonna go to hell because we sin. None of that is true. We all go to heaven when we die. Heam proves that. That's why there's such a big cover-up."

I want to reach across the table and slap her. Instead, I pick up a piece of asparagus and chew on the tip.

"Of course, it would suck if you overdosed and still came back," she says, and she leans in closer. "Did you see that film they made us watch in health class? That guy with all the Heam scars all over his chest? I'd rather die than be scarred like that. Just disgusting."

"It beats dying," I say, and suddenly the restaurant doesn't look beautiful anymore. It looks cramped and claustrophobic. The rushing waterfall sounds more like a steady static of screaming. The candles at each table flicker and heat waves vibrate around them. "I could deal with a bit of scarring, I guess."

"Not me," Paige says. "I'd hate to be that ugly."

I'm sweating. I can feel the drops slipping down my skin to pool inside my bra. I pick up my napkin and pretend to wipe my lips, drawing it quickly over my forehead when Paige isn't looking.

Thankfully, she changes the subject. We spend the rest of the meal talking about school, mostly about our dislike for certain teachers and courses.

"What about that guy I saw you at the party with?" Paige asks me as we wait for the waiter to bring us the bill. "The one with the glasses? He's not from Sebastian."

"I wasn't with any guy with glasses," I say.

Paige shrugs. "Blond hair? Kinda bookish. Maybe I'm wrong. He didn't really look like the kind of guy you'd go for, ya know? Just hanging around and hoping you'd talk to him."

Blond hair? Glasses? I think of the red-umbrella girl and her missing brother. Arnold Bozek fits that description. But he most definitely wasn't at the party with me. Chael was.

"You talked to him right here. Under this light. I saw you two together. I called out but you turned and ran. Why? Why are you keeping him from us?"

I feel like I've been given a novel with some of the plot ripped out.

When we leave, Paige pays with a credit card and gives me a ride back to school.

I decide I do like her even if the Heam conversation got a little too heated for my taste. It's not her fault. She doesn't know my secrets. And maybe if I were a regular teenager, being heavily scarred would be the end of the world. Maybe if it hadn't happened to me, I'd have the same opinion. It's hard to tell. I keep forgetting I'm not like them.

"We should do this again," Paige says.

"Sure," I say, although I don't think I will. No matter how lonely I get, I need to remember the truth.

I'm not one of them.

No amount of pretending will change that.

———◄─╂─►———

That afternoon, there's a tap on the door and Mr. Erikson goes over and opens it. No one pays much attention; most students use this precious moment to secretly text their friends or lay their heads down on their desks.

I'm doodling on the top corner of my notebook and not paying attention in the slightest.

"Faye?"

Oh lord, no.

I glance up and Erikson is looking at me with a very sad expression. A few students turn around in their seats to study me. Whispers start up.

"You're wanted in the office."

I knew it would eventually happen. I've been too careless. Grabbing my books in one sweep, I get up without looking at anyone and walk out the door, my head held high.

There are two male teachers waiting for me. One of them is my biology teacher, the other I don't know. Both of them are much taller than me. They take a spot on each side of me and the three of us start walking.

Mrs. Orman sent muscle. Now, that's not good.

A few students are in the hallway and they watch me go by. Even they can tell something bad is going down.

Dead Girl Walking.

No one greets me in the office. The vice principal and her secretary actually keep their heads down and their eyes averted as the two male teachers march me toward Mrs. Orman's office. The biology teacher doesn't even bother to knock on the door. He opens it and I'm roughly shoved inside.

"Faye."

Mrs. Orman sits at her desk. On the table is my file, of course, a big heaping manila folder with all sorts of ugly secrets hiding inside of it. She told me once she even kept it apart from the other students', heaven forbid someone should try to break into the office and accidently find it.

She motions to the seat opposite her but I don't accept it. Instead, I turn around and look at the door. Sure enough, the male teachers are standing guard, their backs to us. They're here to make sure I don't do anything stupid.

Oh boy. This is going to be bad.

"Sit down. Sit down." She waves at the chair.

"No thanks," I say. "I prefer to stand."

Mrs. Orman shrugs. She crosses her hands over her chest and stares at me for several seconds.

I stare back.

"I gave you a chance, Faye." Mrs. Orman begins what I'm sure is going to be a long lecture. "No one else wanted you. I know this. I know that your adoptive father applied to almost all the schools in the district. They all turned you down for good reason. And why shouldn't they? Why should a school risk its students' welfare for a Heam addict?"

I don't say anything. At this point, there isn't anything left to say.

"Once a Heam addict, always a Heam addict," she continues. "The statistics show this time and time again. But I had on my silly rose-colored glasses, didn't I? I was foolish to think that maybe it would be different with you. Such a young girl. How could I not feel pity? I thought maybe having a cop for an adoptive father might make you stronger. I can see now I was wrong."

"I haven't been using," I say. "Not once. Whoever said otherwise is a liar."

"So I agreed to take you in," Mrs. Orman says, ignoring my outburst. "And when I agreed, the school and I set up guidelines. Certain policies we expected you to follow in order to maintain dignity and grace. I told you on your first day, disobey the rules and I'll toss you out in a heartbeat."

I can't comment. She knows. The only question now is how much.

"On Friday night, you were seen in the presence of other students. There was a fight, I believe. I hear you severely hurt another child. Attacked him like a wild beast and had to be pulled off kicking and screaming."

"No," I said. "It didn't happen like that."

"It shouldn't have happened at all!" Mrs. Orman slams the file down on her desk. The whole table vibrates, knocking over a stapler and another stack of papers. "You knew better. I gave you this chance and you embarrassed me. You've made me look like a fool to the other staff. Most of them were against you being here in the first place."

"I didn't—"

"Stop," she shouts, and her voice echoes in the small office. "Don't you dare. When I first heard this, I thought maybe it was just a rumor. It wouldn't be the first time events got muddled. Many of the students like to gossip and I can see how you would catch their attention at one point or another. But then I saw the pictures."

She turns the computer monitor toward me.

There I am.

In one picture, I'm drinking from a beer, a frown on my face.

Another pic has me beating the crap out of Switchblade.

Then she pulls up a YouTube video. Presses PLAY. I finish off Trevor quickly while the others cheer and boo.

Apparently, every single person at that party had their phones turned toward me. And I didn't even notice.

Oh shit. I look at the desk and yearn to bang my head against it. I've been very, very, very stupid.

She takes my silence for guilt and she's dead-on.

"So you don't deny it?"

"I guess not."

"You know the rules!" Mrs. Orman screams so violently that spittle erupts from her lips and across my manila folder. "You are not to have any communication with these students. Not ever. And here you are? Drinking? Fighting?"

I want to explain it to her but there's no point. No one is ever going to take my side here.

"You're expelled," Mrs. Orman says, and I can hear

the delight in her voice. "You will be escorted to your locker and you will clean it out. Then you will leave these grounds and never come back."

I want to protest. I want to scream at her. Can't you see I need to graduate? How important it is to me? It's all I have left.

But I won't give her the satisfaction of seeing me beg. Never.

The bell rings, signaling the end of the lesson. Even from her closed office, I can hear the sounds of students filing out of the rooms and into the hallway.

"You can stay here until everyone is back in class," she says. "I don't need you to cause any more of a disturbance. You've done enough damage."

No, I haven't. She has no idea what kind of harm I can still do.

"You're an awful woman," I say. "I have been an exceptional student the past four years. I've never done a single thing or said anything that would get me into trouble. You're right; I never should have gone to that party. It was stupid of me. Forgive me for thinking that maybe for once I could be normal. But that's not possible, is it? Because people like you will always make sure that people like me are constantly beaten down."

"Now listen here—"

"No. I'm done listening. It's your turn." I drop my books on her desk and they make a satisfying thumping noise. "You want a monster? I think it's time the truth came out."

As I'm talking, I reach up and grab the front of my

school blouse. I yank hard, buttons popping, as the shirt tears away to reveal my scars in all their glory.

"Don't you dare!"

"Enjoy your life," I say, and I turn. Opening the door, both male teachers immediately jump into action, but I'm too quick for them. I shove the biology teacher, sending him flying back against the secretary's desk. The other teacher is dumbstruck, staring at my scars. It doesn't take much to get past him. I just push him aside and start walking.

One of the secretaries stands up to block my way but cowers once she realizes I'm not stopping. I march through the office, ignoring Mrs. Orman's screams for me to stop. I hear someone pick up the phone, probably to call the cops, but I don't care.

I'm done caring.

The entire school is my audience. I walk tall down the halls, heading toward the front doors, pushing my shirt off my shoulders so that everyone can see what I've been hiding. I march along in my bra but there are no catcalls. No whistles from the boys. No, everyone I pass is struck silent.

There are no whispers from behind me.

Only row after row of eyes watching.

I see Paige before she sees me. As I get closer, she turns, curious about whatever is going on that has struck the students dumb.

She sees me and her face instantly goes pale. Clutching her books tightly to her chest, she steps back and against her locker. Her face is covered in curiosity and uncertainty.

I walk past her and the group of friends surrounding her. The girls whisper at each other and someone squeals.

She thinks the scars are ugly. She said she'd rather die than have them. But now, watching her face, I can tell she's wishing she could take back those words.

Different worlds. Some people just aren't meant to be together.

Paige opens her mouth, but I'm not about to give her the chance. I'm not about to let anyone have the last word but me. Keeping my head high, I turn and walk down the hall. I reach the front door, turn around, and give everyone one last good look at my scars.

Still silent.

Turning, I leave.

——+——

I don't tell Gazer I've been expelled. I don't know how to get the words out. When he asks me how my day went, I smile and pretend it was the most randomly boring day in existence.

So I get up every morning, even though I'm exhausted. I train with him and go running before getting into my uniform and heading off to spend the day wandering the streets. Every afternoon I stop by the Heam center and visit with Beth for an hour or so. Her recovery is coming along slowly; she still refuses to open up to her counselor.

No school official calls to inform Gazer. I guess they really don't care. You'd think they'd at least want their uniforms back.

I'll have to tell him eventually. I owe him that much. How am I going to break his heart? Each night I remove the necklace and place it on my dresser. Each night I look at the Celtic knot with its symbols of water, fire, earth, and wind. What a lousy job it's doing. Protection, my ass.

I will tell him. Each night when I lie down, I make myself promise that I will tell him over breakfast.

Each morning I chicken out.

"What the hell did you do to my daughter?"

I'm not crying. I'm not screaming or begging or trying to throw myself into my mother's arms. I'm a motionless doll, left out in the rain and frowned upon. Is it worth it to try to fix me up or easier to just toss me in the trash?

My mother stands at the door, her entire body puffed out against the frame as if trying to barricade it. She's in her stockings and I can see her feet are swollen from a long day's work. Her face is bright red with anger. Gazer is trying to explain to her what happened. But she's not listening very well.

"Do you have any idea what this means?" my mother screeches. She's smoking a cigarette and the smoke snakes its way up along the side of the doorframe. Her hand is shaking. "My husband went to jail for dealing Heam. I can't have this sort of thing in my house. They're still watching me!" She turns to look at me but turns her head away. She can't stand to look at me. "How could you do this to me, you stupid brat? What were you thinking?"

"We can go down to the station and make a statement," Gazer tells her. "Maybe Faye can give a proper de-

scription of the men that did this. I'm an ex–police officer. I assure you, no one is going to accuse you of anything."

"I don't believe you," my mother says. "I know how you cops work."

"Ma'am, she's been through a very traumatic experi-ence. If you'll just let us inside, we can talk—"

"She's lying to you," my mother snaps. "Can't you tell? Damn kid lies all the time. Made it all up, didn't you, brat? Trying to get out of it. Killed that boy next door, didn't you? Shame on you! Shame on you. Bad girl!"

"Ma'am."

I have to give Gazer credit for trying. But the fear is too strong. Even at eleven, I'm aware of this. I saw them take my father away.

"Get her out of my sight," my mother finally says. She tosses the cigarette in my direction and I have to step side-ways to avoid the burn. "I have no daughter. I don't give a damn what you do with her."

She slams the door in our faces and I hear the dead bolt slide into place.

———+———

I don't see her again for several years.

———+———

It's been an entire week and still no Chael. Don't think for a second that I'm still looking for him. Not me. I've moved on.

It's late night and I'm at my usual place by the bar. I've picked up a coffee from the shop down the street and I lean against my streetlight, prepared for another evening of watching.

It does get boring sometimes.

I've been doing double training with Gazer this week. I've been tossing knives like they're going out of style. The dummy in the basement is so full of holes Gazer finally decided to replace it after I severed its cotton-stuffed neck. Each morning I run for five miles without stopping to rest like I normally do. I do push-ups on my bedroom floor each night before I go to sleep. For some reason, the situation at the party has made me that much more determined to kill my enemies.

Graduation is lost to me now.

It's time I step up the game.

I decide that within the next few weeks, I'm going to get my revenge on the next person on my list.

Ming Bao.

Ming never touched me. No, he was the one who killed Christian. He used to be a professional boxer back in the days before getting expelled from the league. Turns out Ming had a bit of a gambling habit and liked to bet against himself and lose his fights. A dirty cheat. He has a reputation for being a tough guy on the street. He's got bigger muscles than brains and that makes him dangerous.

The night we both died, Ming held my best friend down, pinning Christian's arms behind his back while bringing a thick-muscled arm down and across his neck. I can still remember him laughing while Christian struggled and gasped for air.

Ming is mostly Rufus's lapdog. The two of them work together a lot. In the six years since I've been monitoring them, I've seen them go after the children of eight families, do numerous drug deals, burn down two buildings, and kill seven men. Two of the murders were the result of drug deals gone bad. Four were hired hits. One was an innocent victim who happened to be in the wrong place.

I have witnessed these crimes and it has taken every ounce of willpower to stay hidden. Twice I have anonymously called the police but in vain. Both times they've managed to elude the cops. Thankfully, the kids didn't die, although one of them passed on last year, another victim of a Heam overdose. An addiction that Rufus and Ming encouraged.

I have stayed in the shadows for all these crimes. In a way, my revenge will belong to others too. People I've never met. Victims who deserve more.

I want Ming to know what it feels like to have the air knocked from his lungs. I want him to look up at me while I squeeze the last remaining breaths from his body. It'll take some real skill and determination because even I'm not stupid enough to go up against him in a fair fight. My fighting skills may be equal to Ming's, but my entire body weight is probably half of his.

Tonight he's drinking at the bar with Rufus, which is interesting because they don't usually hang out together here. The bar is Rufus's territory. He doesn't like to do business there. Never mix business with pleasure.

This makes me especially curious to know what's going down.

I'm going to find out.

It doesn't take long before the two of them leave the bar. They stop for a few moments while Rufus lights a cigarette. When he looks up, he spots me; his hand pauses with his finger still on the button of his lighter. Shadows flicker across his face.

I step back against the wall, dissolving into the darkness. I've got to get back into the game. That's twice now I've been stupid enough to let my face be seen. Ignoring the way my heart jumps out of my chest, I breathe in deeply, trying to convince myself that it doesn't matter. Sure, Rufus looked right at me, but he probably assumes I'm just another gutter rat looking for some action. In this neighborhood, there's a girl on almost every corner. I get propositioned a lot when I stand here. Some nights I'm beating them off with a stick.

After about fifteen seconds or so, I peer around the corner, still trying to figure out what I'll do if they're coming for me. But they're not. They obviously didn't even notice. They've turned in the other direction and are walking off. I wait about a minute and then follow. They head off toward the docks and I keep a block behind them, prepared to duck into the shadows if I have to. But not once do they turn around to see if they're being followed.

Silly murderers. They should know better.

A few blocks further, they're joined by a third man. Phil Sabado. He's the last on my list. He's about as useless as Trank and twice as dumb. The only reason I haven't paid him much attention is because he had the least to do with our deaths. He mostly leaned against the wall and worked as a lookout. I'm pretty sure he was stoned the entire time. As far as I can tell, he's an alcoholic and a druggie. Even Rufus doesn't pay him much attention unless he needs the extra muscle. He doesn't like Phil. He only uses him when absolutely necessary.

Something must really be going down tonight if he's bothering with both Phil and Ming. I wonder if he'd be including Trank if he were still alive.

When they reach the docks, they turn and move past the darkened offices and around to the back. It's a literal maze of shipping containers stacked up to the sky. I wait till they disappear around the bend before I start following.

It's an arduous task. I can hear them talking, but because of the way the voices bounce off the metal boxes, I can't tell exactly where in the yard they are. I have to take caution at each corner, waiting before I turn the bend. If I get caught, not only will I have to come up with some quick excuses for why I'm here, but I might end up having to run for it, risking my cover and myself in the process. I know I keep repeating myself to the point of stupidity, but it's become my mantra: Don't get caught.

Don't get caught.

Stupidity never wins.

I turn a corner too quickly and suddenly I'm down by the docks. The shipping containers have ended and there is nothing in front of me except concrete and a hell of a lot of dark water.

And a large group of men.

I duck back around the corner again; thankfully, none of them were looking my way. Turning, I go over to the closest container and start climbing. It's not that hard. They're not stacked as high here and it only takes about three of them before I reach the top. Moving carefully along, I creep down the row until I'm right above them. Unless they happen to look straight up, there's no way anyone is going to spot me. I get down on my hands and knees and crawl forward until I'm in a comfortable enough position to watch for a while.

Rufus and Ming are there, along with four other men I don't recognize. Phil stands about twenty feet away and he's picking his nose. Nice. A cream-colored sedan is parked close by. They're talking and their voices are too low for me to hear. It frustrates me immediately because I know they're talking about something that could benefit me. Something really illegal. Why else would they come here of all places to have this discussion?

One of the men goes back over to the sedan and pops the trunk. Removing a briefcase, he brings it over. More talking continues. Voices rise up and I start catching the conversation.

"What the hell is this?" That's Rufus.

"This is all we're giving you."

"That wasn't the agreement."

There is a loud burst of swearing and I lean forward to the point where my head is sticking right over the edge of the container. If one of them happens to look up, I'll be spotted in an instant. Stupid me. I've been so caught up in the actions beneath me; I should have done a better job checking the perimeter to make sure I was alone. I don't even have a chance to react when the hand goes over my mouth.

Not that I would scream. I know better.

The hand yanks me backward and there's a silent scuffle as I'm pulled away from the edge. Twisting my body around, I raise my hands, ready to fend off my attacker, but stop the second I recognize the face.

I should have known. My friendly neighborhood stalker.

Chael.

TWELVE

I open my mouth to complain but he puts a finger against his lips to silence me. I shrug and he motions at me to follow him. Although I'd like to stay put and watch the show beneath me, I'm more curious to follow Chael. I haven't seen him since the night Trank died and I have a lot of questions for him.

I especially want to know why he's here.

And how he knows the last words that were spoken to me before I died.

We silently move back several containers, until I decide we're far enough away that no one is going to hear us whispering.

"What do you want?" I hiss at him.

"Not here," he says. "We need to keep moving."

I plant both my feet on the metal beneath me. I'm not going anywhere. From where I am, I have a good view of the harbor. The blackness spreads out for miles; I can't tell where the water begins and the sky ends. A bit of a breeze pushes my hair in front of my face and I brush a few strands away.

"Just tell me what you want," I say. "Can't you see I'm busy?"

He grabs me by the arm. I can see the fierceness in his eyes. He's very angry. At me? Yes, I think so.

"You need to leave," he says in a low voice. "You are getting involved with something that is far beyond your comprehension. You're going to get yourself killed. Those men down there aren't playing games. They'll shoot you without thinking twice."

"I'm not going anywhere," I say. My blood is beginning to boil and I'm finding it hard to keep my voice down. Anger and whispering never go hand in hand. "And if you think I'm playing a game, you're an idiot. I have my reasons, not that I need to explain them to you."

"God, why are you so stubborn?" he asks.

And the gunshots go off.

We both drop to the ground, flattening ourselves against the container. Someone screams, a high-pitched squealing noise. The gun fires again and the sound shuts off like someone pressed a button.

"Come on," he snaps. The anger is still there but now I see something new in his eyes. Fear. It's real enough that I don't argue or pull against him when he grabs my arm and leads me over to the side of the container.

We climb down, me first, him right behind me. When

I reach the ground, I'm tempted to run off but he's too quick. He lets go from ten feet above and drops gracefully to the ground beside me. Within seconds, his hand is back on my arm and he's pulling me away from the docks.

But this time I fight him.

"We can't," I say. "Those were gunshots. I have to see what they did. Someone might need our help."

"Not likely," Chael says. "Anyone in that group probably deserved it."

"If they killed Rufus, I want to see it."

"You can hear about it on the news. Now come on."

I turn around, twisting my body out of his grip. Grabbing his shoulders, I use my strength to slam him up against the metal container. Dumb move. The noise echoes through the yard.

There are shouts from behind me. I turn to see people coming around the corner. It's too far to tell but there are at least two of them. I can't tell if it's Rufus and Ming.

Chael grabs my arm and yanks me backward. This time I don't have to be forced. I turn and we both begin to run. I hear the gunshot just as something whizzes past my ear and strikes the metal wall, sending sparks flying.

We round one corner, then another and there's nothing but row upon row of metal containers. This place really is one gigantic maze. I should have paid more attention when I came in. I look straight up at the sky but I can't see anything but darkness. I can't even tell which direction we're running in. There's nothing to look at that might give me a clue.

Even Chael seems to be lost. Finally, he slows down after the tenth turn or so and I stand there breathing heavily, trying hard to keep quiet and listen for the sounds of footsteps from behind us.

I hear someone shouting but it seems far enough away that I don't think I need to start running again. I take several deep breaths, trying to convince my heart to stop pounding in my chest.

Chael isn't even winded. He's staring at me but his eyes keep glancing above my head for motion in the background.

"How do we get out of here?" I say. "If you hadn't dragged me all over the place, I probably could have found my way out. You've gotten me lost."

"Right," he says. "It's all my fault."

"It is," I say, although I'm aware there's now a bit of amusement in his eyes. He's not buying my complaint in the slightest. He steps into the center of the row and looks up at the sky. He closes his eyes. It's like he's listening to the night. He stays this way for several seconds, and when I'm about to finally open my mouth, he smiles at me.

"We have to go that way," he says, pointing in the direction from which we came. "We're not that far. Just a few more turns."

"What? Have you got some sort of magic compass in your pants?" I snap at him. "How could you know that?"

"I just do."

"And why did you call me 'honey bunny'?" I say. He looks confused, so I elaborate. "Last time. You called me

197

'honey bunny.' Why that saying in particular? How did you know that both my father and my best friend used to call me that?"

"I know a lot of things."

"Screw you," I say. "I'm getting really tired of this stupid act. You are not all mysterious and powerful. You're just an idiot."

"This isn't the time for explanations."

My hand pulls back automatically. I punch him in the jaw. Hard. He doesn't even try to block it. Instead, his hands drop to his sides and he looks straight at me as if daring me to hit him again.

"Stop trying to mess with my head," I snap. My fingers remain clenched tight.

"I'm sorry."

"No you're not. Now tell me. How do you know about—"

"Hey!"

I turn around but I'm moving too slowly. Fifty feet away, Ming has turned the corner. He stops, brings up his gun, and points it right at me. I can't move. I want to move.

Move!

The gun fires.

Chael throws himself in front of me and he's forcibly shoved back when the bullet enters his body, pushing us both against the container, knocking the air out of me. I see blood spray against the container, a splash of brightness on the dull gray metal.

Ming isn't letting up. He fires again and the bullet hits the metal a few inches away from my thigh.

Chael turns, grabbing my arm, practically yanking it from its socket, and pulls me back and around the corner as a third bullet hits the wall, right where my head was a few seconds earlier.

We run. Chael's jacket is open and I can see the blood pouring from a tiny hole in his chest. His shirt, which was white, is rapidly turning black and wet in the moonlight.

He's not faltering. He should be on his knees with a hole right through his chest. He should be lying on the ground dying. But instead he pulls me along and we take two more turns and suddenly we're at the entrance of the shipping yard. In front of us are buildings, not shipping containers; wide-open streets and not narrow rows.

We take a hard right and then a quick left into the alley. We keep running. Eventually I turn around to look and there is nothing behind us except dirty concrete, rows of Dumpsters, and a few abandoned cars.

Chael slows down but he doesn't stop until we're at least a mile away. I'm breathing heavily and I lean against a burned-out van to try to catch my breath. I've never run so hard in my entire life and I'm suddenly thankful for all those mornings Gazer forced me out of bed and into my shoes. My stomach lurches and heaves and I lean forward, tucking my head between my legs to keep from throwing up. When I finally right myself, the nausea is gone but my vision is still slightly blurry.

Chael is watching me.

"Are you all right?" I ask. I move toward him, wondering where the closest hospital is and if I can even take him there. There will be a lot of questions if I show up carrying someone who's been shot. A lot of questions. Maybe even an arrest. Should I take him to Gazer? Can I even get him that far? We've just run a marathon. He's probably been dripping blood the entire time. How much can he lose before he dies?

"I'm fine," he says.

"No you're not," I say. "You've been shot. We have to get you somewhere. You're gonna die if we don't."

He shakes his head. "I'm fine."

Anger flares up inside me. I step forward, grabbing hold of his jacket, yanking it aside so I can get a better view of his chest. I can see the hole where the bullet tore through his shirt. Even in the darkness of the alley, I can see the blood staining the fabric.

"You're shot," I say. "See! Right there in your chest."

"It's nothing."

"It's not nothing. You're going to die if we don't get help."

Chael puts his hands on top of mine, prying away my fingers. He lifts his shirt so I can see his chest. There's still a lot of blood but no hole. His skin is bare and inexplicably intact.

"But you got shot," I say. "I saw it. There's blood." I hold up my hands and sure enough, my fingers are stained red from where I grabbed his jacket.

"It's okay," he says. He reaches out and takes my hand, pulling it up against his chest, which is hot but not sweaty or bleeding in the slightest. There should be a small hole where the bullet tore through the flesh. But his skin is soft and unmarked. My stomach flip-flops again but not because of the running.

"That's impossible," I whisper.

"I was shot. But I'm fine now."

"You were bleeding."

"I heal quickly."

I nod but I don't understand this in the slightest. My hand stays against his chest, feeling the strength and warmth of his body as he exhales. My cheeks are burning; my pulse jumps into my throat and I want to swallow but I can't. The lump there is suddenly too big. I can't even speak.

"Come on," he says. "I don't think they saw us but we're not safe yet. Let's go somewhere and I'll explain everything."

I nod again and he takes my hand, leading me off into the night.

—✦—

We end up in a park.

Quiet. Safe. Secluded. A good place to talk.

A good place to kill someone too.

Let's hope it doesn't come down to that.

In the middle of the park is a duck pond, or what once was a pond. There haven't been animals or waterfowl here for years. Now it's nothing but a small watery bit of sludge. People have tossed their garbage here and I can see empty cigarette packets and fast-food wrappers.

We sit down on a bench that has suffered years of abuse from past visitors. There are thousands of scratches in the paint where people have proclaimed their love and proven their existence.

BILLY ♥ CAT.

EMMA + DON. TRU LUV 4-EVER.

JEZZZZZ WUZ HERE.

We sit for a while without speaking. Chael doesn't seem to know where to begin. I only have one question. Not really a question but something I need to know. Finally, I decide to take the plunge.

"Christian?"

He turns to me. The way he looks suggests he's not just responding to my voice. No, he's answering to the name.

And suddenly I see it. The green eyes. His beautiful dark hair that covers his ears. It always looked healthy, even when it hadn't been washed. But especially the eyes. I used to spend hours looking at him when I was a little girl. The day after his burial I swore to myself that I'd never forget him. No matter how many years went by.

He's been here all along. How did I not recognize it before?

"You're dead. I know you're dead. I went to your funeral." My words are choked, and as the tears well up, I blink furiously to keep them back. "I saw your body!"

He nods, turning away as if my tears are too painful to see. He looks down at the ground for a long time. His hands rest in his lap and his shoulders hunch over as if he's trying to force himself into a tiny ball.

"Don't do that," I finally say. "Say something."

"You're right."

"About what?"

"I'm dead."

I reach out and touch him and his body is warm against my skin. I touch his cheek and I swear I can feel the blood pulsing through his veins. He twitches slightly and pulls away. He won't look at me and I can't read the expression on his face. So instead I watch his chest as it rises and falls with each breath.

"You're not dead," I finally say.

"Okay, then," he says. "I'm not dead."

"I watched them bury you."

"Was it nice?"

"What?"

"The funeral."

"It was okay," I say, and then shake my head in disbelief. "Who cares about that? It doesn't explain how you're here right now."

"I would have liked to think my funeral was nice."

"Quit ignoring my question."

He pauses for a few moments and stares up at the sky. "I was dead. I came back."

I want to scream at him. I want to jump up and head into the bushes, exposing the hidden cameras that are filming us. This has to be a joke. A sick joke. One of those stupid television shows where they make people believe all sorts of things before exposing the truth. I wait for the film team to emerge from behind the trees to tell me I've been playing a part in some insanely cruel game.

But the park is quiet. Aside from a swing swaying slightly in the breeze, nothing else moves.

"Explain it to me, then," I finally say.

"It's not that simple. Even I don't quite understand everything."

"Try me."

"Let me start by saying that no one told me I needed to return to earth in order to get my wings or some other crap like that. I'm not an angel. I'm not a ghost. If heaven exists, I've yet to see it."

"But—"

"Shhhh," he says. "Let me talk. This is what you want, right?" When I don't respond, he continues. "I'm not going to pretend I understand any of this. I wasn't given a manual or explanation, but a few weeks ago I woke up. I was lying in an alley. It was raining and I was cold. I had no idea how I got there. All I know is that I'd been asleep or something for a very long time. My body was creaky, limited; it took a long time before I could make things work again."

I remember the first night I met him and how he kept touching himself. His cheek. His hair. As if he didn't quite understand what he was feeling. Like he was wearing someone else's body.

"Where were you?" I ask. "Heaven?"

"No," he says. "At least, I don't think so. It's all fuzzy.

204

I remember a blur. A lot of darkness but not bad. Peaceful. Quiet."

I look straight into his eyes but I can't tell if he's lying to me or not. And why am I even contemplating the afterlife when everything else he's telling me is ridiculous beyond belief?

"Prove it," I say. "Tell me something only Christian would know."

"I kissed you once," he says. "I shouldn't have done it but you pushed me into it. You were very persistent. It was Christmas and you'd somehow managed to find some fake mistletoe. You put it on the edge of the sofa because you couldn't reach the top of the door. You always were such a tiny thing."

My throat has closed up. The tears are pouring down my cheeks now and I'm not even bothering to wipe them away.

I remember.

"You told me you wanted to play hide-and-seek," he continues, and the image of me hiding behind the couch fills my mind. "And when I found you, you said I had to kiss you because of the mistletoe. Come to think of it, I'm not even sure if it was the real thing. It might just have been a bit of Christmas tree wrapped in tinsel."

"It was part of Mrs. Tisdale's wreath," I say. "I stole it earlier that day. I stuck some cranberries to it with superglue."

Chael laughs. "Either way," he says. "You were sitting there, begging me, no, demanding I kiss you. So I gave you a small kiss."

"And then you told me I better not tell anyone," I said.

"I was thirteen," Chael says. "You were eleven. I was embarrassed about what the guys at school might say."

I laugh and it comes out more like a huge sob. "I never would have blabbed. I was madly in love with you."

Chael stands up and walks a few feet away from the bench. He stares out at the duck pond, his hands tucked tightly in his jacket pockets. "Is that enough proof? Do you want me to tell you another one? How about the time you wanted to run away, so you spent the afternoon hiding in the laundry room?"

"It's enough," I say. There's no way anyone else could know the mistletoe story. I never told anyone and I'm pretty sure Christian took it to his grave. It happened a few days before he died.

Chael turns around and comes back to the bench. He doesn't sit down. Instead, he stands at the edge, his hand resting on the wood behind me. "There was darkness. A lot of it. I was alone but never lonely. It was peaceful. Time passed. If I was aware of it, I didn't know. It was almost like everything I knew ceased to exist. It was no longer important. There was so much silence, but that's all I remember. And then one night I came back."

"That sounds more like purgatory," I say. "Not heaven or hell."

"I don't know," Chael says. He opens his mouth but no words come out. He shrugs. "I wish I could tell you more. But I can't remember."

"So what happens next?" I ask. "Do you need to perform some sort of good deed in order to pass on to the next life? Isn't that what purgatory is? You're waiting because you're not ready to get into heaven or some nonsense. Is that why they sent you back?"

"I'm not sure," he says. "But I think it's to save you."

"Me? Why me? I don't need saving."

"It was you who brought me back. Your pain is a sound, and that voice was strong enough that it echoed through all the planes of wherever I was. It was hard not to hear you. Impossible not to respond."

"You heard my pain." Not a question. In fact, the thought is just absurd. My words drip with sarcasm.

"Why does that seem strange to you?" Chael says. "No more unusual than some guy coming back from the dead."

"Yeah, to protect me," I say. "Save it. I keep telling you I don't need your help. What is it going to take for you to believe me?"

"Don't you?" Chael looks right at me. "You're hell-bent on revenge. It's the only thing you think about. You're obsessed. There's more to life, Faye. There is so much opportunity if only you'd open your eyes."

"So that's why you said you're going to kill Rufus and the others?" I snap. "As an attempt to save me? How hypocritical is that?"

"I don't need saving," Chael says. "My fate has already been determined. I've lived it. I'm dead, remember? But you still have a chance."

"How do you know that if you're in purgatory or whatever?"

"I just do."

"God, you sound just like Gazer," I say. "Except he doesn't believe in heaven. He doesn't believe in anything. But he keeps saying that I can determine my future. I have free will. Every choice I make determines my next step. But everyone keeps forgetting. I don't have a future."

"Sure you do."

"No, I don't." I yank down my shirt enough to show him the top of my scars again. "You've been away for a long time. Maybe you've forgotten but things haven't changed. I'm a Heam addict. No one is ever going to give me a job. I'm never going to have a normal life. I couldn't even make it through high school without getting kicked out. I've got nothing."

He looks at my scars for a long time. Eventually I let go of my shirt and the skin disappears under the black turtleneck. Not all of my scars are visible. I want to tell him that but I seriously doubt he'll understand. He's already determined that everything about me can be fixed if I just give up my crusade.

"Scars don't make a person," he finally says.

"They do in this world. Especially when I'm a Heam abuser. No employer is going to hire me once they find out. You know the odds. It's almost guaranteed that I will go back on Heam. The statistics are less than one percent. It's a miracle I'm still alive. Almost no one makes it more than a year or two afterward. I never stop having to fight it either. I mean, right now I want to be high. It never goes away, the constant nagging, the desire. I live with that every single second. Some days I feel as if I could kill every person around me, just to get a hit."

"Your life is difficult," he says. "But still—"

"But? You think there's a 'but'?" I'm shouting now and I can't help it. It makes me angry when people try to make me see the positive aspects in life. It's all a load of crap and no one can possibly understand. There is nothing affirmative in my future. Anyone who tries to tell me otherwise is full of it. Not a single one of these people knows what it's like to live through this.

"There are always choices," Chael says. "You just said it yourself. You never give in to the desire. But it's more than that. If you're going to even refuse to consider living, you'll end up with nothing."

"I've been to hell," I say. "When Rufus shoved Heam down my throat, I died. I didn't get to see the heaven that everyone talks about. I saw hell. I felt it. They ripped me apart. They shoved poles through my chest. You have no idea what that feels like."

"You saw what your mind wanted you to see."

"My brain wanted me to be torn apart?"

"It's more complicated than that. What goes on inside us, even we're not sure sometimes. But everything happens for a reason. You saw hell. It doesn't mean you're going to end up there. Just like the others who see heaven. That may not be their fate either. It's all up to you."

"You're so full of shit," I say.

"I'm sorry you feel that way," Chael says. He kneels down on the ground, looking up at me with those big green eyes.

"What did you see?" I ask. "You took the drug. Where did Heam take you?"

Chael shrugs. "Nothing. Like I said all along. I saw nothing."

There's a long pause while I wonder whether I should believe him. He doesn't really have a reason to lie.

Finally, Chael takes a deep breath. "You're right. I can't possibly know what you've been through. I haven't lived your life. So let me demonstrate to you how things should be. Like how beautiful the world is. Remember the night I first met you again? I told you the sun would look good on you. Will you give me the chance to show you?"

"There's nothing pretty here," I say.

"Let me prove you wrong." He stands up. "It's cold. I should take you home. Come with me?"

"Fine," I say.

We ride the train home in silence. The coach is empty except for a homeless lady and her shopping cart full of treasures. She looks over at us several times, winking at me, giving me the thumbs-up as she checks out Chael.

I laugh and shake my head, making a crazy motion with my finger while pointing at him. The whole experience leaves me feeling melancholy, so I spend the rest of the trip staring out the window into darkness.

At one point, Chael tries to reach out and take my hand but I refuse him. I'm still too stunned to think about this properly. The whole evening has exhausted me. I don't even have the strength to ask him any more questions. All I want now is to crawl into my bed and turn out the lights. I won't look at any photos tonight. I have the feeling it will only make the tears come again and I'm so tired of crying.

I let Chael walk me back to the church.

"Meet me tomorrow," he says. "At noon. I want to take you somewhere."

"Where?"

"It's a secret," he says. "But you'll like it. I guarantee."

"Okay," I say. "Meet me at the station."

"Good night." He picks up my hand and squeezes it but I'm too tired and wary to respond.

"Christian?"

"No, don't call me that anymore. I'm not Christian," he says. "But I was him. A long time ago. Christian is dead. There's no bringing him back. My name is now Chael. But I have Christian's thoughts and"—he pauses and looks right at me—"I have all his memories."

"Okay," I say.

"What did you want to ask me?"

I shake my head. It's not important. He turns away and I watch him disappear into the darkness of the night. I dig my key out of my pocket and head inside.

I'm numb. I don't know how to change that.

Sleep. No dreams. I really don't want to dream tonight. I can't bear what ghosts might come visit me.

THIRTEEN

Morning.

I've been up since five. My hair is soaked. Bits of wet strands have escaped my ponytail and are hanging annoyingly in front of my eyes. Gazer stands in front of me with punch pads protecting his hands. Mine are wrapped in tape to prevent my knuckles from popping and to support my wrists.

Fifty punches with the right. Fifty with the left. Uppercut. Jabs. Hooks. Sweat pours down my chest, soaking my shirt, and the cotton sticks to my scars. Every now and then Gazer throws something back at me so I can block it. I duck down and pull to the side like I was born to do this. I keep my hands raised perfectly to protect my face.

We continue on for a long time. I love this kind of workout. I don't have to do anything except move my body. I can shut down my brain. Who has time to think when the endorphins completely take over? Move to the right. Block the left hook. Jab. All my movements join together into a single performance. I'm dancing. My own demented version of ballet. And this stinking church basement is my stage. All my enemies surround me in the audience, waiting, terrified for the moment when I'll call them up to tango with me.

Gazer brings his knee up and that's my sign to put my all into it. Right. Left. Left. Side kick. Step back and cover my face to avoid his jabs. Block. Kick.

Finally, he puts down the pads and signals for me to stop. I'm panting heavily and I didn't even notice until now. I go over and grab the water bottle and take several long swallows. I wipe my face down with a towel. So much sweat.

I feel so alive.

"Impressive," Gazer says as he goes over to wipe down the pads and put them away. "You actually knocked me back a few steps today. I almost couldn't keep up."

I swallow more water. The pounding in my chest begins to slow as my body takes a break. "Not bad, huh? Now, that's a workout."

"Indeed." Gazer comes over and picks up his mug of coffee. It's probably gone cold by now but he never seems to mind. "Bit more like that and we could even put you in the ring. You could probably go pro."

"Not a chance," I say as I start to unwrap the tape from my wrists. "No drug users allowed, remember?"

Gazer shakes his head. "That's always your answer to everything, isn't it?"

I don't want to get into this. Instead, I decide to change

the subject. Anything to steer away from the "What do you want to do when you grow up" talk that never ceases.

"Why don't you believe in heaven?" I take another drink of water and shrug, as if this conversation means nothing to me except as small talk.

"That came out of the blue," Gazer says.

"Just thinking about it," I say. "Don't you ever wonder if your wife and daughter are up there looking down on you? I mean, it's a nice thought, isn't it?"

"Lovely, yes," Gazer says. "But just a thought." He puts down his coffee mug beside some stray dumbbells. "There's no validity to it. I guess it's the scientist in me."

"You were never a scientist. You were a cop."

"Semantics, girl."

I give him a grin.

"I guess I look at the world and how it came into existence," Gazer says. "We're a small planet stuck in a galaxy. There are billions of other galaxies out there. I guess I have trouble believing that one creator could invent all of this. I look at mankind and think it makes more sense that we evolved from the ooze than were created out of God's image and then Adam's ribs. The Bible was not written by God, it was written by man. It's a lovely piece of work but I think it's fiction."

"There has to be more than that," I say. "I know you came from a Catholic family. You were raised that way. You told me."

"There is," Gazer says, and he gives me a look that suggests he doesn't want to go any further. But he sits down on one of the chairs and rubs his fingers through his hair,

214

which is pulled back into a ponytail. There are a lot more white strands than brown. Gazer may still be only in his late thirties but some days he looks much older. Especially when he frowns like he's doing now.

"I lost my faith when my wife died," he says. "I stood by her hospital bed and I watched the life fade and there was nothing I could do to help her. They'd put her on Valium to help with the pain. She should have just slept her life away. But when her time came, she opened her eyes and looked right at me. Except I don't think she saw me."

"What did she see?"

"I don't know. There was pain there. And fear. Lots of fear. I saw the terror and she opened her mouth to tell me something but she couldn't speak. All she could do was grit her teeth. Then she was gone."

"I'm sorry," I say.

"I think that's when I lost God," Gazer says. "I don't understand how anyone can look at something like that and still believe in such things."

"So you believe there is nothing after we die," I say. "Don't you find that depressing?"

"Not really. Just like going to sleep and not dreaming." He stands and picks up his empty coffee cup. "I'm going to go get a refill and you should get in the shower. You don't want to be late for school."

I wait till he disappears up the stairs. His words echo in my mind.

Just like going to sleep.

Only you never wake up.

No, I can't believe that. Because if I did, that would

215

mean I'm just going insane and Chael is nothing but a fig-
ment of my memory. And I'm pretty darn sure I'm not that
crazy.

Yet.

—+—

"What if they could come back?" I ask Gazer after I've
showered and changed into a uniform I'm no longer supposed to wear.

"What do you mean?"

I reach forward and grab an apple off the table, trying to remain as nonchalant as possible. "I mean, what if
you woke up one day and found someone at your doorstep
who'd died. Just as if nothing happened. Back from the
great beyond or whatever it might be."

"That's not possible."

"But what if it were?"

Gazer puts down his newspaper and gives me a sad
smile. "I don't even want to think about that."

"Why?"

"Because I think I'd be ashamed if she could see the way
I turned out. She's been gone all these years and I'm still
waiting for her. But that's something that's never going to
happen, so I don't know why you're wasting your thoughts
on such things. What-ifs aren't real. You'll drive yourself
crazy reliving moments the way you wish they could have
been. What if I had been there for her? I wasn't. There's
nothing I can do to change that."

"But what if they could come back? Don't you ever think about it?"

"No." Gazer purses his lips and I can tell he's getting annoyed at me. "It's no different from how I already live. I should have moved on but I can't. Every morning I wake up looking at the empty pillow where she should be resting. Sometimes I even believe I can hear her voice. But what I do isn't healthy. She would have hated to see me like this. This is why I can't stress enough that you need to forget about revenge. Life is too short, Faye. Don't waste it on nothing. Don't be like me."

"That would be easier to believe if I had something to waste," I say, grabbing my books and heading out the door before he can give me another lecture.

—————+—————

Of course it's raining again and by the time I get to the train station, I'm soaking wet. I should have brought an umbrella. I go into the bathroom and change into the clothing I shoved in my backpack. Then I toss everything in a day locker so I don't have to cart it around. When I go back outside, Chael is waiting for me under the awning. He's wearing a black leather jacket and a pair of nice-looking jeans today and I briefly wonder where he gets his clothing from. He's also wearing a fedora that pushes his hair flat against his forehead. When he came back from the dead, did they give him an allowance? A gift certificate for the Gap?

He smiles at me and for a second I'm eleven again and there are no monsters under my skin.

"Are you ready?" he asks.

"Where are we going?"

"It's a secret."

"Then let's grab a cup of coffee for the road," I say. "I had one hell of a workout this morning. I'd hate to get there and sleep through everything."

"There's a place along the way," he says. He holds out his arm for me, as if he's leading me off to the Queen's Ball or something. I take it and he guides me down into the dark train tunnels.

It takes about half an hour to reach our destination. We don't talk much, mostly because every time I try quizzing him on where we're going, he refuses to say a word. It is fun, though, and I find myself relaxing. Chael is in a good mood and it's a nice change from the seriousness of the night before. Sometimes I find myself on the verge of teasing, but I pull back just in time. I'm worried that he might take it as flirting. Can you hit on a dead guy? I think that's a boundary I really don't want to cross.

Finally, we reach a stop I'm not familiar with and Chael stands and tells me this is it. I've never been here before. I always thought it was just a middle-class suburb. The kind of area I have no business being in.

We ride the escalator up to the top and step outside. I was right. There's nothing but housing here.

"You're taking me to someone's house?" I say with a smirk.

"We have to catch a bus," he says mysteriously.

So we do. The bus is packed but we still manage to find a seat at the back. We ride for a while through a residential area with the occasional strip mall and nothing else. It's a nice neighborhood. There are no all-night liquor stores or strip clubs. No Heam dealers or gutter rats on the corners. I look out the window but the glass is fogged and I can barely see anything because of all the rain. After fifteen minutes or so, the housing thins out and suddenly we're in the country. Well, okay, not the country, but there are a lot of trees.

"Where are we?" I ask.

"The university."

Of course. I should have known this. Not that I've ever been here before but I knew it existed.

We get off at the next stop. The campus stretches out around us. Old mismatched buildings made of stone line the street, hidden behind century-old trees. It's quite pretty, even with all the rain. Such a refreshing change from the city. I can't even remember the last time I saw so many trees. All around us are students who struggle under the weight of book-filled backpacks. They are rushing in all directions and most of them look like the worst thing in their lives is whether or not they're late for class.

They all look so healthy. So wholesome.

Such a different world.

Suddenly I feel very small in my old jacket and jeans with the tear in the knee. I wonder if they can tell I'm not one of them. How can they not? I'm shabby and uncultured. I don't accessorize well. My hair isn't full of expensive products that make it shine. I could go on and on all day. This is the type of place where Paige will end up after high school. Girls like her will fit in without even trying. Girls like me will be the sore thumbs. A group of students rush by in a flurry of umbrellas and book bags. Chael presses closer against me to let them pass. But if they notice my differences, they don't say anything. They talk loudly to each other, giggling and sipping on water bottles and from coffee cups. Mostly they ignore us as we walk along, Chael protectively sticking close to my side as if he can read my thoughts.

We continue to walk along the road and I watch everyone, trying to ignore the jealousy that burns in my chest. They're so carefree. Well, most of them. Some look a tad stressed, probably on their way to take an exam or maybe they're simply late for class. I step off the sidewalk to let a student riding a skateboard zip past me. Her hair is tucked underneath a baseball cap and she keeps her face down to protect herself from the rain. Her cheeks are rosy and her top is low-cut, showing off wet skin. What I wouldn't give to be able to wear something so deliciously brazen without having people stare at me in fear and disgust.

I glance over at Chael and he's watching me intently, almost as if he's reading my mind. My cheeks burn and I look away, concentrating on the buildings. It's one thing to be jealous of these kids with their bright futures; it's another to have to admit it openly. I don't want Chael feeling sorry for me. Not right now.

"We're here," he says after a while.

"Where?"

"Come on," he says, turning off the sidewalk and onto

a path that leads to one of the newer buildings. It's several stories high and made almost entirely out of glass. The windows are fogged up and I can't see inside. There's a big sign outside the main door.

ARBORETUM

He opens the door for me and holds it as I walk through. Inside, a big information desk is positioned in the middle of the room, with another glass entrance beyond it. A very tiny woman in a blue uniform watches us as we approach. Chael pulls out his wallet.

"Two, please," he says.

He pays the money and gets tickets in return. I stand beside him, cold and wet, wondering if I should go to the bathroom and try to dry myself off a bit before we go inside.

"Come on," he says.

Beyond the glass doors is a jungle. The humid air hits my face, instantly bringing warmth to my clammy skin. Hundreds, no, thousands of plants of all different kinds and sizes cover the entire space. I can hear water in the distance, maybe a waterfall of sorts, and there's a cobblestone path that leads off into all that gigantic greenery.

It's insanely beautiful. There are colors everywhere. Brilliant red flowers I don't recognize are to the right of me. To my left are cacti, long and slender, prickly to the touch. We follow the path slowly; every few feet I stop to stare at something new. A palm tree reaches down with its long fronds, tickling the top of Chael's hat. I bend over to sniff something that looks like a lily, although I'm not fully sure. I've never seen a lily before except in books. For all I know, it could be something else. Maybe an iris? Not a rose. I know those.

There are signs everywhere. *Amaranthus caudatus. Rhopalostylis sapida. Spathodea campanulata.* Words I couldn't possibly pronounce properly or remember, even if someone tried explaining them to me over and over.

I touch the soft dainty petals of a *Eucharis grandiflora.* It's softer than a baby's skin. The scent reaches my nose, making it tingle and itch slightly.

"It's so beautiful," I say.

Chael doesn't say anything. He reaches out to gently stroke the pins on a cactus that's almost as tall as him.

There are metal love seats beside the waterfall. It circles the room, a man-made stream of crystal-clear water. Chael sits down and waits while I dip my fingers in the coolness and then lean over to sniff some daisies. He leans back and closes his eyes. For a moment, I'm distracted and turn away from the flowers.

With his eyes closed, I can study him without him knowing. I can admire the way his hair curls slightly at the back of his neck. His jaw is firm, his lips slightly parted. I can see the top row of his teeth. He is exactly the way Christian would have looked if he'd been given the chance to grow up.

I don't understand how I didn't see it before. Maybe because I wasn't looking? But now that I am, he's exactly how I remembered him. Sure, the muscles are better developed; he was thinner when he was younger. He's more filled out now. His jacket is open and I can see the shirt pressing against his chest. It rises and falls as he breathes. His legs are lean and long, stretched out before him and crossed at the ankles. He always had long legs, but when he was thirteen, they looked skinny and awkward. Now they're muscular and pressed tight against his jeans.

Chael opens his eyes and catches me watching him. He smiles and winks and I look away in embarrassment. Oh, great. I wish I were better at this sort of thing. I should have winked back or tossed my hair over my shoulder in a flirtatious manner. Instead, I've managed to act like a shy little girl with a schoolboy crush.

I force myself to head over to where he is and I sit down next to him on the bench. His fingers tap lazily on the metal.

"So what do you think?" he asks.

"It's beautiful," I say. "I never knew there were so many flowers. It's almost overwhelming."

"Yeah, I thought you'd like it."

I nod, leaning over to put my hand back in the water. The rushing noise fills my ears and I close my eyes for a moment and listen to how pretty everything sounds. The coolness on my fingers, the perfume in my nose—I could spend all day here and probably be begging to come back the next morning.

"I was right. It looks good on you."

"Huh?" I open my eyes.

Chael points up at the ceiling, where bright lights shine down on us. "The sun. It looks good on you."

"It's artificial."

"Close enough."

I tilt my head back and let the air warm my face. It feels good. The sun in the city is never like this. Never this fresh. I dip my hand in the water again and try to catch it between my fingers. Light reflects off the drops and my skin sparkles like crystals. I touch my face, tracing wet circles on my cheeks. I want to remember this moment because it's been too long since I've felt this good. If I could get away with it, I'd kick off my shoes and jump into the waterfall and sit there until I'm wrinkled all over. I'd close my eyes and imagine myself on a tropical beach. Lying on the sand, letting the salty air dry my skin while I drink something fancy like a mai tai or piña colada. I'd wear a bikini because there wouldn't be anyone around to see me. No one for miles. Just me and the ocean.

I open my eyes and squint under the greenhouse lighting. Now it's Chael who is watching me but he's not smiling. The look on his face is hard to read.

"What?" I ask.

"Just watching you," he says unabashedly. "Your cheeks are wet."

I pull myself upward until I'm sitting rigidly enough to break my back. I wipe my fingers on my pants and then use my shirt to dry off my face. I must look like an idiot, playing with the water like I'm a little girl all over again.

"This is nice," Chael continues. "It's good to see you happy. I was beginning to worry about you."

"Sorry to disappoint," I say. I wish I could argue with him and come up with a million ways to prove him wrong. But he's right. I haven't been happy. To say otherwise

224

would be a lie and I never was good at lying to him when we were kids. He could always see right through me.

"Don't say that," Chael says, and suddenly he's very close to me. He's shifted on the bench until we're practically touching. "There's a lot in this world to be happy for. You just haven't found it. You should look in a mirror more often because when you smile, you're beautiful."

I can't look at him. So I stare down at the stream of water as it rushes away in a continuous loop. Kind of like me. Moving constantly but never getting anywhere.

"We should move on," Chael finally says. "There's something else I want to show you."

I stand up to leave but my attention is drawn to some orchids over to my left. I bend down and sniff the petals. So beautiful. I run my fingers along the stem and then touch the damp earth below. When I'm done, Chael reaches out to take my hand and this time I let him. His skin is warm and his fingers wrap around mine, making me feel safer than I've felt in a very long time.

—+—

Another area in the back of the arboretum. There is a screen covering the door and Chael pulls it back so I can step inside.

A butterfly room.

I've never seen so many. Or ones of such bright colors. Stepping beside a tree, I look straight up and the ceiling is a tangle of vines and green leafy branches. It's like being in the middle of a rain forest. And everything is alive. Above my head is a multitude of pink, blue, orange, and purple fluttering wings.

The ground is soft beneath my feet and I watch where I step, careful to make sure I don't accidently squish something. There is a ledge lining the wall and flowers rest in pots. Butterflies feed off of them, their small feelers twitching as they move their wings gracefully. When I look closer, I can see dozens of tiny cocoons mixed in amongst the plants. I even spot a caterpillar as it creeps along a daisy's petals.

One of the butterflies floats beside my face, coming to rest on a vine that drifts down from the ceiling. It's huge, almost the size of my hand. Its orange-and-black wings stretch out, quivering as it tries to attract a mate.

"It's a monarch," Chael says. "Some people call it the wanderer butterfly. They migrate thousands of miles each year. Many of them die along the way, never finding what they're looking for."

"He's beautiful," I say. I want to reach out and rub my finger against that velvety softness but I know that's a bad idea. His wings are fragile and even the slightest touch can hurt. I don't want to imagine the guilt I might feel if I end up injuring him for no reason except my own selfishness. That would be unfair. Everything deserves to live, no matter how small and helpless.

"Did you know some of them are territorial?" Chael says. "Butterflies may look harmless but they can be quite mean. They'll fight to the death if another gets in their way."

I look up and watch as a purple butterfly with red-tipped wings moves across the room to perch on top of Chael's head. It makes me grin and suddenly I'm laughing, wondering if it might end up doing something unsightly on his black hat. The thought of Chael covered in butterfly poop suddenly has me laughing so hard there are tears streaming down my face.

And I can't stop laughing, because those poor things travel so hard and long to search for something they know they're never going to find, and it's such a stupid metaphor for how I'm living my own life that I can't break the image of myself floating along in the wind, powerless to stop, unable to do anything as the dust brushes off my body and I fall to the ground.

"You're crying."

"I'm suddenly feeling sorry for myself," I say as I angrily brush away the tears. "Don't read into this. It doesn't mean a thing."

"Sure it does." He leans closer until the thinnest butterfly wing couldn't get between us. "It's okay to be vulnerable, you know."

I shake my head.

"You've really changed," he says, but he doesn't say it in an insulting way. "When you were younger, you used to look at me with such openness. Now you're trying to close yourself off to the world. I wish I could have been there to watch you grow up."

"You were cheated," I say.

"I was," he says, and his face is so close I can feel his breath. "I was just like you. I wanted to do so many things.

227

So many wasted plans. I wanted to protect you. Even when you were little. There was such a bond between us. I thought it could never be broken."

"I thought so too."

"When they attacked us that night, I wish I could have been stronger. I wanted to tear them apart for touching you. I wanted to kill them. But I wasn't tough enough. I couldn't do anything to save you." He pauses and looks right into my eyes. "I never meant to leave you."

"I know." The tears are still flowing but I can't raise my hand to wipe them away. My body has lost all ability to think for itself. I can only look at Chael as he looks down at me.

"But death couldn't break our bond."

"I don't want you to leave me again," I say. "When you were gone, I was all alone. Empty inside. I can't go through that again."

"I won't. I'm here for you right now. This is our moment."

When he kisses me, everything around us ceases to exist.

FOURTEEN

I'm too happy. Even Gazer is looking at me suspiciously every chance he gets. I can see he wants to attack me with questions but he's holding back. He's respecting my need to keep this secret.

I'm not ready to share Chael yet.

With good reason. I still don't know what any of this means.

It's Friday and I've made it through another week of pretending to go to school every morning when in reality I've been spending it elsewhere. Mostly I've been down at the Heam center, hanging out with Beth. She's not doing well. She's lost weight, which is appalling since she is so tiny to begin with. The secondhand clothes she's been given swallow her whole. Her eyes are always bloodshot, as if she's wiping away the tears the second she hears me come through the door.

The counselor, Ramona, tells me that she doesn't think

Beth is going to survive this. She's seen this too many times before. It's just a matter of counting the days till she runs away. If she escapes, it won't be her parents she goes to. But I'm holding strong, refusing to believe it.

"She's very lucky," Ramona says. We're standing by the front doors and she fiddles with her clipboard. "There are a lot of children that come through here. They don't have people like you."

"Me? I haven't done anything."

"You've been here for her," she says. "That's a hell of a lot more than most of these kids have. A lot of times they're completely isolated from society. Even their own parents disown them."

"I can't imagine," I lie.

"But you've been a good friend to Beth," she continues as she taps the top of her clipboard with her pen. "Tell me. Have you ever considered getting into this line of work?"

"What do you mean?"

"Heam counseling." Ramona leans in closer until her lips are practically pressing against my cheek. "Beth told me about you. I know you're a survivor. I don't give a damn what the government and all their statistics say about abusers. I believe that some can still get clean. You're living proof. With your experience, you'd be perfect for the job."

"It's pointless. That sort of thing requires training, right? No university will take me. Do you know how hard it was to even find a high school?" I pause. I don't want to admit to this woman that I've been expelled. We're not that close.

"I might be able to get you into a specialized training program," Ramona says. "The pay wouldn't be as good without a degree and you'd have to volunteer first. But it could lead to a good job."

"I'll think about it," I lie.

Ramona smiles and nods. As she walks off to do her rounds, I can't help admiring her for being a good woman. She sees these children for what they're worth and not for what they've done. The world needs more people like her. Even if she is a bit naive.

Five minutes later, Beth and I get situated for our daily chat.

"I'm not as tough as you," Beth says. We're sitting outside in the garden, a pitiful place with two droopy trees and a few dying bushes. The ground is hard and lifeless. Grass might have grown there a million years ago but now everything is barren. We sit on a metal bench and it reminds me of being with Chael, surrounded by the plants at the arboretum. Well, maybe not quite, but my imagination is kicking in. I try to push away the thoughts. It won't do Beth any good to see me happy. Not when her hands are shaking so badly she can't hold the hot chocolate I brought her from the shop down the street.

"You don't have to be as strong as me," I say. "You have to be as strong as you can be."

"I can't stop thinking about it," she says. She picks at a paint flake that's peeling from the bench.

"I know."

"I dream about it. Seeing heaven. I close my eyes and

it's there. I can't understand why I should stay here on earth when such a place is waiting for me. It's horrible here. So cold." She picks a dying leaf off the bench and crumbles it between her fingers. "I want to be warm again."

"It's an illusion," I say again, repeating the exact same thing Gazer always tells me. We've had this conversation at least ten times this week. "It's not real. You know this."

Beth nods. Then she says something new. "I don't care what's out there when I die. But I think it can't be worse than here. Nothing is as bad as being here."

"What about Joshua?"

"He'll get over it. He understands."

I take a drink of my coffee, trying to pretend that her talking about killing herself is completely normal. Inside, my stomach is an icicle. I've got to remember to tell the therapist about this before I leave. Maybe they can put her on suicide watch or something. Sure, they're short-staffed, but they should be able to come up with something.

"Don't you think he'll miss you?" I finally ask. "I know I will."

Beth turns to me and there's anger in her eyes. "Don't be mean, Faye," she says. "You know what it's like. I see the hate in your eyes too. You don't want to be here either."

"That's not true," I protest, but it's weak. She's right. Even I have my bad days. I won't pretend that I've never thought of dying either.

"It is true," she says. "No one can understand it. I thought you would."

"Beth," I begin. "Killing yourself isn't the answer."

"But that's what you're gonna do," Beth says. "You told me yourself. You're going to get revenge and they'll probably kill you for trying. What you're doing is the same as me. Don't try and pretend it's different."

I open my mouth to argue but decide otherwise. She's right. I never should have told her about my revenge. I thought it might cheer her up. I can see it was a big mistake. Now she's going to use it against me.

"It's not the same," I finally say.

"Go away," she whispers. "I don't want to talk to you anymore."

When I don't move, she gets up and runs inside. I sit there in the garden for a bit, trying to ignore the droopy trees. It seems that the rain is pushing them down. Water isn't enough. Things need sunlight to grow.

Finally, I go inside and try to find the counselor before I head out. But she's nowhere in sight.

———+———

"She hates me," I say. It's later that evening and I'm sitting with Chael in the coffee shop down the street. I always pick here because it's close to where Rufus sits at the bar. He's there tonight. I checked earlier. I need to get back into my routine. I've been distracted this week.

"She doesn't hate you." Chael holds on to my hand, turning it in his, fingers tracing the lines along my palm. It tickles but I don't pull away.

"She does."

"She's right, though."

"Don't start," I say, pulling my hand away in annoyance.

"I'm not doing anything."

"Sure you are," I say. "You're just looking for another excuse to get into it about my revenge. I'm not stopping and you're not going to fight my battle."

"It's my battle too," he says. "And you're right."

"About what?"

"That it's not my revenge. It's both of ours. And I think we should look at it from that perspective."

"As in?"

He reaches out and takes my hand again, squeezing tightly. "I think we should do it together."

"No way. You'll find a way to make sure I get nothing." I try to pull away but he's holding on too tightly.

Chael leans forward as if he's going to whisper in my ear. Not that it matters. The diner is empty and the waitress is watching a television program behind the counter. The volume is up on the miniature flat-screen and we could shout at each other and she probably wouldn't notice.

"I know you're more than capable of taking care of yourself," Chael says. "But I've been thinking about this a lot lately. I think we should work together. That way I get my revenge and I get to make sure no one hurts you in the process."

"You mean that?" I look right into his eyes, but it's impossible to tell if he's lying. His gaze is strong and intense. He looks completely serious.

"Rufus is mine," I finally say.

"And Ming Bao is mine," he says. "A kill for a kill. Ming took my life. Only fair that I get to return the favor."

"What about Phil?"

"We'll flip a coin."

I giggle and cover my mouth with my hand. This conversation is so absurd. But at the same time, it feels normal. Maybe it is the right thing to do.

"Okay," I say, and I take a sip of coffee to try to remain nonchalant. "Suppose I agree to your partnership. How do we go about doing this? How do I know you'll keep your word?"

"I haven't lied to you yet." The sides of his lips are curling up. He's as amused by this as I am. "I never lied to you when we were younger."

"You lied all the time," I say. "You lied about seeing the Easter bunny that one time. And you lied about the rabbit you said you had."

"That was silly kid stuff," he says. "This isn't."

"I don't know," I say, and I really don't. This is a new thing for me. I need time to think it over. I've spent years plotting this revenge. For me. For Christian. It never occurred to me that he might come back to join me.

Changing the plan was never part of the deal.

"Come on," Chael says, reading my mind. "Let's get out of here and go for a walk or something. You don't have to answer right now. Take your time."

I nod. Chael tosses some bills on the table.

"Where do you get your money?" I ask as I slip on my jacket. "I mean, you came back from the dead, right? Did God give you a wallet? What about the clothing? I keep meaning to ask you about it. And where do you sleep? Is there a Heavenly Hotel I don't know about?"

Chael smiles but something dark flashes behind his eyes. It's only there for a second but I see it. He turns to leave and I grab his arm.

"I really want to know," I say.

"I get by," he says.

And that's it. He turns and walks out before I can even open my mouth. Great. My new boyfriend is probably out there jumping people on the train or robbing liquor stores in his free time. Not the kind of guy I want to bring home to Gazer, not that I would. Gazer wouldn't believe it anyway. He only ever met Christian after he was dead on the alley floor. He can't see what I see. He'd only see the illegal parts and think I'm being scammed or something. He might even call the police. Robbery is a big deal. The worst part is, I can't condone it, but I can't demand that Chael stop either. I'm not exactly an angel myself. It would be hypocritical of me to expect my boyfriend to toe the legal line when we're talking about murder every other minute.

Outside, Chael is waiting for me underneath my streetlamp. The light reflects off his damp hair, giving him that funny glowing halo look.

"Do you want to see my place, then?"

"Huh?"

"My place," Chael repeats. "Where I live. My humble abode. I'm more than happy to take you there." He looks back at the bar, where Rufus is drinking away his pathetic life. "But not tonight. Maybe tomorrow?"

"Why not tonight? It's still early. Gazer won't be expecting me home till later."

Chael looks back at the bar again but no one is coming out. "It's the maid's night off," he says. "I'd hate for you to see it right now. It's a bit messy."

I can see the waitress cleaning our table inside the coffee shop. She takes Chael's money and puts it in her pocket as she picks up the empty coffee cups. Turning, she pauses and looks out the window at us. I smile and nod but she shakes her head and goes back to her work. It worries me; I can't help wondering if she's been eavesdropping on our conversations. No, I tell myself. She'd have called the cops by now if she had any idea of what we were planning.

Chael suddenly swears under his breath and I turn back to him. We're not alone. I have an excuse. At least I was distracted. No idea why Chael didn't catch it in time.

"Why are you doing this to me?"

It's the girl with the red umbrella, only she doesn't have it with her this time. She's standing right in front of us, her arms filled with flyers showing her missing brother. Arnold Bozek. Funny how I can't remember most of the counselors' names at Beth's shelter but I can't forget his.

"What's the matter?" I ask.

But she's not looking at me. She's eyeing Chael and her face is a mess of emotions. Chael won't even look at her. He stares at the ground, his head down in shame.

"Why?" she repeats. And then louder. "Why?"

"What's the matter, sweetheart?" I ask her.

She turns to me and there is enough hatred in her eyes

to kill a thousand Heam dealers. "Stop it!" she snaps. "You're just as bad as him." She turns back to Chael. "Why won't you come home? We've been looking for you every night and you've been here." She sneers in a way no child should. "With her."

Now I'm more than confused. I look at Chael but he's still looking at the ground. Does she think Chael is her brother? How is that possible? Even a blind man could tell the difference.

"You need to come home," the girl says. "Mom isn't mad at you. She's crying all the time and it's your fault. Why won't you come home? We need you."

"I'm not who you think I am," Chael finally says. "I'm sorry, but I'm not him."

"Yes you are!" She throws her flyers on the ground and they immediately begin to soak up rainwater. Arnold Bozek's face becomes blotchy and smeared as the ink runs.

"Listen to me." Chael kneels down on the wet cement and puts his hands on the girl's shoulders. She tries to yank away from him but he holds firm. "Look at me," he says, and his voice sounds harder than usual.

The girl won't look at him. There are tears in her eyes and her nose is running. Her face scrunches up tightly, her mouth puckering into a tiny rosebud. She looks down at the ground defiantly, her eyes holding firm on the mushy fly-ers. I stand beside them stupidly. I want to stop this. I want to grab Chael by the arm and pull him back. But I need to hear what he's going to say. I think the girl does too.

"Look at me," he repeats, and finally her eyes move up

toward his. There are years of pain in those eyes. She's different from the first time I saw her. She's aged a lifetime in the course of a few weeks. Losing someone you love does that to you.

"Chael." My voice is weak. "I don't think you should—"

"You need to go home," he says to the little girl, effectively cutting me off. "You need to give up this search. Your brother is gone. He's dead. His soul is gone. There's no bringing it back. I'm sorry but that's the way things are."

"You're lying."

"I wish I were," he says. "But it's the truth. Staying out here each night is only going to bring you more pain. I'm not who you think I am. You must believe this."

She nods.

"Arnold must have been a good brother," Chael says. "Obviously or you wouldn't still be out torturing yourself every night. He's gone and you need to move on."

"But you're him." The girl is sobbing uncontrollably now. The tears and snot meet at her chin and the rainwater attempts to wash away the mess. Her eyes are bright red and she looks at me for only a second before returning her gaze to Chael.

"I'm his shell."

I'm confused beyond belief. What are they seeing that I'm not? There is a puzzle here and I'm missing a few pieces. Hell, I'm missing most of the box. I want to ask but hold back; better to wait until the whole ordeal is over.

The girl finally manages to get the sobs under control.

She sniffs several times and I hand her a worn tissue that's been in my jacket forever. She wipes her face.

"Did he suffer?" She hiccups and blinks at the same time.

Chael shakes his head. "I don't believe he did."

"Do you get to talk to him?"

"No. He's gone someplace where I can't follow."

"Does he miss me?"

"I'll bet he does."

The girl gives a faint smile and I wonder where her umbrella is. This is the first time I've ever seen her without it. I can't believe I didn't notice until right now. She looks odd without it. Older.

"Are you an angel?"

Chael smiles. "Something like that."

"Will you give him a message for me?"

"I can try."

"Tell him I'm mad at him," she says. "And I love him. I wish he could come home. I miss him."

"I'll do my best to pass it on."

The girl sniffs a few more times and then she does something completely odd. She throws her arms around Chael, her tormenter, and holds on to him tightly. He doesn't hug her back. I'm not sure if she notices.

"I think it's best you go home now," Chael finally says when he manages to pry her away.

"Okay," she says. She turns and walks off, turning around several times to look back at us as she fades into the distance. Chael stands up and watches her until she turns the corner. Only then does he look at me. The hardness is still in his eyes but there's something else there too. Pain.

"Why does she think you're her brother?"

Chael reaches out and takes my hand. He doesn't say anything but starts walking. I have no choice but to follow. We cross the street and head down the block in the opposite direction. Finally, he stops in front of a pawnshop. He puts his hands on my shoulders and turns me toward the window.

There are security bars protecting the glass. Behind them is an arrangement of old guitars, electronic equipment, and mechanic tools. One of the video cameras is turned on and it's feeding directly into a television.

"Look," Chael says.

It takes me a moment to realize he's talking about the television. The camera is directly on us and there are two bodies staring back. One of them is me. The other isn't Chael.

It's Arnold Bozek.

I turn and stare at Chael in amazement. The real flesh-and-blood Chael. His longish dark hair, dampened by the rain. His bright green eyes. Sharp cheekbones. Then I look back at the screen. There's Arnold's blond hair. His glasses. His cleft chin.

"What the hell?"

"I took his body," Chael says. "When I came back. The real Arnold is gone. I'm in his shell. You're the only person who sees me as Christian. Everyone else sees him."

"But why?"

"I don't know. It could be because you're the only

241

person who remembers me. Maybe you're supposed to recognize me. If you'd seen Arnold, you wouldn't have figured it out."

"I would have eventually," I say, but I doubt the words as they leave my mouth. The way Chael looks at me suggests he is thinking the same thing.

I look back at the camera and study the dead boy's image. No wonder Paige didn't have a clue what I was talking about when I asked her if she'd seen Chael. She saw something completely different. Arnold's features aren't nearly as attractive as Chael's. He doesn't stand out as much with his glasses and mousy hair. He probably went through life as someone no one remembered. A person quickly forgotten.

Except for a sister who misses him dearly.

"I'm sorry," Chael says. He puts his arms around me and I watch Arnold Bozek place his chin on top of my head. I watch Arnold's arms circle my waist, pressing against my jacket.

"It's okay," I say. "It's weird, though."

"It just didn't seem that important," Chael says. "I knew immediately that you were the only one seeing me for who I truly am."

"How could you tell?"

"The way you first looked at me. You may not have realized it but you recognized me that first night. I saw it in your eyes. But your brain refused to believe. You needed time to work everything out."

"I thought you were weird," I say with a laugh. "You

looked so out of place. You kept touching your face like you didn't recognize the touch."

"The bodies we wear," he says. "They're not the ones we always want. They get damaged. Used. It's who we are on the inside that counts. The person waiting to jump free."

I reach out and run my hand along my chest, feeling the scars beneath my shirt. Yes, I understand that all too well. What I wouldn't give to wake up one morning and find myself in a new body. One that isn't damaged.

But would it be worth it? Or would I end up like Chael, constantly touching my skin, wondering what feels wrong and why I can't make it right?

"Come on," he says softly. "I'll take you home."

Afterward, when he kisses me goodnight just outside the church doors, I can't help reminding myself that those aren't really his lips I'm kissing. Those aren't his arms holding me tightly.

But the warmth is his. I'm sure of it. It may be a dead boy touching me, but it's Chael's energy that keeps me warm. His spirit.

He kisses me again and pushes his body against mine, pressing my back up against the bricks. I like this feeling of being trapped by his strength. It makes me feel secure. I don't want it to end.

But my brain just won't turn itself off, no matter how much I try to ignore the questions beating around inside my skull.

Finally, I force myself to draw back and look up at his

eyes. He playfully leans down to brush his lips across my forehead. When he goes for my lips again, this time I turn my head. It's not that I don't want to; it's just that I have to ask.

"How long can you stay like this? In this body. Isn't it technically a loaner? When do you have to give it back?"

"I don't know," he says.

"That's your answer to everything."

"I didn't exactly get an instruction manual." Chael brushes a bit of my hair back from my face. His fingers are soft and wet from being in the rain. "Maybe I have forever, or maybe I just have tonight. I'm not going to waste it worrying about tomorrow. Right now, this moment." He leans down and kisses me again. "This is all I need. Tomorrow is a million miles away."

"But what happens when tomorrow comes?"

Chael nuzzles his face against my neck. His body is tense. I can feel his hard muscles pressing against my chest. He trembles slightly and that only makes me try to hold him tighter.

"We've got to appreciate what we've got, Faye," he whispers into my ear. "No one knows how much time they have left. Let's just enjoy every shiny moment."

"I don't want to lose you."

"Even in death, we never truly get lost."

I want to believe that, so I will. At least tonight.

FIFTEEN

"You're smiling again."

I look up from the coloring book I've been doodling in for the past half hour. Beth is giving me a quizzical look.

"Am I?"

"Yes," Beth says. She turns around in her chair and looks over at Chael, who is off in the corner trying to hold a conversation with a Heam abuser who is also a paraplegic. An addict who, two months ago, tried to take a short walk off a freeway overpass when he didn't have any more money to get high. Even though he can no longer feel his body, he can still feel the urges. The last time I was here, I could hear him screaming from his room, begging anyone to help get him high—or put him out of his misery.

Chael insisted on coming with me today when I came to visit Beth. I made the mistake of telling him that Ramona suggested I'd be good in the therapy business and he wanted to see me at my best.

My best? Right. I can't save a flea from an itchy cat.

"You're happy," Beth says without taking her eyes off of Chael. "He's making you smile again."

"Yes," I say.

Beth picks up a green crayon from the table. Coloring is a bit young for her but she wanted to do it. She said it calms her and she enjoys it. She's much better than me. I've spent the last half hour trying to make the black-and-white sky look blue and all I've managed to do is color outside all the lines.

"That's good," Beth says. "You do a lot of things for everyone else. You deserve this." She turns around again and I swear there's almost a hint of a sparkle in her eyes. "And he's really cute."

I grin at her.

We continue to work on the coloring book. Beth presses very softly with her crayon, making her page turn a series of pretty pastels. My blue sky is uneven from where I've pressed too hard. It's a wonder I even made it to high school.

From across the room, Chael continues to speak softly to the addict in the wheelchair. I can't hear what he's saying but it must be working. The boy is nodding and I'm pretty sure he's crying. But not in a bad way. Either way, he's calmer than I've ever seen him before. A few of the other kids have come over to join them. There is now a circle of young drug addicts sitting by Chael's feet and listening to whatever stories he's entertaining them with.

Chael looks at me from across the room and blows me a kiss. I cover my smile with my hand and look down at the table.

"Do you think there's still beauty in this world?" Beth suddenly asks, and I pause to ponder the question. Should I answer truthfully or should I lie? Will it make a difference? Beth is so impressionable; I don't want her thinking that the future is going to be ugly.

"If you asked me that a month ago, I probably would have said no," I tell her. "But I was in a completely different place then."

"You're happy now," Beth says.

"Yes," I tell her. "But you can't rely on others for your own happiness." My fingers absently stroke the Celtic necklace that Gazer gave me. "I think I've started to learn a few things lately. I've spent so much time being miserable and bitchy I've forgotten that there was a part of me that could still enjoy simple things. I thought I enjoyed my hate. I thought I could look at everyone who hurt me and take pride in knowing I would get revenge. But now I'm not so sure."

And when I say these words, I know they're the truth. It takes so much energy to hate. I feel like I've been floating at the bottom of the sea for too long. Good God, at the rate I'm going, I'll be writing greeting-card poetry before long.

"I like the moon at night," Beth says, looking down at her crayons. "I like the way it sometimes manages to find its way through the clouds. I like the raindrops on the leaves in the garden. And I love the way a bakery smells when you go inside."

"All completely enjoyable," I agree.

"And I think that maybe I want to stick around a little longer and see the summer again."

I smile at her and my heart lifts up inside my chest.

"Ramona says there's a school that will take me and I can continue to live at the clinic for as long as I want." She picks up a pink marker and starts to doodle on her chewed fingernails. When she's done, she lifts her hand to the light and admires her work. "I think I want to do that."

"Now I'm extra happy," I tell her. I get up and go around the table to give her a hug. She throws her skinny arms around my waist and pulls me tight. When I look up, Chael is watching me. He smiles and winks.

Afterward, we walk home hand in hand.

"She's coming around," I say happily. I kick at a pile of mushy leaves in the gutter and giggle when they stick to my shoes. I want to twirl around and pirouette in front of the parking meter. I want to jump up on top of the burned-out car and scream to the world.

"You were brilliant," he says.

"So were you," I say. "I think Ramona is in love with you. The way she gushed and begged me to bring you back tomorrow."

Chael grins and throws his arm around my shoulder, pulling me in close.

I helped her.

Maybe Ramona is right. This could be my calling.

For the first time in ages, the revenge doesn't press against my mind, reminding me of where my place is.

I feel free.

Paige is waiting for me when I get home.

Now, that is something I never expected to see. Paige may be a lot of things; I can think of a lot of choice words I'd use to describe her. But gutsy? Brazen? Nope. Never saw that one coming. And she's determined too. She refuses to get out of the way when I try to push past her.

She stands her ground by the church steps, shivering in her brand-name jacket. In her left hand is an umbrella that's managing to keep most of the rain away; the other hand holds a slightly damp-looking envelope.

"What do you want?" I ask cautiously.

"I want to talk to you. Please, Faye."

I go around her but she steps in front, blocking me effectively. She leans against the door to make sure I can't try to sneak past.

"My father is an attorney," she says very quickly. "I told him what happened. Everything. He already knew about the party, so it's not like that was a surprise. And then I told him about what the school did. It's cruel."

"It doesn't matter. I was on a scholarship. They had the right to end it."

"No they didn't," Paige says exasperatedly. "As I said, my dad is a lawyer. He's agreed to take on the case. He says what the school did violates your civil rights. He's pretty sure he can get you back in. And he's not going to charge you either. He's doing it for free."

"Huh?" Yep, that's right. I'm speechless.

"He's drafting the paperwork right now," she says. "And I've got these." She holds up the envelope and hands it over to me. "Open it."

It's heavy and unsealed. I open the flap and reach in, taking out at least twenty pieces of paper. It's a petition. And there are a lot of signatures on the pages. Hundreds of them. I sift through the sheets and it's all the same thing. Name after name after name. Some of them I recognize. Most of them I don't.

"It's the entire school," Paige says proudly. "Except maybe one or two. Everyone signed."

"For what?"

"For you to come back."

"Huh?" I swear, my IQ has dropped fifty points.

"The students are upset," Paige says. "The school tried to cover it up but everyone pretty much knew all about it by the end of the day. And Mr. Erikson's gone. He resigned in protest. We're gonna try and get him back too."

"Mr. Erikson's gone?" I put my hand out on the rail to steady myself. I can't believe it. I mean, I knew he was against what the school was doing but I never thought he'd quit his job. That seems so extreme.

"Yeah," Paige says. "So now we're going to fight to get you both back. I've spent the past few days gathering all these signatures. There's eight hundred and ninety-seven. Not bad, huh?"

"Why are you doing this?"

"Because I'm an idiot," she says without missing a beat. "Come on, Faye. I know I said some wrong things and I can't take them back. I'm not always the best at making the right decisions. Look at Jesse. Can I pick them or what?" She laughs bitterly. "I've always been the girl who gets everything she wants. The spoiled little rich girl. Don't look so shocked. I'm quite aware of what I am. And as you know, I've got no problem using that to my advantage."

I can't help smiling. This is the Paige I know. It's funny to hear her speak so blatantly about it.

"And I guess it took this to make me really appreciate it," she says. "When I saw your scars. And then the way you looked right at me and everyone else when you walked down the hallway. You were so proud. Like an Amazon queen. I know I can be a bitch most of the time. But at that moment, you made me feel so ashamed of myself. I would have done anything to take it all back. And then later Mr. Erikson told us about all the rules you had to follow. We spent the entire class talking about it. It's not fair. They had no right to treat you that way. Because of a drug?"

"That's just the way it is," I say. "Heam addicts aren't exactly liked out here, in case you didn't notice."

"You don't look like an addict to me. When was the last time you actually took Heam?"

"When I was eleven."

"Eleven?"

"It's a long story and I'm not going to share. But it wasn't my fault. And I've never touched the drug since." I look right into her eyes as I say this. I don't know why, but suddenly it's very important to me that she believes me. Maybe it's because no one has ever stood up and fought for me before. All those signatures. I can't believe they all signed the petition.

"I can't expect you to trust me after all I've done to

you," Paige begins. "So you don't have to. Everything I'm doing should be proof enough. And you don't have to do anything. I've got it all taken care of."

Is she being honest with me? I can't tell. I want to believe her but that was my problem in the first place. Just like I wanted to believe I could get an education without ever having a problem. I think back to our lunch and when she talked about how dying would be better than having scars. Is it possible that she's simply trying to make good on her words? Is the guilt real? Or am I just some new project for her to take on? Something to look good on a college application?

"Do you really live here?" Paige finally asks, breaking the silence and my thoughts. She looks up at the church in awe. She's actually impressed. I find that funny, considering I was so amazed at her place. I guess that's what happens when you lead completely different lives.

"Yeah," I say. "Do you want to come in?"

"I'd love to."

I unlock the door and we're greeted by silence. Thankfully, Gazer isn't home. So I give her the whole tour. The living area that's surrounded by empty pews, the kitchen with our bipolar refrigerator; I even show her the basement with the broken-down gym equipment. Eventually we end up in my bedroom. I try not to act embarrassed because there are clothes on the floor and my bed's not made. I'm sure her room would be the same if it weren't for the maid.

"I love this place," she says. "It's so beautiful." She sits down on my bed and bounces up and down a few times. "You're so lucky."

"Me? Your place has a pool and, like, twenty bedrooms. We don't even have heat half the time."

"But a church has character," she says. "Anyone can live in a big house. How many people get to say they live in a cool place like this?"

"Most people get weirded out by it."

"Not me. I'd kill to live here. It's so unique. You've even got stained-glass windows. So pretty."

I can't help it. I laugh. But not in a mean way. I think of the few people who have been here over the years and most of the time they react the same way Detective Aggett did when he was here. They get nervous, as if they're offending God or something. No one has ever called this place pretty.

There is definitely more than one side to Paige. But which one can I trust, if any?

"Anyway, you can keep that," Paige says as she points to the envelope still in my hand. "It's just a copy. Dad's got the real deal and he's going to use it when he files the complaint with the school."

I open my desk drawer and toss the signatures inside. Best not to leave it out in the open. I still haven't told Gazer I've been expelled. If Paige actually follows through on this, then I might figure out what to say.

"So what do you think?"

"It's probably a waste of time," I tell her. "You're trying to change the laws. That's not easy to do."

"They need to fix things," Paige says. "They're biased. This whole damn world is biased. Times are changing. Everyone deserves a chance. Just think. Getting you back in school could be the first step."

I can't help smiling. She'd make a great politician. She's obviously got a flair for the dramatic. I understand why she's doing this now. I've officially turned into a cause. There's something wrong and Paige is determined to right it. I guess I can't complain. I think of Beth and her skinny arms and how her parents treat her differently now that she's got her own scars. Let Paige fight. It's not just for me. It's for Beth and Chael and even Arnold Bozek. It's for the thousands, if not millions, of people out there that need more help than this world is willing to give them.

If Paige has her way, she'll probably change history. Thinking about all this actually makes me like her a little bit more.

"I should probably go," Paige says as she gets up off the bed. She actually holds out her hand to shake mine as if we've come to a truce. "Is there anything else I can do?"

I look down at her perfectly manicured gel nails and an idea comes to me.

"Actually, yes," I say. "There is something."

Half an hour later we're at the beauty salon and a lady with an eyebrow ring and a purple-and-black spiked style is lathering up my hair. I shouldn't have let Paige talk me into this. All I wanted was for her to take me to the place so I could buy Beth a gift certificate. I promised to take her out tomorrow and do something fun and I was thinking along the lines of getting her nails done, maybe a pedicure too. I think it will do wonders for Beth's self-esteem to have a girls' day out.

But Paige has managed to convince me during that

short car ride that the one thing I need in the world is a new hairstyle.

"You look beautiful already," she says. "But this will make you gorgeous."

I'm such a sucker.

"So what do you want done?" the stylist asks as she tousles my damp hair.

I look at her spiked style and try not to cringe. "Nothing major," I say. "I don't want to lose the length. But I do have a date tonight. Maybe something nice?"

The stylist picks up her scissors. "I know just what to do with you."

I try not to look too worried as she begins to cut.

———◆———

Paige drops me off with promises to keep me fully informed of her new goals. She'll let me know the second the school responds to her father's petition. And she plans to take it further. Maybe the newspapers. Or television reporters. But small steps first. I won't lie and pretend that the thought of seeing Mrs. Orman's face when she gets the complaint doesn't make me feel all warm and bubbly inside.

Paige actually asks me if I'm willing to go have coffee with her sometime. Part of me thinks she's just looking for some new way to slum.

I'm still not going to put her on my friends list just yet, but I say yes because deep down inside, I really do think she wants to change. Maybe I'm a glutton for punishment but only time will tell. And helping me get a new hair-style and a manicure sure did up her Brownie points a bit. I won't admit it out loud but I actually had fun.

Back at home, I sit by the fire with Gazer while we both try to keep warm. It's raining more heavily than usual to-night and the church seems engulfed by a cold draft that just won't be tamed. The fire crackles and sputters and I toss in another log and glance up at the clock. It's just a bit after seven. I promised Chael I'd meet him at nine. He's going to show me his apartment tonight and I must admit, I'm dying of curiosity to see it. I pick up the poker and shove the embers around.

"Are you expecting someone?" Gazer asks, his eyes peering from the top of his book. *Moby-Dick*. A classic. The pages are worn and swollen from constant creasing.

"No, why?"

"Because you keep looking at that clock every other minute," he replies. "Either you're expecting time to stop altogether or you're waiting for someone."

"Neither," I say, and I pick up my book. A cheap ro-mance, nothing nearly as deep or exciting as what my men-tor would ever read. I've been turning the pages for over an hour but I can't say I've read a single word.

"Are you going out tonight?"

"Yes," I say, trying to sound nonchalant. "In a little while."

"Who is he?"

I look at Gazer and he's staring at me intently. There might be a twinkle in his eyes or it could be just the fire reflecting in his pupils. I can't tell.

"What makes you think there's a boy?" I ask.

Gazer chuckles and I toss my book at him.

"You're transparent, Faye," Gazer says. "Completely, utterly transparent. Of course, having a new hairstyle might have something to do with it."

"Is it that terrible? I knew I shouldn't have let her use the curling iron." I jump up, ready to run to the bathroom and try to dismantle it bit by bit. There's a lot of hair spray. What if it doesn't come out?

"You look beautiful. You're going to knock him flat on his back. Figuratively speaking, of course."

I laugh but my hands sneak up toward the top of my head to make sure the curls are still in place.

"I hope I'd approve of him."

"You would."

"Does he have a name?"

"Chael." I don't offer him a last name and I pray he doesn't ask. I don't actually know. I guess I could use Bozek.

"Sounds like a gentleman. When will you bring this Chael by?" Gazer picks up my book and studies the cover. He wrinkles his nose and tosses it back in my direction. Gazer still can't fathom why anyone would want to read something that doesn't involve philosophy or has been written in the past century.

I stand up and stretch. One last glance at the clock and I decide it's time to get ready. "I didn't think you'd want to meet him."

Gazer grins. "Of course I want to meet him. Someone's got to be here to walk you down the aisle."

I make a big show of rolling my eyes before retreating

to the coldness of my room. I spend a lot of time at the mirror trying to tie my hair up in a way that won't get it wet or ruin the curls. Thankfully, the hot water is working and I'm able to have a shower. The water burns against my back, sending steam off my body and leaving my skin a nice pink color. Afterward, I quickly dress myself in a pair of nice jeans. Standing in my bra, I dig around in my closet until I find a tank top. Chael isn't ashamed of my scars, so neither am I. There are no more rules for me to follow. After that, I add a sweater for warmth that can come off later if need be.

Don't get me wrong. I'm not planning on doing anything I shouldn't be doing tonight. I'm not there yet. But at the same time, I'm ready for a little more.

I let my hair down and thankfully it didn't get ruined during my shower. I swear, I've never put this much effort into making myself pretty before. It's exhausting. I put on a bit of makeup, smudging my cheek with mascara twice before finally getting it right. I'm just not experienced enough at this sort of thing. I ignore the twinge of pain when I think about how my mother used to sit at her mirror and apply her face. I used to hang out on the bed and watch her, fascinated with the way she expertly used those tiny brushes to make her eyes appear twice as big and a thousand times more exotic. That was back in the days when my father was still around and she was happy.

"Don't open your eyes," she'd say as she used the brush to apply the tiniest amount of blue shadow around my eyes. "Just a bit more. Okay, take a look. You look like a fairy princess."

I was always enthralled by the way my eyes looked with shadow on them. I felt so grown-up. I know it's such a cliché but I truly felt different. Transformed.

Only, princesses usually didn't have secondhand clothing with holes in the sleeves, but I didn't know enough to care about that. Even Cinderella had her rags for a while. The faded picture on my shirt was of a white stallion and I wore it all the time. I'd never even seen a horse before.

But none of that mattered. Mom had given me one of her older lipsticks and I loved twisting the cylinder over and over, watching the pink column rise up and down from the darkness of the tube.

"Remember to blot it," Mom would say, holding out the box of tissues. I'd reach out and take a handful at a time. Removing the lipstick was more fun than actually wearing it. I liked seeing the color on the Kleenex more than on my face.

"So pretty."

"That's way too much, darling."

"But I like it this way."

"You won't when you're older. But don't worry, I'll show you how to do it properly then."

Now I sit in a dingy room and try to figure all this out on my own. I still find it hard to imagine that my memories are actually real. I once had a mother who loved me and didn't toss me out in the cold, calling me a little slut, and telling a complete stranger to take me away so she didn't have to ever see me again.

But I'm not going to feel sorry for myself. Not tonight. Not anymore.

SIXTEEN

I should have known better. All that work to try to keep those curls curly. Ten minutes in the rain and my hair's stuck to my head. Water is dripping down the back of my neck. I'm beginning to think that maybe it's time to invest in an umbrella. Or at least a hoodie. It's weird. I never had anyone I really wanted to impress before.

Of course, when I see Chael, his hair is just as wet as mine. Funny, on him it just makes him look sexier. There are drops sticking to his eyelashes. He looks like he's crying crystals.

I'm positive I look like a drowned dog.

We meet in front of the coffee shop, but we don't go inside. This is the big night. He's taking me home, wherever or whatever that might be. I'm dying of curiosity, but I don't ask any questions. It's obvious that he's enjoying the suspense game too much. If he pulled out a blindfold and asked me to wear it for secrecy, I wouldn't be overly surprised.

"So are you ready?" he asks with a grin. "I hope you didn't eat dinner?"

"I can always eat," I say. "With the amount of exercise Gazer makes me do a day, I could scarf down a dozen meals and still look this hot."

"I like your new haircut."

"What?" My hands instinctively go up to the tangled wet mop. "How can you even tell?"

"Because it looks different. I've grown accustomed to your 'straight out of the shower' look," he says, and tousles my hair, sending droplets all over my shoulders. "Correct me if I'm wrong, but I think there are still a few curls there."

"Look who's talking."

He takes my hand and leads me off. As it turns out, he doesn't live very far from the docks, where we witnessed Rufus and Ming Bao killing the men.

He finally leads me down a street that appears barren, as if no one has lived there for at least a decade. We walk halfway down and he stops in front of what once might have been an apartment complex.

"Home, sweet home," he says.

I look up at the dilapidated building with skepticism. "People live here?"

"Not really," he says. "It's been condemned by the city. There are a few squatters on the main floor but I haven't seen them around much lately. Mostly just rats. A few birds. A stray cat or two. I've pretty much got the entire place to myself."

"Sounds disgusting," I say, and suddenly I'm wondering what I've gotten myself into. Wall-to-wall dingy mattresses? Burned floors that leak more than my church? What about the ceiling? It looks like it's about to cave in on the top right. What if the place falls down while we're in there?

This is where angels dare to live?

"Come on," he says. "It's not as bad as it looks. You'll see."

The door is heavy and squeaks when Chael opens it. Once we're inside, the smell of mold and dust assaults my senses. I wrinkle my nose and try not to sneeze. It's dark. Super dark. There's a hallway in front of us and a staircase. I'm positive someone's been peeing there on a regular basis. The door shuts behind us with a vibrating thud and suddenly I'm feeling very claustrophobic.

"Take my hand," Chael says. "We have to climb a few flights. There's no banister from the second floor on. Be careful."

We climb for what feels like forever. I try to count the steps but I'm so busy concentrating on where I'm putting my feet that I lose track after sixty-five. It's too dark to see anything, so we move slowly. My feet blindly reach up with each step, trying hard not to stumble. At one point, I step on something lumpy and squishy. It's the only time I'm thankful I can't see. I keep one hand slipped into Chael's and the other reaches out and finds the wall. It's coarse and the plaster crumbles under my touch. The stairs creak and groan under our weight and I try to block out the thoughts of us suddenly falling through and breaking our necks.

Finally, we reach the top and head down the hallway. There's a busted-out window at the end and I can see a bit of a glow from the streetlights. The hallway in front of us is lined with torn carpet and a long row of closed doors. I can't hear a single thing except the sound of our feet.

Funnily enough, as old and dingy as this building is, the doors look fairly strong and secure. Some of them even have locks that look newish. Maybe Chael is wrong and there are more people living here. Maybe that's the new thing to do. Live in a place that's completely disguised as something condemned. That would explain Gazer and my church. No one would ever bother to sneak in and rob the place if they thought no one could possibly live there.

Chael stops at a door and produces a key. It fits the lock easily and the door opens into more darkness. I allow him to put his hand on my elbow and lead me inside.

"Hold on," he says. "Let me find some light."

I wait there patiently until a lighter sparks several feet away. Chael lights candle after candle until the room begins to flicker and glow. He kneels down in front of a faux fireplace and turns on a battery-operated heater. The room instantly grows warmer, chasing away the chill, and I step further inside.

After the long trip up, I never in a million years expected to find this.

For starters, the place isn't just clean—it's impeccable. The floor is concrete, but free of dust. It's obviously been washed recently. In the middle of the room, there's an old rug. A couch that's worn, but looks comfortable. A small table filled with candles. A bed in the corner that's made neatly and even has a few extra throw pillows for style.

I step further inside. The kitchen is to the right of

me. The cupboards are missing the doors but the shelves are free of dust. There are some groceries stacked neatly. Mostly canned food and some crackers. A few dishes, stuff that looks like it was found in secondhand shops. There's no electricity, so I'm assuming the fridge doesn't work. The taps probably don't run either from the looks of the bottled water on the counter.

In the middle of the room, close to the portable heater, Chael has laid out a picnic blanket. On top are two long-stemmed glasses and a bottle of wine. There is also a single pink rose in a glass filled with water.

"What do you think?" Chael asks. He's finished lighting the candles, a few dozen of them on the table, the fake mantel, even on the floor. The glow gives the room a soft cozy feeling. He reaches out and takes my hand, leading me over to the picnic cloth and helping me sit down. Very gentlemanlike. The warm air from the heater hits my back. I take off my jacket and pat my hair down, trying to get rid of some of the extra water.

"I'm impressed," I say. "I like what you've done with the place."

Chael laughs. "It's kinda barren. Could use a woman's touch. Or about five interior decorators. Can't complain, though. It's free."

"How did you find it?"

"I have my ear to the ground," he says. "All I had to do was put the lock on the door. Not that it matters. No one ever comes up here."

He opens the wine bottle and pours me a glass. Believe it or not, I've never had wine before. Beer, vodka, even a few gulps of scotch, but never wine. Gazer isn't much of a drinker and we all know how adept at socializing I am. I sniff at the glass, wondering if I'm supposed to take a sip or a gulp. The red liquid smells faintly of fruit and something else I don't recognize.

"To us," Chael says, and he holds up his own glass against mine. Yes, cheesy as hell, but I'm glad I'm sitting down because I think my legs just got a little weak.

I watch him carefully and he takes a sip, so I figure that's the right thing to do. The wine is thick and bitter in my mouth and I swallow quickly. I don't know what to say afterward. Mmm? Wow? Fantastic? Yuck?

I keep my mouth shut instead and look at the wall. It's smudged with black scuff marks and there's a good-sized crack in the corner but nothing worse than what's in our church.

"I've got more," he says, and he gets up and goes over to the kitchen, where there's a cooler. He brings it over, along with a few paper plates, and starts placing items on the picnic cloth.

Olives. Cheese. Crackers. Strawberries. Grapes. A loaf of French bread along with some hummus for dipping. All sorts of things I really like to eat.

Watch out, I'm about to become a pig.

"I can't believe you did all this," I say as I snag a cracker and place a slice of white cheese on top. I take a small bite and it's delicious. It takes all my willpower not to shove the entire thing in my mouth.

"Try one of these," Chael says, and he holds up something green and weird-looking.

"They look disgusting."

"It's called dolma. It's made from grape leaves. Trust me, you'll like it."

I pick one up and nibble on the end. I'm not sure how to describe the taste. It's like eating pickled rice. But in a good way. "Interesting," I say.

Chael laughs. "Interesting good, or interesting in an 'I'm going to go throw up in the toilet' way?"

"Good," I say with a giggle. I pop the rest of it in my mouth and quickly eat another. We spend the next ten minutes or so sampling the various items that Chael has packed in his cooler. My stomach starts to fill up quickly. I shouldn't have eaten that hamburger earlier tonight with Gazer. Or the French fries and the extra-large Coke. Soon I'm going to be rolling on the floor in a food stupor and there's nothing I can do to stop myself.

That's the great thing about the huge amount of training I do every day. I get to eat like there's no tomorrow.

I take another sip of wine and notice that Chael's barely eating at all. Sure, he's got a piece of cheese in his hand but he's only taken a single bite out of it. I'm pretty sure he ate a few of the dolmas, and when I look at the half-empty container, I know it's true. But right now he's staring off at one of the candles, a faraway expression on his face.

"Are you okay?" I ask.

"Huh?" He turns and his eyes are alight with fire. But distant. He's not really here. Absently he pulls at the strands of hair above his ear.

"You seem out of it."

"Just thinking."

266

"About what?"

"Sometimes I feel like I'm trapped in someone else's dream." Chael puts his piece of cheese down on his plate. "I get disorientated. Blurry. I stare at things but they don't really seem to be there. Does that make sense? Maybe it's just a weird reaction to whatever's happened to me. Maybe it's life's way of telling me time is short."

"Your life was short but now you've got a second chance."

"Yeah, I guess so."

He looks so sad that I want to take him in my arms and pull him close. But who would end up comforting who? He's very much like me, tough on the outside, confused beneath the surface. When we were younger, he didn't come off as strong or sensitive or haunted. He seemed normal. But then again, so did I. Can we really overcome our past with this new future?

"What do you think it means?"

"I don't know." Chael shifts his entire body over a few inches, until he's super close. He puts a hand out against my leg and pulls me toward him. "I want so much to take care of you, Faye. I want to take your pain and free you from all the monsters that live under your mattress. You've been so happy these past few weeks. But it's not gone, is it? I can't make you forget."

"I am happy," I say. "I can't begin to express how wonderful it is to have you back. But I've wanted this revenge for half my life, it seems. You can't just show up out of the blue and expect me to change my mind."

"You have a chance, Faye. It's right there in front of

your face, but you're not seeing it. Look at the way you work with Beth. You're a natural and you could make a great life for yourself working with Heam addicts. You could have a future."

I shake my head. I can feel tears threatening to drop from the corners of my eyes. It's all a lie. Why can't he see that? Everything he says sounds great when we talk about it over candlelight. But in reality? It's never as simple as he's trying to make it. I have no future. I have shadow demons waiting for me. I have an elevator in hell with my name written all over it.

I wish I could convince myself that my thoughts are fake and that there is no heaven or hell like Gazer believes. Like Chael wants me to think. But neither of them was there with me.

It may not be real to them but it's real to me.

And whatever I did to deserve this hell, I truly believe that bringing Rufus and the others down might absolve me a little. If I can save one life, one measly gutter rat that might otherwise fall into Rufus's clutches.

What about Beth?

"It's not that simple," I finally say because Chael is looking at me. I wish he wouldn't put so many demands on my shoulders.

"It is."

"And what happens if you do save me?" I ask. "Do we get to live happily ever after?" The bitterness is strong in my words. It stains my tongue.

"Yes."

"Just like that?"

"Just like that."

I stand up and walk over to the window to look outside because if I keep sitting on the floor in front of Chael, I'll probably burst into tears. The window is closed and slightly grimy but I can still see the ground below. No one is on the streets. It's silent.

Chael wants me to be something I'm not. And if he's going to force me to pretend, it's not going to end well. Why can't he understand that I just can't turn myself off? People are more complicated than that. I'm too far gone. Asking me to give up my obsession is like asking me to cut off my head. Yes, maybe I could be all those things he wants me to be, but eventually my anger will push back up to the surface. You can only wear a disguise for so long before the mask starts to decompose. I can't just smile and wish away six years of my life.

"Why can't I have my revenge and my happily-ever-after too?" I finally ask.

"Because it will destroy you."

"You don't know that."

"It'll eat you up inside. Unless you're a monster to begin with, taking a life destroys you. It's like cancer, festering in the furthest corners of your mind. Getting into every nook and cranny. There's no escape."

"I'm a tough girl, I can handle it."

Chael comes over and wraps his arms around me. He's so amazingly warm. I lean back into him, feeling the rise and fall of his chest as he breathes.

I wish we could stay like this forever. Every moment is simple and pure. It would be easy to forget everything else. I can see why people search desperately for love. It's comforting. It makes you feel secure. Safe.

"I don't want to lose you, Faye," Chael says. "And I will fight for you, even if you end up hating me forever."

I turn around in his arms and look up into those bright green eyes. "I could never hate you."

"You haven't seen everything I'm capable of."

And then he leans down and kisses me.

We don't talk much after that. After a while we lie down on his bed and hold each other tightly. My hair has since dried and Chael twirls his finger around my curls, winding and unwinding them over and over. I trace my hand along his chest, feeling the smoothness of his muscles. We kiss some more.

I'm not sure exactly when I fall asleep but I'm in his arms and I feel secure.

I feel loved.

I sleep and there are no dreams. Nothing but warm darkness washing over me.

—+—

When I wake up, I'm alone.

It takes several minutes to remember where I am. The strange room looks disjointed and spooky without the light. Chael must have blown out all the candles. The portable heater is still on, but he's turned it down so it only gives off a faint amount of heat. That's fine. The room is warm enough.

But where is Chael?

I get up, trying to shake the sleepiness from my mind. I walk over to the bathroom to take a look since it's the only other room, but there's no Chael.

I sit back down on the bed and replay our last conversation in my mind. Why would he go and leave me here alone? That makes no sense. He never mentioned having to do anything tonight.

Unless . . .

I grab my phone and check the time. It's a little after two. Closing time for the bars. Is it possible that Chael went after Rufus?

You haven't seen everything I'm capable of.

Holy crap.

I cross the room in two strides. My fingers wrap around the door handle but nothing happens. I pull hard but the door won't budge.

I've been locked in.

That rat bastard!

I twist the handle in both directions and bang on the door. I put my ear against the metal and try to see if I can hear anything on the other side. Nothing. So I go over to the wall and do the same thing. No televisions blare from next door. No voices chatting. Not even snoring.

I try the window next but it's sealed tight. No matter how much I pull and yank on it, the glass won't move an inch. I run my fingers along the side looking for secret locks but I come up empty-handed. The only way I'm going to get through is to break it and I'm not there yet. Besides, it's pointless. The street below is empty and I can't imagine anyone is going to come strolling along any minute. It's too late at night. Even if I managed to find someone, it'd probably be a drunk or a gutter rat too scared to get involved.

Chael was right to pick this place. There's no one to hear me scream.

I could call someone. Chael didn't take my phone. But who? There's no way I'd call Gazer and he's pretty much the only person I ever contact. I'd rather die than admit to Gazer that I got locked into this situation like a fly drawn straight into the beehive.

So stupid of me. I should have never let down my guard like that.

I go back and try the door again but now I'm starting to feel ridiculously foolish, like a chicken with its head cut off. Resigning myself to the situation, I finally go back over to the bed and sit down. There's nothing I can do except wait.

I'm going to kill him when he gets back.

No, not kill. That would be too good for him. I'm not against a little bit of torture at this point.

If he kills Rufus, that'll be it. I'm not sure if I can come back from that. Chael said he wants to take my revenge in order to save me. But he's right about one thing. If he does this, he'll make me hate him. And forever won't be long enough. There have just been too many years of resentment and long nights plotting revenge. I've built up too much rage. I've invested a lot of time in this. What will I do if it's taken away?

Is having my hatred good enough as long as he thinks he's saving my soul?

I pick up the wine bottle and take a long drink. Sitting back down on the bed, I position myself so I have a good view of the door.

If there's one thing living this life has taught me, it's patience. I can wait till Chael gets back. It's not like I'm going anywhere.

—+—

Although I've been dozing for the past hour, I hear the creak of the key in the lock. Instantly I'm off the bed and at the door before he manages to open it an inch. The second his body pushes through, I'm at him, hands raised, smacking him against his chest and arms.

"You bastard!" I shout. "How could you do this to me? I trusted you."

"That was your first mistake, I guess."

I smack him again and he doesn't even try to protect himself. He steps through the doorway and off to the side, leaving the entrance wide open.

"Relax."

"What did you do?" I grab hold of his jacket and shake him. "Tell me!"

Chael refuses to look me in the eyes. Instead, he glances down at the picnic cloth, which still holds plates of abandoned food.

"It's done."

I scream. And not some high-pitched squawk. A deep mournful sound escapes my lips. The moment I've been working up to for six years is gone with two words. All the fight inside of me, the anger, the suffering, pulls against my brain, trying to focus and find meaning.

The worst part is I'm also relieved.

"I hate you," I say to him. "You took everything from me."

"I gave you life."

"Fuck you!" I storm back over to the bed and pick up my jacket. I shove my arms into the sleeves, accidently kicking the cooler in the process. "That man took away my life. He made me what I am. All I had left in this world was revenge and you stole that too. You're no better than him."

"If you'd killed him, everything you know would end. There's no coming back from that. You may think you're tough and you've done a great job building up that safety bubble, but trust me, this would find a way to get inside of you."

"I wasn't planning to come back from it."

"You are nothing but a selfish little girl," Chael spits at me. "You say he took away your life? You're still alive. He *killed* me. So boohoo. You had a crappy childhood? He destroyed mine. So go ahead and talk about how you'd rather be dead because at least you still get to make that decision. I would have given anything to be with you. To be a part of your life, the very one you want to end. You've got no one to blame for that. You could have lived all this time. But all you've done is focus on your hate and self-pity. All I did was die."

I pause, coat sleeve only halfway up my arm. "That's not fair."

"Yes, it is."

"No, it isn't." I stamp my feet, fully aware of how childish it is. "Look at you. You may have died but you came back. You don't have any scars. You don't have the addiction clawing away at your brain. So you missed a few years, big deal. You could go out tomorrow and get a job and anyone would hire you because there's not a single trace of Heam on you."

Chael doesn't say a word. He stands there with his hands clenched into fists by his side. I march up to him and glare right into his eyes. He instantly looks away and moves over to let me pass. I shove by him and out into the hallway.

I don't look back.

——+——

He had no right.

The revenge was mine. I worked hard for that. How could he turn around and take it?

The rain continues to fall and it doesn't take long before my hair is wet and sticking to my scalp again. Who cares? There's no one worth looking good for anymore.

I walk in no particular direction and after a while I find myself back at the bar where Rufus goes. Wait. Change that. Used to go.

It's almost four in the morning and the place is closed. The neon sign is turned off and the windows are dark. Will anyone mourn Rufus tomorrow when they get the news? Will they toast with their beers in the air to honor his memory? Or will they never find out? People disappear all the time and are never found again. Maybe they'll mourn the loss of sales. Rufus was quite the drinker.

I wonder where Chael killed him. Is his body hidden behind one of the thousands of Dumpsters in this city, or did he get more creative and dump him in the water? Maybe he's folded neatly into one of the trunks of the abandoned cars that litter the streets. If I'm lucky, the rats will pick at his flesh until there's nothing there but bones. He deserves that. I hope he's in that elevator right now with the metal bars piercing his skin and the shadow demons sliding across his tongue and down his throat to tear apart his insides.

Even hell is too good for that man.

I stand under the streetlamp and look up as the raindrops splatter across my face. The light glows against the gray clouds. I wish they would go away so maybe I could see the stars. You almost never see them in this city and if you do, they're pale and washed out. I once read that if you go out into the forest you can see millions of stars and if you stare at them long enough, they begin to dance. I'd like to see that one day.

I wish I could take back my words. Chael's partly right. I am being selfish. But it's my right. I wasn't seeking revenge just for myself but for Chael too. He seems to think I've forgotten that he was once dead but I remember it every time I look in his face.

True love never dies, even if they come back.

I can't even begin to count how many times I've fantasized about killing Rufus over the years. The countless times I've plotted out the details in my mind or even scribbled in notebooks when I'm supposed to be paying attention in class. I've come up with some far-fetched ideas and others that seem like the perfect murder. I've thought of countless accidents and simple plots that require a single gunshot or knife to the throat.

But I've never thought beyond that. Not once.

Chael thinks I'm selfish and that I forgot about him but that's not true. There's a reason why I never replaced my nightstand and why I continued to trace Christian's initials in the melted wax that covers the top.

Because my revenge was also his.

And now it's gone.

Is it really so bad that Chael reclaimed it for his own?

I kick the lamppost once as hard as I can, ignoring the pain in my toes. I deserve this. I spin around to kick it again but something else catches my attention. Across the street, I can see someone walking toward me but it's too dark to see their face.

If it's Chael, I should probably apologize. Perhaps I've been looking at this from the wrong perspective. Instead of being selfish, I should be thankful that Chael did the job. Besides, there's still Ming Bao and Phil Sabado. They're not nearly as satisfying but I guess I can't be choosy at this point.

I look up at the approaching figure, ready to open my mouth and call over to him. It's got to be Chael.

He comes into the light.

My vocal cords freeze. My mouth remains wide open.

It's not Chael.

It's Rufus.

SEVENTEEN

Rufus crosses the street and moves toward me. I can't seem to do anything except stare at him. Is he a ghost? After everything I've seen, I can't dismiss that idea without solid evidence.

Solid evidence? Ghost? Right.

The stupidity paralysis doesn't break until he's right on top of me. Grabbing hold of my jacket, he shoves me sideways and up against the wall. His arm presses down on my throat, pinning me to the brick. He brings his face in close and studies my face long and hard.

Then he pulls out the gun and holds it right between my eyes.

Fear. Icy, burning, confusing, leg-numbing terror crawls all over my skin like a thousand chewing insects. I can't move. I can't breathe. I stare down the barrel of the gun.

"I don't know you."

My eyes flicker over Rufus's face. He's got his face right

up against mine. He presses harder against my windpipe and I start to see stars. The dancing type. But the second the edge of my world starts to darken, he eases off a bit and the air rushes back down my throat.

"I said I don't know you." Rufus turns his head to the side and then back, rubbing his cheek against his shoulder, and his eye starts twitching. His gin-blossomed nose is almost pressed against mine. I can smell the rank alcohol on his breath.

He continues to wait, so finally I manage a little nod.

"So if I don't know you, why the hell do you keep turning up like a bad penny?"

"I don't know what you mean." I finally manage to get the words out. My throat burns from where he pressed against my windpipe and my voice is barely more than a whisper.

"I've been seeing you for some time now," Rufus says. "You always standing here like some sort of whorish gutter rat. But you're more than that, aren't you? There's a reason why you're here. You look familiar. Have we met before?"

"I don't think so."

"Are you one of Trank's girls?"

The terror keeps me from laughing. I'm far too old for Trank to have been interested. The thought of him willingly touching me makes me shudder in repulsion. I shake my head as much as I can.

"You're not a cop." More of a statement than a question.

I cough twice. My throat feels like it's been torn to shreds.

"But you're someone. Why else would you be follow-ing me? At first I didn't think much about it," Rufus says, ignoring my pathetic coughs and splutters. He's talking more to himself now, not even looking in my direction. The gun, however, moves until it's planted against my jaw-bone. "But then some of my buddies have gone and got themselves killed. And I hear stories about how this young girl managed to beat the crap outta some of my boys the same night Trank gets himself broken up. So I'm trying to figure out who's going after my men. And all of a sudden I remember you. Why is that?"

"No idea."

"And then tonight another one of my men bites it and here you are."

"Who?"

Chael lied to me. He killed someone but it wasn't Rufus. Ming? Phil? I open my mouth to speak but Rufus shoves me against the wall again and my head cracks hard against the brick. He raises the gun until it's right against my teeth.

This is it. I've failed my revenge. All that training and I'm useless. I can't even raise my leg high enough to kick him. I should have done better. Gazer taught me to defend against everything. A gun isn't any more threatening than a fist. So why did I freeze and why can't I fight back?

Gazer was right. I'm not ready.

"I don't like coincidences, girlie, and you're turning out to be one, don't you think?" Rufus smiles at me but there's no light in his eyes. The weapon moves downward, tracing an invisible line along my neck and then back up to my forehead.

"I didn't do anything," I finally manage to say.

He holds the gun up for what seems like forever before finally pulling it back a few inches. Suddenly he releases his grip and I collapse to the ground before my legs manage to regain balance. I land in a deep puddle and cold water assaults my lower body. Rufus kicks me hard, right in the side, and pain shoots through me, reducing me to curling up into a ball and trying to bite back the tears as they threaten to fall.

I'm not tough at all. It's all been an act. How could I not know this?

"Your face is familiar and I never forget a face," Rufus says. "You were there the other night at the docks. Why?"

"I wasn't there."

"Don't lie to me. I saw you outside the bar and then at the docks. You and that dorky kid with the glasses. I thought I shot him but I missed. You're not as invisible as you think."

"I'm not following you," I gasp. "I swear."

Rufus kicks me again. My right leg spasms in the wet puddle.

"Who are you?"

"No one."

Another kick.

I raise my voice as high as I can. "No one!"

Wham.

Again.

I'm going to pass out. I can't take this pain. It's horrible. Even a Heam addiction is better than this.

I need Chael.

Bright lights turn the corner and start heading in our direction. A car. Maybe a cop? Can I ever hope to be that lucky?

Rufus's gun quickly disappears into his jacket pocket. He kneels down on the ground and grabs me by the hair. Lifting up my face, he whispers right in my ear. "I'm going to figure it out. Then I'm coming for you. Don't you forget it, bitch."

He slams my head against the wall one last time and then disappears into the darkness. I lie there, half against the wall, stars swimming in my eyes and pain throbbing through every single muscle in my body. I watch the car as it moves past. It doesn't slow, but continues on. The driver didn't even see me.

Panicking, I struggle to my feet. I have no idea how far Rufus got. If he's close enough to see the car go by, he might come back to finish the job.

I've got to get out of here.

My legs won't work. They refuse to hold my weight. So I start to crawl on my hands and knees. I have to get away. My fingers are numb from the cold rain but I can't stop.

I make it over fifty feet before my legs stop shaking. I don't look back. If Rufus is coming after me, I don't want to see. I push myself up on one knee and manage to get into a standing position.

It's not until I'm several blocks away that I allow myself to cry out in pain before collapsing in a doorway. I stay there for half an hour, curled up against the wood, trying to keep quiet as the tears roll down my cheeks.

Finally, I force myself to get up and slink through the streets as quiet as a mouse to try to make it home before Gazer wakes up.

This is my own fault. There's no one to blame but myself.

I wasn't on my guard. The one thing Gazer keeps telling me is that I constantly have to be aware of my surroundings. I allowed my emotions to take control of my brain. I screwed up tonight, big-time. I've paid the price. My ribs feel like they've been through a meat grinder.

I won't make that mistake again.

—+—

I wake up late, realizing instantly that Gazer hasn't come in to check on me. Concerned, I listen to the church, waiting for a telltale sound that he might be puttering around in the kitchen or reading by the fireplace.

Nothing.

Did I screw up again? Maybe Rufus followed me home? No, I was careful. I checked every few minutes to make sure no one was behind me. Is it possible I was outsmarted again? What if he came while I was sleeping and did something to Gazer? What if Rufus killed him in retaliation for what Chael and I have done to him?

This wasn't part of the plan.

I roll out of bed, ignoring the stabbing pain in my stomach and rib cage as I force my muscles back into action. So sore.

It takes me a while to climb down the stairs. Partly because I'm trying to be quiet but also because my limbs are stiff and screaming at me with every step. I slip on the third step from the bottom and almost tumble the rest of the way. I manage to grab the banister at the last second, clamping my teeth down hard to keep from screaming.

So much for a graceful entrance.

"Faye?"

Gazer. I come around the corner and he's by the fireplace, a cup of coffee in his hand, several books stacked on the table in front of him.

"Why didn't you wake me up?" My voice sounds like gravel and I swallow twice, trying to force the spit through the sandpaper that is my throat. I plop down in my chair, hoping the pain doesn't show on my face. I should have looked in the mirror first.

"Thought you deserved a day off," Gazer says without so much as glancing in my direction. "Obviously, I was right."

Relief overpowers me. Gazer is safe. I'm safe for the moment. I'm sure even Chael is safe right now, although he's still in the doghouse as far as I'm concerned.

"How was your date last night?"

"It was good," I lie. "Casual. We just went for coffee and talked a lot." I decide to keep the date window open. I may be able to use it as an excuse in the future. Also, pretending I'm happy is easier than coming up with a story to cover the truth.

"I'm glad to hear that," Gazer says. "Not that I worry, but I'm always here if you need to talk."

I force myself to smile. "I know."

"There's still some coffee in the kitchen," Gazer says. "We're almost out. I'm heading to the store this afternoon to pick up some more. I've left a list on the counter, so if there's anything else you need, be sure to put it down."

I stand, ignoring the wobbly knees and the stomach spasms. Coffee sounds perfect. Then a nice hot shower. I'll be as good as new.

"Faye?"

I pause and look back at him. Gazer is staring right at my face.

"Are you sure there's something you're not telling me?"

I almost burst out laughing. Where would I begin? The list keeps growing every day. But I keep my face impassive and shake my head.

"Everything's fine," I say.

"Okay," he says, but I can tell he doesn't believe me.

———◆———

When did I start lying to Gazer? I can't remember. I once told him everything but that was back when things were simpler. Before Chael. Before Beth and Arnold Bozek and Paige LeBlanc. Way before I got thrown out of school for something I didn't do, and now the entire school is fighting to get me back and I can't tell him about that either.

He'd like that one. Gazer always says that one day people will start fighting for equality again. But fighting for me? I never saw that one coming.

Rufus knows me now. Okay, so I said that would be the biggest mistake I could ever make. How large of an error is it, though? It's not like his face lit up with joy and he yelled out "Holy crap, you're Faye!" He doesn't remember the little girl and boy he left on the pavement all those years ago. Have I really been so arrogant to assume that he would? That he'd take one look at me and remember such an insignificant event?

It was the worst event of my entire life.

For him, it was just another day.

A few more gutter rats bite the dust.

Okay, Rufus, this is it. You may know my face but you don't know who I am. That's fine. When the time is right, you will remember because I will tell you. But I'm not going to make the same mistake again. It was very stupid of me to be so vulnerable. I see that now. I've been harboring this crazy idea that I've been invincible because of all my hate. I got careless.

It won't happen again.

My fingers trail along my stomach, wincing at the tender spots from Rufus's boots. What was that nonsense he was spouting about never forgetting a face? If that were true, he would have remembered mine.

I look at my face in the bathroom mirror. Wiping the steam off the glass, I examine my eyes and cheekbones to make sure there are no bruises. Nothing. My stomach is purple and black and so is part of my rib cage.

I can deal with that.

I slide my fingers across my scars. The skin is soft and slightly tighter than on the rest of me. The red spiderweb veins thrust away from my heart and along my chest and across my shoulder. They're not really ugly. It's a pattern, actually, and not a horrible one. Why have I spent so much time hating them?

No more.

I am done pretending to be someone I'm not.

I will stand up and fight and I will win.

It's time to take my revenge no matter what Chael and Gazer say. Afterward, I will march myself straight to hell and accept whatever punishment the afterlife decides to dish out.

Leaving the bathroom, I get dressed quickly, pulling on my jeans and a black sweater with a high neck. I pick up the switchblade I keep buried in my drawer and put it in my back pocket.

I should be carrying this all the time. I guess I've gotten so used to people leaving me alone that I didn't realize I still needed it. The blade presses against my butt and I'm comforted knowing it's there.

I grab the gift certificate for the hair salon off the table. First things first. There's not much I can do in the daytime, so I might as well spend the day saying goodbye to Beth. I just hope that what happens to me won't affect her rehabilitation. Just because I am choosing a different path doesn't mean she needs to end up like me. I know that now. She could be anything she wants. A teacher. A doctor. An artist. Anything she sets her mind to.

I'm living proof of that.

No one can ever accuse me of not going after what I want.

———+———

"What do you mean she's gone?"

I'm sitting in Ramona's office and the counselor is at her desk, forcing a cup of coffee and some stale cookies on me. I should have suspected it was bad news when she asked me to join her first. I just thought maybe she had the information on the courses she was trying to persuade me to take.

Heam counselor my ass. They'd be stupid to ever let someone like me get involved with helping people. After all, once a gutter rat, always a gutter rat. They never change. They can't once it's in their blood. They'd kill their own grandmother for another journey to heaven. Why would anyone trust me with a job? I can't even keep a single addict from running away.

"She went out her window last night," Ramona says. "She was there when the night staff checked around midnight, so she must have taken off after that. I'm sorry, Faye. I know how much you care for her. This isn't your fault."

"But she was doing so well," I say. "She said she wanted to go back to school. She was even talking about how her parents might consider letting her come back home."

"Yes, she was having a good stretch. Sadly, they don't last very long. You know this." Ramona opens up a folder that's sitting beside her coffee cup. "I've contacted her parents but they haven't seen or heard from her. I also tried her friend Joshua. He said he'll go around to all her favorite places and keep an eye out but there's not much else we can do."

"Except wait for her body to show up." I'm trembling so hard I can't hold on to my coffee cup. It slips through my fingers and hits the table with a dull thud. Coffee spills everywhere. "Shit!" I jump back from the chair, wincing as the hot coffee hits my jeans.

"Here!" Ramona rushes over and grabs some paper towels. Together we clean up the mess.

"I'm sorry," I say.

"It's not your fault."

"I meant the coffee."

Ramona smiles at me. "I know."

I wipe down the mug, marveling at how it didn't break even after I dropped it. I toss the towels in the trash and remember the gift certificate. It rests on the table, now stained brown and slightly curling. It's ruined. I pick it up quickly and shake it, sending droplets in all directions. Ramona hands me some more paper towels and I try to sop up the remaining liquid.

"They will probably still accept it," Ramona says. "It's not too badly damaged."

Of course, the certificate is made out in Beth's name. We both stare at the lettering.

"I'll spend the afternoon looking for her," I say. "I'll do whatever it takes."

"It can't hurt," Ramona says.

"Do you think it's possible she didn't drop? Maybe she

just wanted to get away for a bit. Sort some stuff out inside her head?"

Ramona sighs. She comes over and puts her hand on top of mine. "Maybe," she says. "It has happened in the past. But you need to understand, Faye. The odds are against her. But if we're lucky, she'll have her hit and come back tonight or tomorrow."

"The odds are also greater for her to overdose," I say. Not that I need to say it. We both know the stats well enough.

"She's not dead yet," Ramona says. "Let's just keep saying that instead."

—•—

The next few hours are spent looking for both Beth and Chael. Beth for the obvious reasons. Chael because I need to find out who he killed.

I avoid the bar and Rufus's other hangouts like the plague.

Beth isn't anywhere. She's disappeared into the city, where all the other missing gutter rats go. I ask around but no one's seen her.

A ghost child.

I find Chael at the coffee shop. I look in on him from the window and he's reading a book, his shoulders hunched, arm resting on the table as he randomly turns pages. There's a coffee cup in front of him and half a dozen empty creamers and sugar packets are strewed across the table.

I stand there in front of the glass and think about how

the waitress sees him as a completely different person. She doesn't see the shiny hair that he's still absently tugging on or the sharp jawbone. No one else sees the green eyes except me. In reality, Chael's eyes are buried with him in the cemetery, decayed into dust and nothing.

And yet Chael is here.

He's been waiting for me. From the looks of it, he's been there most of the day.

I open the door and step inside.

Chael immediately looks up. I go over and sit down because the waitress is already bringing over the coffeepot and a clean cup for me. The other diners don't pay me much attention; they continue to eat or read their newspapers, whatever they have to do to get through the day.

So I sit down in front of Chael because it's the least offensive thing I can do. It's expected of me. I'm not about to interrupt everyone's lives because what I really want to do is throw a hissy fit.

Nope. I can do better than that.

The waitress pours me a cup of coffee without me having to ask. I've become that predictable.

"Anything else?" she asks, although she already knows the answer. She's turning to walk away before I can even get the words out.

"I'm good."

I don't say anything to him. I have no idea what to say. I didn't plan this far in advance. Even though I've been combing the streets all afternoon for him and Beth, I haven't thought of a single thing to say to him.

He doesn't say anything either. He closes his book and

places it on the seat beside him. Grabbing a creamer, he pours the contents into his coffee and mixes it up with his usual amount of sugar.

We continue our stare-down.

A couple come in from the cold and order hot chocolate. They sit at the booth across from us and spend their time holding hands and whispering to each other. The girl is pretty and is wearing a nice pink furry hat. She giggles a lot. An old man gets up and pays his bill in loose change. A family comes in. The waitress wanders over and tops off our coffee.

Finally, I decide to break the silence. Otherwise, we might be here all day.

"I know you didn't kill Rufus. I saw him. He's alive and well." I keep my voice low enough so as not to disturb the other patrons. For obvious reasons, I'm not going to mention that Rufus flattened me to the ground in seconds or that my ribs are still hurting something fierce. Chael's on a need-to-know basis.

Chael shrugs.

"Who did you kill?"

"Phil Sabado." His voice is barely more than a whisper. The spoon bangs against the mug as he stirs absently.

"How'd you do it?"

"Do you really want to know?"

"No."

"Fine."

"You lied to me."

"Yes."

Simple. None of this "It was for your own good" or "I

was only protecting you" crap I've come to expect from him. I like this straightforward honesty; I only wish he'd given it to me before.

"So why'd you lie?"

"To keep you from going after him. If you thought he was dead, you'd leave it be. How'd you find out?"

"I'm a bad penny," I say, ignoring his momentarily confused look.

I could be angry at him and start screaming. I'd probably terrify the couple and the family ordering cheeseburgers but I don't care much about that. I want to be furious and slap him several times, asking how he thinks he can lock me away like a wounded bird when I've already proven to him time and time again that there is nothing in the world that could ever keep me from my destiny.

But I don't. It's no longer in me.

"You can't save me, Chael," I say. "I know you want to but you can't. It's not that simple. You can't just kill someone on my behalf and make it all go away. Oh God." I put my hands on my head because suddenly the reality of everything makes the room start to spin. "That sounds so crazy. It's like I'm talking about taking a trip to the mall instead of life."

"Faye." Chael looks at me and his eyes are wet and filled with longing.

"No," I say. "Let me finish." I pause, unsure of what I want to say next. I reach out and take his hand. "I can't let you put this burden on yourself. You said you heard my pain from across the planes. Now I'm here in front of you telling you that I don't want you taking my sins."

"It's not the same thing."

"Yes it is," I snap. "I don't want you being damned because of something I can't get over. Because of my mistakes. I don't think I can continue living with that guilt."

"It's too late for that."

"You lied to me," I say. "And I know that it wasn't easy for you to do. I get that. But that's just the first step. I can't handle this anymore. I care for you too much. I've always loved you, from the moment I met you so many years ago. Losing you once was hard enough." I reach into my pocket and drop some change on the table. Not enough to pay for the coffee but I don't care. Let my mysterious boyfriend pay for it—however the hell he gets his cash. "I want you to leave me alone."

"If that's how you want it," Chael says. He won't even look me in the eyes.

"I mean it."

"Sure."

This isn't going how I expected. I stand stupidly for a few seconds before I remember I'm supposed to be making a dramatic exit. I get up and head over to the door. Outside, the cold air hits my face and I pause to do up my jacket.

"One last thing," Chael says as he opens the door and comes up from behind me.

"What?"

He doesn't say anything for a few seconds. I wait impatiently, tapping my foot loudly just to be clear.

"If you had one week left in your life to do anything at all," he begins, "would you spend it with the person you loved or would you hunt down the ones who signed your death warrant?"

I pause.

"Because in your case," he says, "I've got to do both. I'd much rather have spent this time just loving you."

"What do you mean by one week?" I ask with a shaky voice.

"Just a figure of speech," he says. "One year. One day. One single minute. Who knows what time we have left?" He looks up at the sky and the clouds in all their gray glory. "For the record, I've always loved you too."

Then he's gone. He turns the corner and I watch him disappear from my life.

EIGHTEEN

I'm being followed.

I picked up the hint a few blocks back but every time I turn around, the street is empty.

But someone is there. I can feel it.

I walk a little faster. I'm a few blocks away from the subway. If I can get there, I might be able to wait on the corner for the person to show themselves.

Who is it?

Rufus?

Chael?

No, probably not Chael. I think I made it clear enough that I don't want to see him right now. Unless he knows about Rufus attacking me. Maybe that's why he was so obedient tonight. He's planning on using me to get what he wants.

I listen to my feet slapping the pavement, and just beneath that sound I can hear an echo behind me of someone else.

I whip around again and this time I'm rewarded with a glimpse of that someone ducking into a doorway.

Ming Bao.

Oh crap.

So Rufus sent someone to follow me. Well, that's not so bad. I've got my knife tucked away and I'm prepared this time. But Ming won't be an easy adversary. I always figured he'd be someone I'd have to get a secret jump on. I'm not sure if I can take him in a fair fight.

I turn and start walking even faster. If I can make the station, I should be okay. I'm not taking the coward's way out. I'm going to be practical. It's still daylight. He's not going to jump me right now. Neither of us wants witnesses. If I'm going to fight him, I'm going to make sure I have the edge I need to win.

I have to make sure I can lose him before I get close to home. I won't put Gazer in harm's way. It's a bad idea to have your enemies know where you sleep.

Ahead of me is a massive Catholic church, the only one in this neighborhood. Its bells start ringing as I approach. The hollow empty sound echoes through the street. I can feel the sound reverberating through my sneakers.

Mass is starting. Apparently, God still lives in this church.

Up ahead I can see people walking up the cobblestone steps and in through the wooden doors. The majority of them seem elderly; they carry canes and wrap heavy jackets and winter shawls around their shoulders. Their hands are gripped tightly on the banister as they climb. Some of them have family with them. The priest stands at the top of the stairs, greeting everyone and shaking their hands as they enter his home.

So different from my church.

I have this crazy urge to go inside. I've never been to a mass before. It also would make an excellent hiding spot from Ming. I can't imagine he'd dare to follow me inside. I pause at the bottom of the steps and an old couple glare at me. I know exactly what they're thinking.

You don't belong here.

And they're right. I don't belong in their world any more than they do in mine.

Someone tugs at my jacket sleeve. I look down and there's the red-umbrella girl peering up at me. I look at her in surprise and then notice she's not alone. She's standing with her mother and a few other people. Her family? Her mother is wearing a black dress and a veil over her face. Does this mean she knows that Arnold Bozek is dead? Did the little girl tell her? Are they holding a prayer service for him?

No one will pray for my soul. But I'll still be just as dead.

"Are you coming here tonight?" the girl asks. I scan her face for anger but there is none. She looks different. Peaceful. Sad, yes, but serene. "Do you want to sit with me?"

I glance back to see that Ming is still at the end of the block but not getting any closer. He's waiting to see what my next move will be.

"I'm not sure if I'm allowed," I say without taking my eyes off of Ming.

"Everyone is welcome," the girl says. "Otherwise, it

wouldn't be a church. Come and sit with me." She takes my hand and leads me up the stairs. Her mother looks me over, but doesn't seem to disapprove. She follows behind us and I wonder what she's thinking.

The priest reaches out and shakes my hand. I smile but my knees are shaking.

The inside is so different from my church. This one isn't dripping water in the corners and the pews aren't covered in dust. The altar area isn't full of books and a fireplace but instead has all the things you expect to see in a church.

The statue of Christ. His sad eyes look down at his worshippers as blood drips from his pained wrists.

The stained-glass windows are gleaming. Sparkling. Someone must clean them weekly with loving care.

The congregation waits patiently, listening to the two rows of gospel singers. They're wearing long robes and smiles on their faces. One of the ladies must be at least ninety years old and her voice is still strong and sweet.

It's beautiful.

We sit down in a middle row and the girl continues to hold my hand. Her feet are restless and she kicks at the air.

The girl's mother leans toward me. "It's good to meet you. How do you know Jessica?" She nods in the direction of her daughter.

I don't get the chance to answer. "She helped me hand out flyers," Jessica says, although I'll probably want to call her the red-umbrella girl for the rest of my life.

"Oh, you knew Arnold?" the mother asks, and tears fill her eyes. "That's so nice of you. They're praying on his behalf tonight. We still believe he'll be back any minute. He's just lost. He can't find his way home."

Oh man, I can't take this. The optimism in her eyes is unbearable. The way she makes it sound as if Arnold took a wrong turn on his way home from class one evening. Maybe she thinks he's wandering the desert looking for the meaning of life. I look down at Jessica and she's staring at me with a look on her face that suggests she's crossing her fingers and toes in the hope that I'll keep my mouth shut. She hasn't been able to tell her mother yet. Heaven forbid I give up that secret.

"I'm sorry," I say. "Excuse me, please." I'm up and out of my seat in an instant. I should have known better. I push my way past a few silver-haired ladies who are trying to remove their heavy raincoats. I nearly knock one of them over in the process, that's how desperate I am to get away.

I make it to the lobby and pause. Ming is waiting for me outside. I need to find a back door to slip out.

"I'm sorry," a small voice says from behind. Jessica.

"It's not you, it's me," I mutter. I see a sign leading to the basement, where the bathrooms are. Maybe I can crawl through a window.

"I know she's scary," Jessica says. "Mom refuses to believe. I tried telling her but she won't listen. She won't listen to anyone. We all knew Arnold had a drug problem. He'd been taking Heam for at least six months. But she wouldn't believe that either. She's happier with her head up in the clouds, as my dad used to say."

"Sometimes it's easier that way," I say.

300

"She has her good days. Some better than others. I stay home from school sometimes and sit with her so she won't feel so alone."

"That's very nice of you."

"I'm glad you told me," she says. "I wanted to know. I didn't believe you at first, but I do now. Your friend—the one in Arnold's body. Is he going to be here for good now? Do you think he'd mind if I hang out with him now and then? I know it's not really Arnold and I'm not gonna pretend he is. I just want to see him now and then."

"You'd have to ask him," I say. "But I don't think he'd mind. He's very nice that way."

"Is he dead too? I mean, did he die and come back?"

"Yes," I say. "We knew each other when I was your age. I was with him when he died. I'm not sure how, but he came back to me."

"You love him, don't you?"

Am I really so transparent that a child can read my deepest thoughts? "Yes," I finally say. I don't see the point in lying to her. Lack of love isn't what's keeping me away from Chael. It's really the other way around.

"Maybe Arnold will come back like he did." She looks around as if wishing it might make it so. But I doubt Arnold's going to be walking up the church steps anytime soon.

"I don't know," I say. "I don't think this sort of thing happens very often."

"You're lucky," she says. "God must have thought you suffered enough if he was willing to send him back to you."

I'm not sure if God had anything to do with it but I'm not going to burst Jessica's bubble. Whatever made it happen isn't important. The fact that he's still here is.

From deep inside the church, organ music begins to play. Jessica turns around, drawn by the voices of the choir. "I should go back in."

She doesn't invite me to join her. I think even she can figure out that it's making me uncomfortable.

Without warning, she throws her arms around me and gives me a hug. I can feel her tiny body pressed against mine, her bones that are fragile and cold from many hours in the rain. Reaching down, I hug her back, trying to take away all that cold. She's just like Beth. I pray she never tries Heam and follows in her brother's footsteps.

I stand there for a few minutes after she's gone, listening to the choir first and then the voice of the priest as he begins the sermon. I miss a lot of the words but that doesn't matter. It's soothing. I think of Jessica inside, sitting next to her mother, probably holding her hand in comfort.

There's a hollowness in my stomach that makes me think of my own mother. She didn't believe in God, so it's not like we ever went to church together. But I would have liked to, now that I think about it.

I miss my mother. As much as I hate her and loathe everything she ever did to me, I still wish she were around. I guess every girl wants her mommy, no matter how big she grows. No matter how hard and far she's thrown from the nest.

Turning, I head downstairs and into the women's

bathroom. From there, I'm able to jimmy a window wide enough to slide through. I end up in the alley, where I'm able to give Ming the slip long enough to head for home.

—+—

I spend the rest of the night at home, back in my own church, where the brick walls comfort me and keep me protected. I know I should be looking for Beth but I can't make myself go back out there again. Here, I'm safe. No one can hurt me. Every time I go out, I risk seeing people who either want to kill me—or worse, want to help me deal with all my problems.

Why won't they just leave me alone?

In the morning, I have to drag myself out of bed and into my gym clothes. It's not raining today, which is a miracle in itself. I run my miles without complaint or even coherent thought. That's the best thing about training. I can turn my brain off.

Gazer is waiting for me in the basement when I get back. I can hear him puttering around, moving some of the equipment or something from the sounds of it. I pour some coffee and head down.

"It's good to see you're awake this morning," Gazer says. He's tinkering with the ancient treadmill. His tools are out and scattered across the floor. I don't know why he's bothering. It hasn't worked in ages. "I was beginning to think you'd given up on your training."

I sit down on the table beside him. "Nope. Just needed a few days off."

Gazer turns the screwdriver a few times and grunts as an answer. I take a drink of coffee and wait.

"Seems to me you've given up on a lot of things lately," Gazer continues. "You sure there's still nothing you want to tell me about?"

"Like what?" I say, coffee cup frozen halfway to my mouth. This is going somewhere. Gazer never repeats himself unless he already knows the answer.

Gazer gets up off the floor and tosses the screwdriver on the table beside me. Taking a rag, he cleans his hands before turning to face me. "I know about school, Faye. I know they kicked you out. What I don't understand is why you've been continuing to wear that outfit for the past few weeks to deceive me."

I look down at the floor. I should have known he'd figure this out on his own. The school probably called him the day it happened. "I didn't know how to tell you," I say. "I know how much it meant to you that I graduate."

"Me? How about *you*? Isn't that what you wanted?" Gazer throws the rag down in disgust. "This was the one thing in the world you wanted. Or am I wrong? Was that just some ploy to make me happy?"

"No," I say. "I did want to graduate. It's not my fault."

"Nothing is ever your fault."

"It isn't!" I jump down off the table and go over toward the punching bag. If I get the urge to hit something, I'm going to make sure I'm close enough to it. "It was because of the stupid fight at the party. It's probably got a million hits on YouTube by now. Of course the school found out about it."

"People can be deceiving," Gazer says. I'm not sure if he's talking about the kids at the party or me.

"I'm trying to fix things," I say. "Paige. This girl at school. She's got her father putting together some sort of legal petition. She's trying to get me back in."

Gazer shakes his head. "It won't work," he says. "We signed papers in order to get you in. A legal form. The school had a right to dismiss you without reason or warning. We agreed to it."

"I tried, Gazer," I say. "I really tried. You have no idea how difficult it was."

"Not hard enough," he says. "But you've had no trouble keeping yourself busy since."

"What's that supposed to mean?"

"I heard about Phil Sabado. I guess that doesn't mean much anymore. You missed out on the graduation, so you decided to head straight in for the kill now, is that it? Didn't take long at all."

"That wasn't me," I shout. "That was . . ." I pause here. Gazer doesn't know about Chael. No need to bring him into the equation. There'd just be too many questions I'm not willing to answer.

"You've changed so much, Faye," Gazer says. "Or maybe it's that you haven't at all and I'm just finally seeing it for the first time. I've tried so hard to believe in you; I guess I was wearing blinders this whole time."

"You're the one who taught me to kill."

"I taught you how to defend yourself," Gazer says. "So let's get to work, then." He gets into an attack position. "Come on. This is what you want, right?"

Gazer comes at me before I even have time to respond. He goes to put his arm around my neck and I block him. But he's too quick. His leg wraps around mine from behind and I go flying onto my back. Hard.

"Come on," he says as he bounces up and down to keep loose. "You wanted to learn how to fight. I didn't think that was a bad idea. You were so helpless. Giving you the power was supposed to make you stronger. Give you more confidence. Make you want to live again. But all it did was fuel your hatred. You were the one who was supposed to take that power and use it for good."

"They took my life," I snap. I get back onto my feet and he comes at me again. Two left jabs and then an uppercut. I block the moves easily. I throw a punch back and he gets my arm. Pulls me forward, upsetting my balance, and once again my body hits the padded floor.

"There you go again. A broken record. The only person who took your life is you, Faye. You had your second chance. You blew it."

I get up off the floor and cross the room because I don't know what else to do. My legs are shaking and I want to punch something so badly that my hands clench tightly into fists, digging my nails into my skin. Gazer is making me look like an idiot. He's turning my anger against me. I can't think properly. I'm fighting like an amateur.

"What are you going to do now?" Gazer says from behind me. "Two down, two to go. Ming and Rufus are left, right? Okay, so what happens after you kill them? Do you think things are going to be instantly fine and dandy? Is the world going to improve?" There's a long pause. "I'm not going to help you this time. If the police come, I won't lie to them."

"I don't want you to lie," I say. "I want them to catch me."

"So they'll arrest you? Give you a death sentence? Then you can head off to that hell you're positive awaits you?"

I whirl around, my fists rising up to my face. Defensive mode. "Stop trying to make my thoughts stupid."

"I don't have to do that," Gazer says. He comes at me a third time and I manage to get out of his grasp and avoid the floor. I can hear the whoosh of his arm as it barely misses my face. Concentrate, girl! Don't let him get under your skin. That's how they beat you.

Gazer comes in hard again but finally I catch a lucky break. I grab his arm in mid-punch and jump out of the way, bringing him along with me. He goes down to his knees and I bring up my leg to kick. But I stop at the last second as I'm trained to do. If this were a real fight, I'd finish him off.

But this isn't real, right?

Gazer gets up off his knees and goes over to the table and sits down. Picks up my coffee cup and looks to see what's inside. Taking a long drink, he puts it back down on the table. He's breathing heavily. "I killed the man that murdered my wife and child."

"What?"

"I killed him. After I left the force. I hunted him down. It was a calculated move on my part. I was obsessed with finding him. It took me two years."

"You never told me about this," I say.

"It's not something I wanted you to hear," he says.

307

"But you're ready now, even if you won't listen. Killing him didn't change anything. My wife and daughter were still dead. Shooting him didn't make the pain go away. It didn't remove the memories. It gave me no satisfaction. Revenge is only revenge and nothing else. Listen to one who's been there, Faye. You're never going to find the peace you're looking for if you go down this road."

"I'm not you."

"No, you're not. Did you ever wonder why I took you in, Faye? Why I spent all these years training you to defend yourself? Some people might find that weird. They'd probably call me a creepy old man if they really knew what goes on here."

"No, they wouldn't."

"Sure they would. I've made you a killer." Gazer rests his arms on the table. "I can still remember all those years ago. You were so small and fragile. You begged me to help you grow stronger. All I wanted to do was protect you. I thought if I taught you to defend yourself, you'd never feel frightened again. You want to know why I keep saying you're not ready?"

I shrug.

"A warrior must accept forgiveness for his enemy before he can truly become a warrior. It's as simple as that."

"I guess I'm not that simple."

I turn and head for the stairs before Gazer can respond. I don't stop till I'm up in my room and I've slammed the door for good measure. I lie down on the bed, sweating heavily, but I barely notice. I stay there for a long time, listening to my heart beating wildly in my ears.

I'm not Gazer.

I'm not Chael.

My actions are going to be my own.

I'm so tired of everyone telling me what to do.

—+—

I spend the afternoon searching for Beth.

She's hasn't checked back in at the center and Ramona is still worried about her. But ten new Heam addicts have arrived in the past few days and the counselor is running around in a panic, so I don't stay long.

Beth isn't at her house. She hasn't been around since the night I found her in the alley. Her mother stands at the doorway, refusing to let me in and only giving curt answers to my questions. I get the impression that she doesn't care much one way or another if Beth comes back home.

Joshua hasn't seen her either. He's been out searching every day. He's called the hospitals but has had no luck. He's even checked with the police twice. He's terrified. He suggests we team up but I point out that if we're separate, we can cover more ground.

It scares me that Beth hasn't even tried to contact Joshua but I don't say that to him. He still has hope.

It's around dinnertime when I reach the townhouse. The lights are on and I stand outside for about ten minutes before I finally get the courage to go up and knock. It's a strange sensation, like having to ask to attend your own birthday party.

I can hear someone running over to answer. She flings open the door without even bothering to look through the peephole. Not a smart idea in this area.

The girl in front of me looks to be about four years old. Her hair is long and brown. She smiles at me instantly, full of trust, showing me a set of tiny pearled teeth. She's wearing a shirt with a faded picture of a white stallion. I'll bet she's never seen a real horse before either.

"Hello," she says, and her voice is familiar. She sounds just like me. My heart tightens in my chest.

"Is your mother home?" I ask.

"Sure, hold on." She escapes back into the house, hollering at the top of her lungs. "MOM! THERE'S SOMEONE HERE TO SEE YOU."

"How many times have I told you not to open the door to strangers?" a voice shouts back at her.

I wait.

The woman who comes to the door is wiping her hands on a dish towel. Her hair is in a tired ponytail. Several strands have escaped and frame her slender face. She pauses when she sees me. If this were a cartoon, her jaw would come unhinged and drop to the floor.

"Faye."

"Hi . . . Mom."

There is an uncomfortable pause as we stare at each other. There are a million thoughts running around my brain but I can't find a way to express any of them. How do you respond to someone you haven't seen in six years? It's not like I can reach out and throw my arms around her in a welcome-home hug. She's not going to invite me in for

310

hot chocolate and tell me how my bedroom is exactly the way I left it.

I promised myself I'd remain calm if I chose to do this. I would not blame her for anything. I would not fight.

Mom drops the dish towel on the side table and opens the storm door. She steps outside instead of inviting me in. The little girl comes running up behind her but she shoos her back in. "Mommy needs to talk to the lady alone," she mutters. "Go finish drying the dishes."

"Who is she?"

"Nobody. Now go!"

"Awwwww." But the girl listens and disappears into the house.

Alone at last.

My mother stares at me, her hands on her hips, her lips pursed tightly. She doesn't even bother to blink. Her gaze shoots straight through me.

"I never knew I had a sister," I say. "What's her name?"

There's a pause where she's obviously deciding whether to tell me or not. "Sophie," Mom finally says.

"She's beautiful."

Mom nods. "What are you doing here, Faye?"

No "How are you?" "Where are you staying?" "How have you been?" Mom never was one for small talk.

"Just wanted to see you," I say. "It's been a long time."

"It has." She looks me up and down. "You look well."

"Thanks."

She sits down on the steps and motions that I should sit beside her. So I join her on the cold cement and we stay that way for a few minutes.

"You look really good," she finally says. "I'm sorry, but I never expected to see you again. I thought you were dead."

"By all odds I should be," I say.

"Where are you staying?"

"With Gazer. The man who rescued me. He adopted me. You must remember. You signed the papers."

She nods. "That was a long time ago."

"Six years."

"So much has happened since then." She sighs and I can see how the years have caught up. There are new lines creasing her forehead and in the corners of her eyes. And her hair is turning gray now.

My mother is growing old.

"Sophie's father is dead," she says. "Work accident three years ago. So it's just her and me. She doesn't know about you. I didn't know how to tell her. So if it's okay with you, I'd rather leave it alone right now."

I nod like I understand, but I don't.

"I did everything I could," she says. "I'm sorry but you have to realize how scared I was. When you came to the house with the scars . . . I was still on probation because of your father. I didn't know what to do."

"I'm not here looking for closure," I say. "You don't have to say anything or apologize. There is no amount of sorry that can take it back."

Anger flashes in her eyes. "I had no choice."

"There's always a choice."

"If you hadn't done something so stupid in the first place."

"I just wanted to see you one last time," I say as I stand up. "I'm happy that I have a sister." I look back at the house and I can see that Sophie is watching us through the window. She's the princess in the tower, with the same second-hand clothing that I used to wear. I see that my mother is wearing running shoes with holes in the toes and that her shirt has been washed so many times it's almost transparent.

Reaching into my pocket, I pull out the thousand dollars that Trevor gave me for the fight all those weeks ago. I hold it out to her.

"What's this?"

"Help," I say. "Take it."

"No." She stands up. Her eyes dart back and forth on the street to make sure no one dangerous is watching.

"It's not illegal," I say. "I earned it fairly from a job. If you don't take it, I will go inside and give it to Sophie. Buy her some new clothes. I guess I was wrong when I said I wanted nothing. Consider this my closure."

She finally holds out her hand and I press the money firmly into her palm. Her fingers shakily close around it.

"Love her," I say. "Even if she screws up."

I turn and head off into the night.

—+—

I walk and I walk. There's nowhere to go.

When I see the sirens, I know instantly what they mean. I have no idea how I know—I just do. I start to run, closing the gap between me and the red flashing lights.

One ambulance at the end of the street. A police car beside it. The officer is talking on the radio. He doesn't even notice me as I approach.

I remember this alley.

I turn the corner and head toward the medics. They're not rushing. They've got their equipment, but bringing it out was a wasted effort. The only necessary item is the stretcher but they're not using it yet. They must be waiting for the green light because they're standing around talking to each other. One of them lights a cigarette and spits in the gutter. The other wrinkles his nose and comments on the stench of urine.

"Gonna smell like crap all night now," he says.

The alley stretches out before me. I first met Beth here. She was hunched in the corner with Joshua between the metal Dumpsters and the wall. I almost missed them because they were so well hidden. I remember how they were huddled together, secretive gutter rats, trying to survive the pain of living. Searching for heaven.

"Hey!" One of the medics notices me. I ignore him and push my way past and in between the Dumpsters.

The child in front of me is curled up in a small ball. In her hands is the small empty vial that once held strawberry-flavored poison.

She's so pale.

Beth lies with her back against the brick wall. She's only wearing a thin shirt but she's not feeling the bitter cold.

Her lips are blue. Just like her eyes that stare out into nothing but darkness.

NINETEEN

"Hey! You can't be here." One of the ambulance attendants tries to grab my arm but I shake him off.

"I know her," I say. "She's a friend."

Kneeling down on the cold cement, I'm thankful that it's not raining, because that would be too much déjà vu for me to handle. It was pouring the first night and Beth's eyelashes were wet and shiny.

She was lifeless too back then.

This time is different.

She's been here awhile. The rats have nibbled at her fingertips and her hair has leaves and bits of garbage stuck in the fine blond silk. Her eyes are dull and filmed over.

A day, maybe? Two?

I've walked down this alley twice since I've been looking for her. Why the hell didn't I think to look behind the Dumpsters? It would have been the most obvious place to look. It should have been my first choice. So why not? Maybe because I was afraid that I would find this?

Clutched in her small white hand is the empty bottle of Heam. I wonder where she got the money to buy it. It's possible she stole from someone at the center. I wonder if Ramona would have told me. Or did she sell something of value? Maybe Joshua gave her some money the last time he came to visit. Of course the "how" doesn't really matter anymore. She's still dead. Poor Beth. She tried so hard but the addiction managed to eat away her last ounce of willpower. The war was too strong inside her and the bad guys won. I wish I could have taken her pain away and put it inside of me. I think I could have been strong enough for the both of us.

"You don't want to do this, Faye."

I remember almost doing the exact same thing six years ago. In fact, I tried doing it three times over the years. But Gazer always came after me. Always. This time he found me in the basement of the church, the bottle of silvery evil clutched in my hand. I'd managed to get it from one of the gutter rats who dealt over by the schoolyard.

"You don't know what it feels like," I said. "I wish I were dead."

Gazer knelt down beside me, gently reaching over and taking the bottle from my hand. I wanted to kick out and scream, bite him, whatever it took, but in the end, I simply handed it over. That's the problem with Heam. It takes all the fight out of you and replaces everything with emptiness. Pain. Addiction.

"I love you, Faye, and I don't want you dead," Gazer said after a while. "I'm here for you always. We will get through this together. You're never alone."

"I can't make it turn off," I said. "I can't make it go away."

"It will always be a part of you," Gazer said. "So let's find a way to use that addiction to your advantage. Let's reclaim your own body for yourself. Let's give you power."

"Can we do that?"

"We can try."

"Miss?" The police officer has come over. "Do you know her? What's her name so I can call her parents?"

His voice is kind and soft and I think he's probably a lot like Gazer was when he was a cop. I turn and there's no anger or boredom in his eyes.

"Beth," I say. The tears are falling freely now and I wipe them away with the sleeve of my jacket. "Her name is Beth Vincent. I don't have her phone number but I can tell you where she lived."

The officer nods and pulls out his notepad. I give him the information. I wonder how Beth's parents will take the news. Will they be relieved? How about my own mother? Would this have been better? Maybe I should have died all those years ago. How different everyone's lives might have ended up.

When I see Ming Bao watching me from the end of the alley, I know what I have to do next. Rufus and Ming probably didn't give Beth the drugs personally but Rufus is to blame. He's the middleman in this neighborhood and all the Heam dealers go through him. As far as I'm concerned, every time a child dies on these streets, they are somehow involved.

Chael thinks my life would be better if I gave up on my revenge. But this isn't about me anymore. Anger, bright hot and red, spreads throughout my body. I allow it. I close my eyes and let the hatred in. It builds, removing any traces of doubt I've been feeling these past few weeks.

I nod curtly to Ming and turn away. I start walking down toward the docks. I have no doubt that he's going to follow me. Someone like Ming won't be able to resist such an easy target.

This revenge won't just be for Christian and me. This will be for Beth. For Jessica. For Joshua and all the others who have suffered. For my mother. My little sister that I never knew existed until tonight.

You see, Heam doesn't just affect those addicted. No, it goes further than that. Just like the scars on my chest, it spreads out, its weblike branches touching everyone and everything in its path.

I'm going to make him pay.

—+—

The water is dark and endless. I stand on the dock, looking out into the bay. I'm feeling very peaceful. The wind blows against my face. I can smell the saltwater and decay of the ocean in front of me. A seagull calls out somewhere above me and another one answers it.

I breathe deeply.

And again.

Then I turn to face him.

Ming stands about twenty feet away. He's smiling. He blocks the path that heads into the maze of containers. There's nowhere for me to go.

That's okay. I don't plan on running.

A switchblade appears from beneath the folds of his jacket. Ming steps forward, inviting me into the fight. I smile back at him. I can feel the weight of my own knife in its sheath. It waits, tucked away in the small of my back. I won't use it yet.

Ming may have the extra weight over me. He may be a professional boxer and he always fights dirty. But none of that matters. I have the strength. I have the souls of Beth and the hundreds of gutter rats he's already destroyed. I have the power of the afterlife on my side. I've seen hell. I've seen everything there is to fear. Now there's nothing left for me to be afraid of.

Men like Ming deserve to die.

He lunges forward without warning, raising his fist to try to punch my head, but I'm quick enough to duck to the side, barely dodging both the blow and the slash of the knife. I spin around, raising my foot, kicking him in the back of his knee. He staggers but doesn't go down.

He comes at me again and I'm too slow. The first punch slams into my cheek, bringing fresh tears to my eyes. The second punch knocks me back several steps and I stumble, refusing to go down. I dodge the next few blows, bad move on my part. I should have been watching my feet. My shoulders smack against the metal container. There's nowhere else to go.

Ming throws his body against me, pinning me to the wall, using his weight as a weapon. Several punches slam into my already-wounded rib cage, leaving me breathless and gasping for air.

I see the glint of steel coming in from the right and I barely manage to squirm out of the way before the knife pierces my skin. It tears the fabric of my jacket as I shove Ming as hard as I can. He steps backward and it's my turn.

Uppercut to the jaw. Ming's head snaps backward but he's agile enough to block the next three punches. I crouch down and kick at his kneecap but my foot hits only air. Ming comes in again and I'm beginning to notice a pattern. Either he's so arrogant that he thinks I'll never beat him or he's just a crappy fighter. I'm beginning to understand why he fights dirty.

Ming always uses his left hook first.

Time to get rid of that knife.

I dodge the blow and throw myself at him. We both go flying backward onto the ground. Luckily for me, Ming takes most of the fall. I land right on top of him. I go straight for his hand, grabbing at the blade and slamming his knuckles hard against the pavement. He grunts but doesn't let go of the weapon. He bucks his body upward, sending me straight into the air and onto my knees. It takes a second for me to get my balance.

"Was that gutter rat your friend?" Ming says. He's smiling as he climbs to his feet. He's barely winded at all while I'm panting like I've run a marathon.

I don't say a word. My mouth is full of blood. I turn

and spit, clearing my throat, trying to remove the metallic taste from my teeth.

"Who do you think sold her the drugs?"

He's trying to get under my skin but I won't let him. First rule of fighting. Never lose your cool.

"Shut up," I finally say. "Neither of us is here to talk."

His smile grows even wider. He raises his switchblade and lunges at me. I duck to the side, managing to land a kick to his hip. Grunting in pain, he brings his hand around and the knife slices through my jacket. My skin burns as the blade cuts the fabric and hits flesh. Another punch sends me back and I fall hard, landing on my now-bleeding arm.

Ming doesn't let up. He's on me again and the blade is going straight for my throat. I manage to block him and there's a tense moment where the blade almost sinks in. But I twist my body around and punch him in the head in order to get away. I scramble to my feet, trying to pretend that I haven't slowed down.

I'm swaying. Dizzy. The last blow to my head has stunned me a bit.

Ming knows. He moves in and I do the only thing I can. I run.

He's fast but I'm faster. I race through the containers, wincing when I turn a corner too sharply and my shoulder bangs against the metal wall. Right. Right. Left. I can hear Ming a few containers behind. Our footsteps pound the pavement and the noise becomes confusing.

Ming's lost me. I can hear him several rows down,

swearing loudly. His fists slam into a metal wall in frustration.

I move to the end but don't round the corner. I'll wait for him to come to me. I pull the knife out and hold it tightly in my hand.

I can fight dirty too.

It's not long before I hear his footsteps grow louder. He's coming straight for me and he's running. He won't have time to stop himself.

Readying myself, I wait until the last possible second. I spring out from behind the container and throw myself against his body, slamming the knife into his chest.

Chael's chest.

I try to stop but the momentum's taken over. The knife hits home, burying itself into Chael's body. I let out a short shout of surprise and Chael's hand shoots out, covering my face.

"Be quiet," he says.

"Oh God, oh God, oh God," I whisper. I've let go of the knife and the handle is sticking straight out of his chest.

Chael looks down and then back at me. He grabs the knife and yanks it out with a quick motion. I swear, my stomach lurches at the squishy sound that follows.

"I'm so sorry," I say. I quickly press my fingers against his wound, trying to keep the blood from pouring out.

"I'm fine," he says. "You know this can't hurt me." His hands encircle mine, pulling me closer to him.

"Why are you here?" I ask.

"I heard your pain." He looks me over to make sure everything is fine. When he sees my face, he reaches up and gently touches my lip. "I followed it to the ambulance. I saw Beth. Then I felt your physical pain and it led me here."

"You can't have him," I say. "Ming's mine. He killed Beth."

Chael doesn't get a chance to respond. We both hear the noise behind us at the same time. Ming is running toward us, knife raised, and he's probably going to try to kill the first thing he stabs. Chael pushes me out of the way and I turn as Ming slashes down at me. I grab his hand at the last second and manage to use his own momentum to slam him into the container. His fingers smash against the metal and he releases the switchblade. I bend down and grab it.

Chael gives me a sad look but doesn't do anything. He backs away and lets me finish the job.

Ming gets the first punches in, rapidly, one right after the other. My face begins to burn. I manage to land a blow squarely on his nose. I feel the cartilage break beneath my knuckles. He throws himself against me, fingers clawing at my hand as he tries to reclaim his weapon. I bring my knee up and shove him off me. He hits the ground, does a quick roll, and comes back for more.

He dives at me. I raise the knife up at the last second and it sinks into his chest as if he's made of jelly and not flesh. When I feel the metal scrape bone, I let go in disgust.

Ming grunts once and collapses on top of me. His mouth opens and blood splashes against my face.

It's over.

Chael is there instantly, pulling Ming's body off of me.

I scramble backward on my legs and hands until my body hits the container. Sitting there in shock, I watch as the last of Ming's life disappears on the concrete ground.

It doesn't take long.

Then the tears come. They pour from my eyes and I don't do anything to try to stop them. Chael comes over and helps me to my feet. He wraps his warm arms around me and holds me for the longest time.

I cry for Beth. I cry for the thousands of nameless gutter rats I've seen over the years. I cry for Gazer and his dead wife and child and the revenge that didn't solve his problems. I cry for my mother and the sister I never knew I had until tonight. I cry for Arnold Bozek and his sister, Jessica. And I cry for Chael, who should be holding me with his own body and not one that makes him feel like he's on borrowed time.

Most of all I cry for me.

I killed someone tonight. I took his life.

Finally, when all the tears are gone, I pull gently away from Chael, who has been holding me all this time without saying a single word. Without speaking, he reaches down and tears a strip of his shirt away and hands it to me.

"I don't have a tissue," he says.

I try to laugh but out comes another sob. Pressing the cotton to my face, I wipe away the blood and the last of the tears.

"How do you feel?" he asks.

"Stupid," I say. "Dumb. Empty."

"You're not."

I look down at the dead body of Ming Bao. A pool

324

of dark blood has spread beneath his back, staining the concrete, leaving a mark that will take a long time to wash away.

"He deserved it," I say. "He killed you. He took you away from me."

"Yes, he did."

"I don't feel any better," I say. "I thought I would but I don't."

"That's not how the healing process works," Chael says. He puts his arms around me again and pulls me close. But suddenly I'm repulsed at the idea of him touching me. I shove him back.

"No," I say. "Don't act like it's okay. It's not."

"I didn't say it is," he says. "But you'll heal if you allow yourself to."

"He won't." I go over to the body and kneel down beside it. Ming's eyes stare up at the sky. He looks peaceful. Younger. As if all the anger and violence has been erased from his eyes.

I wonder where he is now. Is there his own personal hell waiting for him? Or is there nothing but darkness? Is he being judged? I hope so.

In reality, I haven't done a thing. Tomorrow another man will take his place, standing on the street corners, peddling Heam to the gutter rats. I could go out with my knife and kill them all, but more will just pop up in their places. In superhero movies, the masked man always stops the bad guys and saves the world. They stick to that version of happily-ever-after. No one points out that the sequel isn't far behind. Or the trilogy. And so forth.

A never-ending problem. Suddenly my revenge seems rather small.

What exactly have I achieved?

"So that's it, then," I say as I turn around and get up off my knees. "Now I'm really going to hell."

Chael smiles. "You just don't get it, do you?"

"What do you mean?"

"Life isn't that black and white, Faye. Death isn't either." Chael comes over and takes my hand and it's so warm. My own fingers are icy cold. "You are a good person. You can't live your life trying to undo all the wrongs done to you. Or me. All you can do is go on and make a difference in the lives you've yet to meet."

"But I saw hell," I say.

"You saw what you needed to see," he says. "Do you remember that night? Ming gave me the drug first. You fought like a wildcat. The last thing I remember before I died was you screaming my name and begging me not to leave you."

"Did I?" I say. "I don't remember that."

"It was the guilt and fear that sent you where you went," he says. "And if there's one thing I know, our life is never written in ink. We can change our future. Free will, Faye. You choose your own path. You are in charge of your future, even in death."

"I want to go home," I say. Suddenly I need to see Gazer. I need to give him a hug and tell him how truly sorry I am about his wife and child.

"I'll walk you home," Chael says.

"Stay with me," I say. "For tonight."

"Absolutely."

—+—

We don't talk much on the way home. There are no words to describe how I feel. Chael holds me. We get a few odd stares from people but I don't care. We must look a mess, both covered in blood. What amazes me the most is that no one bothers to ask if we're all right. No one calls the police. They avert their eyes and look everywhere but at us.

No one cares.

There's something really wrong with this picture. Have we become so jaded that we can't be bothered? Is it possible to make people care again? How can I make them listen?

We need our pain to be heard.

It should be shouted from the rooftops.

My anger is gone. I have no idea where it went but I'm not mourning it.

We get off at my stop and I duck into a gas-station bathroom for a few minutes before going home. I stand in front of the sink with an insane amount of paper towels and try to remove the last traces of blood. Considering I just got my ass almost kicked, I don't look that bad. My lip is slightly swollen but not enough that Gazer will see. I dab at the dirt on my jacket and rinse my mouth out a few times with tap water. My hair is a mess but I manage to comb it out a bit with my fingers.

Finally, I decide this is the best I'm going to get, so I

turn out the light and head back to Chael. He's been in the men's room himself and has managed to clean up a bit. He's even turned his shirt around so the ragged hole isn't visible.

We walk slowly and at some point he takes my hand and I allow it. When we reach my church, I hold on tighter.

We go inside. Gazer is sitting by the fireplace. I look at the clock, surprised to see it's just a little past eight. For some reason I feel it should be later. When Gazer sees I'm not alone, he puts down his book and stands to meet us.

"Gazer," I say. "This is Chael."

I'm so nervous, you'd think I was introducing the Queen of England to the Dalai Lama or something equally ridiculous. Chael steps forward and holds out his hand, and Gazer, after a moment's pause, extends his own to meet it.

"Pleased to meet you," Gazer says. His face is a mixture of surprise and pleasure. I've shocked him. I can't help feeling a little happy about that.

The men exchange a bit of small talk. I don't add to the conversation. What can I say? Gazer, this guy is dead so don't get too used to him. He might not be around much longer or he might start rotting in the living room. He's a good man. He's almost as smart as you. I love him and I can't say that to you either because it's too personal. I'm not ready to share. But when I am, you'll be the first to know about it.

As it turns out, I don't need to say a thing.

"Maybe I'll go down to the bar and hang out with some of the old boys," Gazer says after a bit.

I open my mouth in surprise but Gazer just winks. I

leave Chael to admire Gazer's book collection as I follow my adoptive father to the door.

"What are you doing?" I say. "You never go out for drinks. Ever."

Gazer grabs his coat and hat and puts them on. "Always a first time for everything," he says. "And I feel like celebrating."

"For what?"

"Your life," Gazer says. "When you left today, Faye, I was positive I was never going to see you alive again. Instead, you show up with a boy on your arm and your eyes are glowing. I don't know what happened tonight but I'm just thankful. So I think it's time for me to move on too. Go out and see some of my old friends. I've been a hermit for too long."

"A new outlook on life? That's always a good start."

"I don't want to know what you did tonight, so don't tell me," he says. "I'm just glad you're home. And I better not have to remind you not to do anything that might annoy me in my absence."

"No wild parties. No drugs. No fun. I get it."

"Not funny, Faye." Gazer looks back toward the living-room area, where Chael has sat down to read the back cover of a thick novel.

"I'm sorry," I say. "But he's good. You'll approve. He's taught me a lot of things."

"Oh?"

"I'm not better," I say. "Not even close. But you're right. You're always right. The two of you are very similar. It kinda freaks me out a bit."

329

"Nonsense," Gazer says. "There's no right or wrong. Everyone is different. You just needed to find out on your own."

"I'm tired of being angry all the time. Sometimes I just want to forget everything. Be empty. But that wouldn't solve my problems either." I swallow hard and take a deep breath. The tears are threatening to come back out again. I try to concentrate enough to keep them away. "Do you think I'll ever be okay?"

"Don't know." Gazer puts his arms around me and hugs me tightly. "But I'm glad you're sticking around to find out. Now go pour that man some tea or something. I'll be back in a few hours." He pauses and shakes the door handle. "I think we're going to have to fix this. Lock's going to break right off any day now."

I close the door behind him and head back to the main room. Chael is done looking through Gazer's book collection and is now admiring his vintage vinyl.

"He's got just about every single big band from the twenties and thirties," he says. "And this record player is amazing. It's got to be at least forty years old."

"More like fifty," I say. "I grew up listening to that stuff. I know most of those records. I swear, Gazer should be at least ninety years older than he really is. He loves all that stuff. I'm going to make some tea. You want?"

"Sure," he says without even looking at me. He's too enthralled by Bing Crosby's greatest hits. I wander into the kitchen, wondering what I've gotten myself into. They say girls marry their fathers. In this case, my ghostly boyfriend's musical taste is way too much like my guardian's.

Am I ever going to live a normal life?

When I come back five minutes later with tea, Chael's managed to figure out the record player and Frank Sinatra is blasting out a ballad.

"Dance with me," he says, taking both mugs of tea and placing them on the table. I start to pull away but he gets his arms around my waist and soon we're both laughing as we step on each other's feet.

"I feel like I should be more upset than this," I finally say as he spins me around.

"Why's that?"

"Um . . . Ming?"

Chael pulls me closer and I sink into his arms. He's so very warm and soft. I lean my head against his shoulder.

"What about Rufus?" Chael asks. "What are your plans for him?"

"I don't care about him anymore," I say. "I really don't." I pull my head away and look right into Chael's eyes. "Why is that?"

"You said earlier that you feel empty," he says. "And I think that's true. But that's because something's been removed from you. All that hate is still there but maybe it's not."

"No," I say. "It's still there. But it feels different."

"Maybe you're learning that you can channel it somewhere else. Make a difference in the world. Create rather than destroy."

I think of Beth and imagine all the other Beths still out there. All those gutter rats that have been rejected by everything warm and loving. Pushed to the point of addiction because they've lost any chance of real happiness. The world is a hard place. Can one person make a difference? Can I?

"You need to refill yourself with something other than pain." Chael leans down and kisses my neck gently. "Let's start by giving you some really good memories."

His lips meet mine and everything melts away.

It's surreal. I almost feel like I'm watching a movie in which I'm the star. This isn't a happy ending. I killed a man tonight and now I'm dancing. That's wrong. I shouldn't be this happy. Rufus is still following me. Now that I've killed Ming, he's going to come after me with a vengeance.

But all those nagging thoughts refuse to stay in my mind. I'm ignoring them because I don't want them.

What's wrong with me?

I push Chael away. The room's gone suddenly cold. He comes closer again and puts his arms around me. I allow it only slightly.

"This is wrong," I insist.

"You're punishing yourself again," he says.

"I should be." The tears are back again, threatening to fall.

"You're allowed to be happy."

"Not like this."

Chael reaches out and runs a finger along my cheek. "It takes time to heal," he says. "It won't happen overnight and I'll help you get through it. I'm here for you. I'm not going anywhere. We've got all the time in the—"

A gloved hand stabs a needle into Chael's neck. Silvery

liquid speeds through the tip and into the skin. Chael's green eyes widen as he struggles to get the last word out.

"World," he says.

Then his entire body shuts down. As he falls away from me, all I can see is a look of surprise staring up at me.

"Dumb bitch."

The words are there and it takes me forever to tear my face away from Chael. I know that voice. I've heard it a million times in my head, playing over and over like one of Gazer's records.

I look up and gaze into the eyes of the monster I've wanted to kill my entire life. Only minutes ago I was ready to give him up. Now he's gone and taken that from me too. How many ways can he destroy me?

Rufus stands before me, smiling like a maniac. He's holding in his hands the needle that, seconds ago, was sticking out of Chael's neck. There's still some silver liquid in the syringe.

Heam is deadly and has plenty of side effects. But it's a drug that is ingested by swallowing. People don't shoot Heam unless they're planning on never coming back. It's like putting liquid nitrogen into your veins. It kills you within seconds.

Chael isn't like most people. Chael's survived being shot and stabbed. He heals quickly. This should be a walk in the park for him. But he's not getting up off the floor. His eyes remain closed. He's not breathing.

Something's wrong.

"You're next," Rufus says. He drops the old needle on the floor and pulls another one from the folds of his jacket.

Rufus lunges at me and I barely manage to snap out of it before I feel his hands grabbing at my hair. I pull back my arm and punch him as hard as I can. I miss most of his face; my knuckles land the blow on the side of his head, but it's enough to make him let go and step back in shock.

He expected this to be easy. He beat me once without any resistance on my part. That's why he went after Chael first. That's why he was cowardly and attacked from behind. Maybe he thought I'd drop to the floor in tears like some sort of hysterical idiot. Nope, not this time.

I hit him again and a well-placed kick makes him drop the needle and retreat in pain. I see his other hand going into his jacket to grab his gun but I don't allow it. I throw myself on the monster, kicking and punching, not giving him a second to catch his breath. The gun flies out of his jacket and I ignore it, choosing instead my fists as my own weapons.

Rufus drops to his knees and covers his head with his hands, trying to protect himself from my blows. I punch around his fingers, finding cracks in his defenses, kicking at his chest and ribs.

He finally goes down and I stop. Rufus curls up on the floor like a baby and suddenly all that fire inside of me washes away. I look at him, a pathetic loser, a wasted man who uses pain to make his life seem useful.

I pick up the gun and aim it at his head. I should pull the trigger and end his life. I'd be doing the world a favor. I've thought about this moment every day for six years. I should be ready for this.

But I'm not.

Gazer and Chael have been right all along. Revenge isn't as sweet as everyone is led to believe. I'm still not complete. In fact, I doubt I ever will be. And I don't want to kill him.

I want to live.

Behind me, Chael's lifeless body waits. There are more important things to do right now.

"Did you figure it out?" I ask. "Do you remember me?"

Rufus spits out blood and refuses to look at my face.

"You killed me once," I say. "Many years ago. A poor helpless child. But you should have made sure I was really dead. I came back. I got strong."

"You mean you're just a gutter rat?" Rufus finally looks up at me. "Holding some stupid grudge because you got addicted to Heam? I've got news for you, sunshine. That's your own fault."

I refuse to rise to the bait.

"You think I'm going to remember every single gutter rat I've given drugs to? Jesus, my memory ain't that good. You're nothing more to me than a thousand other faces." He spits on the ground as if to emphasize his point. "No one cares about you and they sure as hell won't remember you—least of all, me."

"I should kill you right now," I say. "But I'm not going to. I'm not going to give you that power over me. I'm not letting you take my life completely."

Rufus starts to climb to his feet. He sways unsteadily for a few seconds. Then he spits again in my direction. He's still smiling. The bastard is still grinning like I'm not a threat.

335

I raise the gun straight to his head and he flinches.

"Your boyfriend doesn't look so good," he says.

"Get out of here," I say. "And don't let me ever see you again. Because the next time I will kill you."

Rufus looks around like he wants to challenge me but at the last second he decides against it. Even he knows his limits. He wipes some blood away from his mouth and starts walking backward.

"Watch yourself, girlie," he says. "One day when you least expect it. I know where you live now."

"I'll keep the back door unlocked for you," I say.

He stops and takes a step forward. I raise the gun above his head and pull the trigger. The explosion is loud and part of the ceiling sprays bits of brick from where the bullet entered.

Rufus puts his hands over his head and ducks. I lower the gun until it's level with his eyes.

"I said leave."

He opens his mouth to say something but I wave the gun again and he thinks better of it. Rufus turns and heads for the door with me right behind him. The moment he leaves, I lock the door. The knob wobbles in my grip. Gazer was right, it does need fixing. It probably wasn't hard for Rufus to pick it.

I drop the gun into the empty umbrella basket. My arms are shaking so badly I'm amazed I've been able to hold it for this long. I lean against the door, trying to mentally force my heart to stop pounding.

Chael!

I turn and run.

He's still on the floor and I drop down beside him and put my head on his chest. His shirt is still warm, but for how much longer? I can't hear a heartbeat, so I check for a pulse. Nothing. He's not breathing.

I get into CPR position and place my hands on his chest.

One, two, one, two, one, two.

I tilt his head back and breathe air deep into his body.

One and two and three and four. One and two and three and four.

Breathe. Breathe.

"Dammit, Chael," I scream. "Come back to me. Don't leave me!"

The minutes pass. My body begins to cramp and my hands ache. But Chael doesn't move.

I pound on his chest before finally giving up. I sit on the floor beside him, exhausted, both mentally and physically. The music clicks off. Sinatra has left the building.

Reaching out, I take his hand and hold it, trying to will my own warmth to leave me and enter him instead. Tears run down my cheeks.

"True love never leaves," I whisper. "Even in death. You came back to me before. Please come back again. I don't want to be here without you. I can't do this without you."

I have a feeling it was only a one-time thing.

But that doesn't mean I can't go to him. Suddenly I'm off the floor and searching the room for the syringe. I find them both beside the couch. One almost empty. One filled.

I pick up the one with more silvery liquid and hold it up

to the light. Instantly I can feel the ache tugging from my scars. The desire.

It's time to feed it.

If Chael can't come to me, then I'll go to him.

The needle slides under my skin and I push the plunger home. There is a bright flash of white light. My head involuntarily turns up toward the ceiling as my body completely shuts down. In slow motion I fall backward, watching everything around me go blurry. My head hits the floor but I don't feel it.

My vision dims.

Nothing but darkness.

TWENTY

The world stretches out before me in the shape of a dark space. There are no walls, just an endless hardwood floor that leads off further than my eyes can see. There is no ceiling. When I look up, I see nothing but darkness. But there must be light somewhere because I can see. I am surrounded by a dull glow, giving me about ten feet of visible space.

I appear to be in the spotlight.

I'm lying on the floor, my hands scraping against the wood. Maybe once, this floor was shiny and new. I wonder how many people have traveled through here to wear down the finish, leaving nothing but splinters and cracks.

If this wood were sand, there would be a million footprints left behind.

I get up after fully taking in my nonsurroundings. Chael has to be here somewhere. All I have to do is find him.

I start walking. The light follows me. No matter which direction I turn, the glow sticks to me like glue.

My walk turns into a jog.

Then I'm flat-out running.

No matter how far I go, the floor beneath me doesn't change. I'm going nowhere. Eventually I stop, collapsing to my knees, panting heavily. I keep my head down and wait for the inevitable hell that's sure to follow.

The shadows are all around me. I'm sure of it. They're moving in across the floor and they're going to swallow me whole this time. I can feel them getting closer and I brace myself for the pain I know is coming.

—+—

I can't remember how we first figured out that our bedroom windows are side by side. But now that we've discovered it, we pull the screens off the windows every single night and stick our heads out to talk. Mom gets angry because she says I'm damaging the blinds. So we have to be secretive.

Our secret.

"What happened?"

"They arrested Dad," I say. The blue-and-red lights are finally gone. They lit up the entire street, forcing the neighbors to peek from behind their curtains. Mom is still downstairs. She sent me to bed but I hid at the top of the stairs, watching quietly as they read my father his rights and slapped the cuffs on his wrists.

"That's what my parents figured," Christian says. "Mom's gonna offer to take care of you for a bit if needed."

"I don't know," I say. "It's scary. She's downstairs, staring at the table. She hasn't moved since they left. She's crying. I've never seen her cry before."

"Do you think he'll come back?"

I shake my head. "I think he did something really bad. They wouldn't say and Mom caught me listening on the stairs. So I didn't hear."

"I'm here if you need me."

"What if you're sleeping?"

"Hold on a sec." Christian's face disappears from the window. I can hear him jump on the bed. The springs creak. Then I hear a soft knocking noise coming from our adjoined wall. A moment later, he's back. "There. If you need me, just knock. It'll be like Morse code."

"I don't know Morse code."

"Neither do I," he says with a grin. "But all you have to do is knock. I'll know it's you. It'll be like I'm sleeping right beside you."

——+——

I place my hand against the hard wood and start knocking. *I need you. I need you so bad. Don't leave me alone in the dark.* Skin rubs off my knuckles, but I keep going. No splinters in the world can stop me.

"Faye."

"Chael?"

Hands wrap around me, pulling my face upward, and there he is. Chael comes down on his knees so he's level with me. He runs his fingers along my cheek, pushing back the loose strands of my hair. He tilts his head to the side and gives me a sad smile.

"It's really you," I say. And by that, I mean he's in his real body. For the first time since he's come back, he finally looks comfortable in his skin. He looks like he belongs there.

He's beautiful.

"It's me," he says. "Why'd you come? It's not easy to go back from here. Trust me, I know."

"I didn't want to be left behind again," I say. I touch his chest with my fingers, tracing a path along his shirt. He's so warm.

"So you'd rather die than live? Trust me, Faye, you don't want that."

"I want you," I say.

"And you'll have me," Chael says. "But not today. It's not your time. You have to go back."

"No!"

Chael gently places a hand behind my neck. He pulls me forward and kisses me. I dissolve into his arms, refusing to think about anything except this moment. How can he ask me to go back? I can't make it without him. He's my strength.

"Do you see?" Chael says when he pulls away. "No hell. I told you. You hold that control. Everything that happens to you, from here on out, is because of what you think you deserve. This is your heaven. You create it and it chooses you back."

I look around at my empty space full of splintered hardwood. Why on earth would my brain pick such a confusing place? It's the most frustrating puzzle in the world. Or universe. Or afterlife. Where am I?

"Where did you go?" I ask. "When you died. I know you said it was nothing but darkness, but there's got to be more than that." I wave my arm around. "It can't be just this."

Chael leans in and whispers in my ear, "I went where I was supposed to go."

"I don't understand."

"Remember the time we pretended we were on the beach? We transformed the living room into what we used to see on those tourism posters down at the mall? We stared at them forever and imagined all the places we'd explore when we got older. But the ocean was always our favorite. That was my heaven. I was on my adventure and I was there because of you."

"Why me?"

"Because it wouldn't be heaven without you." He takes my hand and helps me to my feet. "Do you want to see?"

"Yes."

"Okay, but only for a minute."

Instantly the dark room grows foggy and the floorboards disappear. I reach out for Chael and he takes me in his arms. I close my eyes tightly until the darkness goes away.

Until I feel the warmth on my face. I smell the saltwater.

My feet are suddenly wet.

I open my eyes.

The emptiness is gone. There's white sand all around

me, stretching for miles. Above us, a seagull flies and I can see palm trees in the distance. Below, a set of footprints races away toward the bluest water I've ever seen. Gentle waves rush over my feet, sinking my toes into the sand. Somewhere in the middle of all this death, I lost my shoes. And I'm wearing a sundress. Blue with pink-and-yellow suns, strikingly similar to the beach towel I used to own. Never in my life have I ever dared to wear anything so summery. Normally, such a thing would look horrific on my pale skin. But when I raise my arm, I can't help admiring how the translucent whiteness has grown tanner.

Chael is wearing khaki shorts and no shirt. His hair falls into his eyes as a soft breeze passes by.

"You helped create this," Chael says. "You invented it the exact same way you built the elevator and all those shadow monsters."

"Impossible," I say. "This is heaven?"

"It's the afterlife," Chael says. "I have no idea if there's a heaven or hell. At least, not the kind religions speak about. As far as I can tell, there's only the place where you think you deserve to be."

"I don't understand."

Chael smiles and takes my hand. "You saw hell because your eleven-year-old mind thought you deserved it. All that fear and terror made you believe you'd done something terribly wrong and needed to be punished. Don't you see? It's our life experiences that matter, Faye. It's the whole 'Why do we exist?' question. We live so that we'll know enough about living. Without life, there is no afterlife to look forward to."

"So you're saying I can change it?"

"You did change it." Chael points behind me and I turn to see the most perfect little beach hut. There's a soft-looking couch on the porch and it looks exactly like the dream world Christian and I talked about all those years ago.

I turn back to look at him. He's holding a yellow-and-white flower. He brings it up to my nose and I inhale the sweet scent. I remember this. I saw it as a child in a travel magazine. I remember wondering how it might smell. Chael brushes my hair back and tucks the flower gently behind my ear.

"I told you the sun would look good on you."

I smile because I'm completely at a loss for words. I don't need them. There's nothing I could say that could come close to what I'm feeling right now. I wrap my arms around him and hold on tightly, resting my head on his chest and feeling the rise and fall of it. Feeling the heat of the sun on his skin. Feeling the strength of his heart, beating against my ear.

"But time is fleeting," Chael finally says. "We have to get you back."

My stomach drops to my knees. "Let me stay with you," I say.

"That's not up to me to decide," Chael says. "You can't get in here early. You have to wait until it's your time. Just like everyone else."

I hold on to him tighter. "No."

"True love never dies," Chael says. "I'll be here for you. When it's your turn, it'll be my arms that bring you over."

He presses his fingers against my heart. "You have to go back for you. Don't think about me. Think about everything you'll truly be giving up."

I close my eyes and instantly see Gazer. If what Chael is saying is true, then Gazer's wife and child are somewhere out here in their own version of paradise. What would it be? The world's largest library? Or the peaceful cottage he told me he wanted to buy one day? The place he planned to retire to with his wife.

Gazer needs me. He loves me. I need him too. He was the one person who cared for me when no one else wanted to.

And what about my mother and little half sister? Is it possible I could get to know them both? My mother made a bad decision and I've spent my life hating her. But here, in all this beauty, I can't hate.

I can see a future.

All the other Beths out there waiting in the dark. Hiding in the alleys, looking into a bottle of silver liquid. I can help them. Ramona is right. I can make a difference.

I can have meaning.

But I can't if I stay here.

I pull back from Chael's embrace. Looking into his eyes, I see nothing but love. I could stay here, forever in his arms. Wrapped inside his warmth. It would be so easy. He's the one I'll never stop loving.

People spend their entire lives searching for the one person who will truly love them back. Their soul mate. That one person who understands them better than they do themselves. How lucky I was to find that love so quickly. Can I really walk away from him again?

Yes, I can. I take a deep breath and the words slide off my tongue. "I'm ready to go back."

"Let me give you something to remember me by."

Warmth flows from his fingers against my skin. A soft pale glow spreads across my chest and into my arms and legs. It grows brighter with each heartbeat. It hurts my eyes but I can't look away.

And I feel it. All that pain. The yearning. The insects squirming around my brain begin to die. The addiction. That desire for Heam that's supposed to haunt me till the end of days.

It's gone.

For the first time in six years, I feel normal.

"There's someone waiting for you," Chael whispers into my ear. "You have to go now. I'll wait for you."

"Me too," I say.

"Go live your life the way you were supposed to," Chael says, and he kisses me one last time. "I've always loved you. That's not going to change."

"I love you too."

The glow inside my body explodes and everything disappears. The never-ending beach evaporates beneath my legs.

And Chael . . .

My eyes open and I'm coughing hard. I can't breathe. Gazer is kneeling beside me, pressing down on my chest. CPR.

Then he's lifting me into his arms and holding me

tightly. We rock back and forth while I struggle for air. My head grows dizzy. The lights hurt my eyes.

I'm so cold.

But I'm alive.

"I thought I lost you," Gazer says. "I was so scared, Faye."

"It's okay," I say. "I'm back." Turning, I look over at Chael but he's no longer on my living-room floor. Arnold Bozek's body is in his place. Or rather, Chael's gone and now I can only see Arnold as he really was.

"What happened?" Gazer asks.

"Rufus," I say. "He had a needle. He stabbed Chael with Heam. I managed to chase him off. I didn't kill him. I could have, but I didn't."

Gazer nods but I can tell he's confused.

"Don't you see?" I say. "I could have had my revenge but I didn't. Even though he killed Chael a second time, I let it go. I took my power back. I didn't want it anymore."

"What do you mean he killed him a second time?" Gazer reaches up and puts his hand on my forehead. "How hard did you bang your head?"

"I'm fine," I say. "I'm better than fine."

My skin is pale and clear. The scars are still there but the tug from the addiction is gone.

Gazer is studying my face, still looking for signs of a concussion.

"One last gift," I say. "I'm whole again."

"I don't understand," Gazer says.

"Let me tell you about it," I say. "Get comfortable. This is a long story. . . ."

In the end, we didn't know what to do with the body. Gazer wanted to call the police but I talked him out of it. Arnold Bozek had been missing for a long time. There would be too many questions to answer. So we took him down to the park and placed his body gently on a park bench. Then we made an anonymous call and waited for the police to come get him.

A Heam addict in life, Arnold didn't have much of a chance. He hurt the people around him and fell into an empty world that didn't care. He'll probably never know how he saved my life. His dying allowed Christian to return to me. I wish I could meet Arnold personally to thank him for everything. Maybe one day I'll run into Jessica again and tell her the entire story. In return, I want her to tell me everything about Arnold. Who he was. What he did. I never want to forget him.

In the end, Arnold finally got to go home and his family got their closure.

Gazer listened to my story but I could tell he didn't really believe me. Not fully. That's okay, I still don't quite understand it myself.

But I know and that's all that matters.

Believe it or not, Paige managed to get me back into school. The signatures she collected and her father's legal action were enough for them to bend and allow me back. They tried to impose the same rules as before, but it was a lost cause. Mr. Erikson decided to give up teaching. It was a good thing too. He's since gone on to start an awareness group that will help Heam addicts finish high school.

Paige was there to make sure my last couple of months at school would be ones I remembered. For the first time in my life, I sat with girls my age at lunch and made friends. We went to movies and parties. We hung out. I even had a few boys ask me out, but I politely said no. It's too soon for that.

Gazer cried when I walked onstage and received my diploma. And although she never stopped to talk, I saw my mother sitting in the back row with a smile on her face. A few weeks later, I got a birthday card in the mail. Inside was a picture of Sophie wearing some brand-new clothes. She's a beautiful little girl. We have the same eyes.

I haven't gone back to visit Mom yet. But one day I will. And I'm pretty positive that next time she'll invite me in.

A few months later, I started college. It was the very one that Chael took me to during our first date. I haven't been back to see the butterfly room or smell the flowers but that's okay. When I'm ready, I'll go.

Paige is taking some courses with me. We study together and we go for coffee on a regular basis. We're both so busy these days.

I'm studying addiction. With Ramona's help, I'm planning to get into Heam counseling. I still volunteer on weekends. Paige joins me too when she's not too busy with homework or exams. Beth may be gone but there are a lot of other girls who need my help.

I want to help.

Gazer is the same. Still reading his books and helping me train in the mornings. The nice part is we've lost the seriousness of everything. The desperation. That complete waste of revenge time. He's still very much the father figure. I'm the one who's a little less stupid. What can I say? It's hard to see the light when you've got so much tunnel vision.

Speaking of light, Rufus won't be seeing it anytime soon. Shortly after Chael's death, Rufus was arrested for the suspicious death of Ming Bao. After his incarceration, a lot more charges suddenly came to light. I'd like to say he's spending his days locked away in a maximum-security prison. But six months into his sentence, he was murdered. Stabbed in the back during a riot. Karma can be a real bitch in a delightful sort of way.

But life isn't perfect. I won't lie and pretend it is. I killed a man. Most nights, I can't forget. Chael was right. That sort of thing changes a person. I got away with it. No one ever came looking for me. Sometimes I can still convince myself that Ming Bao deserved it.

Sometimes.

It's a slow process. There is guilt in taking a life. Guilt and pain that sneak up in the middle of the night, whispering into my ear and reminding me that all killers go to hell. Who was I to judge?

The only thing I can do from here is move forward. I can't forget; otherwise I'll never heal.

Does the afterlife exist? Isn't that the ultimate question? Heam exists because there are always going to be people looking for the afterlife. They want the answers so they'll be less afraid of dying when their time comes. They are the ones who can't handle not knowing. Life has been harder on them than others. Or perhaps it's been too good?

Empty souls. Empty stomachs. Heam doesn't discriminate between those who seek it in desperation and those who try it for fun. But it needs people like me to help them become whole again.

As for the afterlife?

My theory is that just because you can't see it doesn't mean it's not there. Gazer can roll his eyes all he wants, but I know better. It's like having the world's biggest secret, only I can't tell a single soul. No one would ever believe it.

But knowing the answer doesn't make it any easier. The gates of paradise have been slammed shut in my face. For now.

I get lonely sometimes, and at night I'll pull the pillow up against my back to pretend Chael's lying there beside me. I try to remember every last detail. His long dark hair falling into his eyes. The sound of his voice. The way his breath felt against my skin. It makes me happy and sad at the same time. I long for him the way I used to dream about silver liquid.

Addiction is a strange thing. Even with the physical cravings gone, the mental anguish lasts. I'm not sure it'll ever leave me, though certain days are easier to deal with than others. I came across a couple of gutter rats not too long after, and seeing the Heam bottle still brought on a lot of nervous angst in my stomach. In a way, I'm thankful I can remember this. It's important that I never forget. This way I'll be able to be more successful in helping others.

The bodies we wear can only take so much damage. We wear them down and eventually they stop working. But I now know that who we are lives on, even without our bodies. And once in a blue moon, someone can find a way to come back and try to make everything right.

Sometimes when I'm lying in bed at night, I swear I can hear Chael's voice calling to me across the distance. But not in pain. Never in pain.

Chael's waiting for me. I wonder if it gets lonely on that beach all by himself.

And I'll never stop missing him.

One day I'll get there and find him.

But it won't be soon. I've still got too much living left to do.

ACKNOWLEDGMENTS

I started writing *The Bodies We Wear* when I was still living in South Korea. My father had recently died and I was spending a lot of time thinking about life and death. I was questioning my own beliefs and searching for an answer to an impossible question. The idea grew out of my own questions about the great beyond. What if someone could see heaven? What effect would that have on humanity?

Basically, I'm saying this novel wouldn't exist if I hadn't been questioning my father's death. So thank you, Dad. Even if I can't show you these words personally, I'm still inspired by your wisdom and love.

I'd also like to thank Melanie Cecka for having such wonderful advice and ideas. An author is lost without a good editor.

I'd also like to thank my agent, Sarah Davies. She's a fantastic lady and a fellow animal lover.

Special thanks to Julia Churchill, the first to read

Bodies and the first to give me a chance. No matter where she goes in the world, I'll always keep in touch.

Thanks to my friend Kari Brackenbury, who helped me with Faye's workout routine. Her knowledge of personal training has been invaluable. She's also good at torturing me on a regular basis.

And finally, thanks to Adam Fink. I should have thanked you for being you a long time ago.

FAYE'S TRAINING SCHEDULE

	SUNDAY	MONDAY	TUESDAY
Block 1	Warm-up: 20-minute run	Warm-up: 20-minute run	Warm-up: 20-minute run
Block 2	Core Circuits: mountain climbers, crunches, leg lifts	Arm Circuits: push-ups, seated row	Core Circuits: mountain climbe. crunches, leg lifts
Block 3	Weapons Training (Knives)	Core Circuits: duck-unders, candlestick raises and lowers	Parkour Training
Block 4	Cool-down	Yoga	Cool-down
Block 5	Meditation	Cool-down	Meditation

EDNESDAY	THURSDAY	FRIDAY	SATURDAY
arm-up: -minute run	Warm-up: 20-minute run	Warm-up: 20-minute run	Warm-up: 20-minute run
m Circuits: ish-ups, seated row	Core Circuits: mountain climbers, crunches, leg lifts	Arm Circuits: push-ups, seated row	Core Circuits: mountain climbers, crunches, leg lifts
ore Circuits: duck-iders, candlestick ises and lowers	Leg Circuits: weighted squats, leg presses	Parkour Training	Leg Circuits: box jumps, weighted squats, resisted side step
oga	Cool-down	Yoga	Cool-down
ool-down	Meditation	Cool-down	Meditation

FAYE'S WORDS TO LIVE BY

"Every blade has two edges; he who wounds with one wounds himself with the other."
—Victor Hugo, *Les Misérables*

"Appear weak when you are strong, and strong when you are weak." —Sun Tzu, *The Art of War*

"In this hour, I do not believe that any darkness will endure." —J. R. R. Tolkien, *The Return of the King*

"Nobody has ever measured, not even poets, how much the heart can hold." —Zelda Fitzgerald

"You know that place between sleeping and awake, that place where you can still remember dreaming? That's where I'll always think of you."
—J. M. Barrie, *Peter Pan*

"Don't cry because it's over, smile because it happened."
—Dr. Seuss

THE BODIES WE WEAR
A PLAYLIST

1. "Save Me"—Shinedown
Faye in the city

2. "The Ghost of You"—My Chemical Romance
Christian

3. "Alone Together"—Fall Out Boy
Faye and Chael

4. "The Point of No Return"—Immortal Technique
Training for revenge

5. "Love Songs Drug Songs"—X Ambassadors
Beth and Faye

6. "Hanging On"—Active Child
Addiction

7. "Tourniquet"—Evanescence
Heaven

8. "Run to You"—Pentatonix
Faye and Chael's theme song

9. "It Can't Rain All the Time"—Jane Siberry
Theme